I0619397

THE MEMNID

TR GREENWOOD

****

This work is lovingly dedicated to my incomparable Wife and Children whom keep me grounded; and of course to my magnificent Mother for laying the foundation

****

Cover art: *Memnon's Statute* by Bernard Picart

Copyright© 2013

For contact information, please go to:
www.memnid.com

All rights reserved. No part of this publication may be reproduced or transmitted in any form or by any means, electronic or mechanical, including but not limited to photocopy, recording, or any information storage and retrieval system, without the prior written permission of the author and/or publisher.

The Memnid

ISBN-13: 978-0615803401
ISBN-10: 0615803407

TABLE OF CONTENTS

Page

I.   EMBARKING FOR TROY....................................1

II.   ECHIDNA AT THEBES.................................26

III.   THE NEREIDS..........................50

IV.   CHRYSAOR............................76

V.   THE ABDUCTION OF TRITON...............................102

VI.   THE ISLES OF BOLBE.................................125

VII.   ELYSIAN HECTOR.................…..150

VIII. THE REUNION OF MEMNON AND PRIAM...................…............175

IX.   BATTLE UPON THE TROJAN PLAINS...............................199

X.   THE FUNERAL GAMES...............................241

XI.   THE ASCENSION...................269

THE
MEMNID

I. Embarking for Troy

Oh fie the day the Fates[1] ordained!
That Great Memnon, son of the bright goddess dawn[2]
Should depart his exalted lands where his reign is just
And subject loyal comrades to the mercy of the abysmal seas

Into the hostile embrace of trident bearing Poseidon[3]
The Earth shaking son of the long deposed Cronus[4]
For purpose of arriving upon the shores of holy Ilium[5]
Metropolis despised by both Hera and gray eyed Athena[6]

For it was destined prior to your wondrous birth
That Myrmidon Achilles' imminent demise[7]
Never to transpire without receipt of grievous wound
Inflicted by your famed lance and glorious sword

And without hesitation or unnecessary delay
Determination is hastily made by great Memnon
To depart for the Trojan shores, come what may!
Nary a doubt by the goddess born king of lovely Aethiopia[8]

---

[1] three goddesses of fate; Clotho spins the thread of life, Lachesis measures the length, and Atropos determines when to cut the thread of life for all mortals

[2] Eos, goddess of the dawn; mother of Memnon

[3] god of the seas

[4] king of the Titans; father to Zeus, Hera, Poseidon, and Hades; overthrown by Zeus

[5] another reference to Troy

[6] the impetus for the Trojan War is that young Trojan prince Paris chooses Aphrodite as most beautiful amongst the three goddesses, thereby incurring the wrath of both Hera and Athena whom vow to destroy Troy

[7] son of the sea nymph Thetis and Peleus, king of Phthia; greatest of the Greek warriors; Myrmidons are warriors from Phthia

[8] birthplace and homelands of Memnon

A magnanimous decision to intervene in the Great War[9]
By the son of the goddess,[10]handsomest of men!
Immeasurable beauty equaled only by prowess in war
And the name of mighty Memnon forever recited!

Amongst the timeless heroes who sailed to Troy
Some vowing to protect the city, others sworn to destroy
The high walls constructed by Earth shaker himself
At the command of father Zeus and King Laomedon[11]

Sturdy aegis against both mortal and divine foe
Averting the sack of the Trojan citadel by Agamemnon[12]
A prize unclaimed after many years of strife and despair
Suffered alike by both the Achaeans and Trojan battalions

And great Memnon aligns his armies with those of Ilium
A formidable accord with mighty Hector Priamides[13]
The bulwark of the besieged Trojan kingdom
And famed defender of the Scaean Gates[14]

Son of the goddess, is there any man alive not aware of your
Famed lineage? Descended from divine beginnings
For the exalted Olympians[15]are your forebears
Manifested by your awesome beauty and piety

---

[9] another reference to the Trojan War
[10] another reference to Memnon
[11] Poseidon and Apollo, god of light, are ordered by Zeus (king of
all Olympian gods and goddesses) to serve King Laomedon
(father to Priam); Poseidon builds the famed Trojan walls during
this servitude
[12] high king of Greece
[13] son of King Priam, greatest warrior amongst the Trojans and
their allies
[14] famed gate entrance into Troy
[15] twelve deities that were the principal gods and goddesses of the
Greek pantheon

Zeus' beloved son Dardanus, ruler of the Idaean plains[16]
Had a son named Erichthonius, richest monarch on Earth
Whom begat Tros,[17] owner of the swiftest horses ever born
As they were descended from Boreas the north wind[18]

King Tros had three magnificent sons
Ilus, Assaracus, and beautiful Ganymedes[19]
The latter taken as cupbearer to serve lord Zeus himself
And Ilus was father to Tithonus[20] and Priam[21]

Prince Tithonus carried off by the goddess Eos herself
To be her eternal consort at her palatial abode
And granted immortality by father Zeus
At the request of the lovely daughter of Hyperion[22]

Thus Prince Tithonus lives forever
Amongst the ranks of the great Olympian deities
In his mortal life a fierce and handsome warrior
Accordingly he begets an incomparable man amongst men

Such is your lineage, great Memnon Tithonides!
Descended from Dardanus, and great Hector is your cousin
Accordingly obligating the incomparable son of the goddess
To stand in defense of his ancestral homelands

And who could foresee the adventures to be encountered?
On the treacherous voyage to King Priam's metropolis

---

[16] founder of Troy
[17] Trojan king, great grandfather of Memnon
[18] son of Eos; one of the four winds; brother to Memnon
[19] cupbearer to Zeus; carried off to Olympus for this purpose due to his beauty
[20] father of Memnon
[21] king of Troy
[22] father of Eos; grandfather of Memnon and a Titan

From the wondrous shores of lovely Aethiopia, as he and his
Subjects cross the Aegean to assist his besieged kinsmen

Memnon's fame enumerated by his awesome exploits
As he overcomes immeasurable odds
Overmuch for a much lesser man to endure
But capably borne by the son of the goddess

And his concerned mother iridescent lovely Eos[23]
Cognizant of the impending sufferings and strife
That her heroic son would undoubtedly encounter
And his trusty comrades would too endure

Swiftly sets off for the blessed Aethiopian kingdom
To forewarn her redoubtable and exuberant son
Of his destiny if he intervenes in the Great War
And abandon his homelands for the sake of Troy

Her aim to prevent departure from his palatial estates
And though she knows the resolve of great Memnon
To partake of the conflict raging in far away Ilium
And cast himself and his men to the mercy of the seas

Radiant Eos is determined to convince him otherwise
And so intense is her enduring maternal love
That the goddess could not endure any adversity
Enveloping the most revered of her divine offspring

For awaiting at the high walls of lofty Pergamus[24]
Difficulties would beset the Memnon and his comrades
As they arrive in defense of his famed kinsmen
And his ancestral nexus to Hector and pious Aeneas[25]

---

[23] goddess of the dawn; mother of Memnon
[24] citadel of Troy

And as great Memnon commands that preparations be made
For departure from his peoples and enchanting realms
And board the vessels bound for far away Troy
His divine mother suddenly appears before him

As she is witnessed in the halls of Olympus[26]
In all of her iridescent splendor and glory
Her appearance befitting as goddess of the dawn
As beloved Eos tenderly guides her golden chariot

Across the vast and splendidly blue skies
Bringing welcomed light to all below
And respite from the dreaded darkness
As the hopes of the lugubrious are renewed

The goddess gingerly approaches her famed son
As great Memnon stands near the Aethiopian a shore
Gazing upon the scenic view from a high promontory
As radiant Eos takes his strong hands into her own

And begins to express to her godlike son
Her concern for his impending sufferings
At the hands of the divine forces of Olympus
And those of both monstrous and mortal origins

As prophesied by the revered Oracle at Delphi[27]
If he should set for sail for holy Ilium
Becoming a pawn in the battle between the Olympians
Though afforded latitude in determining his fate

---

[25] son of Aphrodite, goddess of love; second greatest warrior amongst the Trojans and their allies

[26] heavenly abode of the Olympians; located atop Mount Olympus in Greece

[27] priestess of Apollo at his temple in Delphi; for those whom solicited, the priestess foretold of future events

And so the goddess begins, "My son, deliverer of joy to my
Heart! Since that day I bore you near the Aethiopian
Foothills to your beloved father, Trojan born Tithonus
Although a mortal, that mighty man won my eternal love

For he was best amongst the men of his generation
Both in physical beauty and prowess at arms
And as I made my trek across the lofty heavens
His presence was most pleasing to my eyes

As he was flushed with youth and vitality
With ease he outlasted his envious peers
As the men of Troy competed in varied sport
Tithonus was the pride of his father King Laomedon

And as he lay sleeping near Scamander's flowing waters[28]
I bequeathed my love to the Dardanian prince
And eternally pledged devotion to lord Tithonus
And bore him two magnificent sons

Both to reign over vast Aethiopia without reproach
To partake of the riches accorded by these lands
Lush fruits, berries, fish, and pheasant
And all manner of venison as deemed fit for nobility

And the aboriginal peoples most splendid
In appearance and physical attributes
Renowned for wondrous beauty and comeliness
Without equal in all realms of the earth

And no foreign armies dare to invade these holy lands
For the devotion of Olympus safeguards Aethiopia
By far the most beloved by Cronus' son
Of any kingdom presently in existence

---

[28] Trojan river god; also called Xanthus

And your famed lance none dare to enrage
For your prowess is known throughout the world
And none can withstand your fury once provoked
For you dexterously overcome any opponent

And since your realms are far from Troy
And the son of Atreus has no designs to come to these shores
For the queen of Sparta is not in an Aethiopian bed
Nor has she eloped to these lovely lands

I implore you in earnest, a mother's anxious request
My darling! Please consider the utter anguish!
I must endure if you were to leave for Troy
To oppose the haughty Argive[29] battalions

For included in their ranks are ferocious men
All with purpose of destroying delightful Ilium
And enslave Priam's demoralized peoples
Seizing the riches of the city for far away Argos

Huge Ajax, sly Odysseus, and arrogant Antilochus[30]
All determined to destroy Ilium for the sake of Menelaus[31]
A luckless mortal whose beloved wife is
Overcome by the Dardanian beauty of Paris

And worst by far is Myrmidon Achilles
Whom you shall surely engage, more a plague than a mortal
For he has thoroughly ravaged holy Ilium
Because powerful gods and goddesses support him

---

[29] another name for the Greeks, referencing the inhabitants of
ancient Argos
[30] captains in the Greek armies
[31] king of Sparta; brother of Agamemnon; estranged husband of
Helen

Even now I can see spiteful Hera,[32]queen of us all
With Poseidon, Athena,[33] and even amenable Hermes[34]
Determined to destroy the most splendid of earthly realms
Due to an ill fated decision of Priam's son

And leave no doubt that Achilles has been forewarned
By his own mother, Nerenian Thetis of the sea[35]
Betrothed to Peleus[36] as his immortal wife
That his fate coincides with your own

That awful man, a terror for many Dardanians![37]
And will surely relish the chance for further glory
Satisfying both his and wretched Ares' lust
For carnage and death, appeasing his bloodthirsty appetite!

And these men are not deterred from assaulting Olympians!
As haughty Diomedes dare to aim his lance[38]
At the divine body of lovely Aphrodite[39]
Without remorse he engages in this forbidden act!

As she ventured to save her beloved son Aeneas
Nourished by her breasts from a tender age
An act any concerned mother would readily perform
Ensuring the safety of her beloved child

And as Ares[40]set out to avenge the wounded Aphrodite

---

[32] daughter of Cronos; wife of Zeus; queen of the Olympians
[33] daughter of Zeus; goddess of wisdom
[34] son and messenger of Zeus
[35] mother of Achilles; one of the Nereids (daughters of Nereus, referred to as the "Old man of the Sea")
[36] father of Achilles
[37] used interchangeably with Trojans
[38] son of Tydeus; captain in the Greek army; one of the greatest warriors after Achilles amongst the Greeks
[39] goddess of love

Against the reckless mortal that injured her
Diomedes, exhorted by gray eyed Athena
Defiantly attacks the war god himself!

Would you too have me harmed by the Achaean[41] steel?
Or have some bold Argive lacerate my own divine flesh?
Such pain and anguish I would gladly endure on your behalf
For I love my renowned son more than myself!

And after the impending demise of mighty Hector
You alone shall thwart the fall of the Trojan citadel
Until Poseidon the Trident Bearer intervenes
A powerful Olympian matched against a mortal!

No, my brave and honorable son!
I must not allowed your beauty to be destroyed
You, the handsomest man in the entire world
My darling favorite, I could not bear your brutal demise!

And it is spoken in all realms subject to the will of Zeus
Of the beauty and intellect of the ravishing Cyrene[42]
And her immense love and yearning that is solely for you
The Libyan queen is just in her undisputed reign

And her unadulterated desires for you are plain
As she forsook the love of her devastated family
Offering comfort to your vast conquering armies
As you established dominion over these lands

Such is the devotion shown to you by your benefactor
As the Queen of Libya[43] bequeaths herself only to you

---

[40] son of Zeus and Hera; god of war
[41] another name for the Greeks, referencing the inhabitants of
ancient Achaea
[42] queen of Libya

Angering her multitude of powerful suitors
And simultaneously endangering her own beloved citadel

And so I beseech you to remain in blessed Aethiopia
And forsake this horrible blood stained conflict!
Take the loveliest lady of these lands as wife
And begat beautiful progeny to eternally rule

And live a long and prosperous life
Blissful and happy all your remaining days will be
And your people will love and honor your just reign
And reminisce of the days of great King Memnon"

And godlike Memnon dutifully replies,
"Dear mother whose divine womb nourished me
Since the day you chose mighty Tithonus
And begat myself and that incomparable Emathion[44]

Great champion of the Aethiopian kingdom
Feared throughout the world for his prowess at arms
Beloved by his people for his generosity and kindness
I would count myself blessed if to possess

A fraction of that mighty man's courage and honor
For he stood strong and unflinching against
The might of Zeus born Heracles[45]
As he endlessly suffered in his Labors[46]

As ordained by Zeus's bitter wife Hera

---

[43] lands located north of Aethiopia

[44] brother of Memnon; son of Eos and Tithonus

[45] son of Zeus; strongest man to ever live

[46] for killing his children in a fit of insanity, Heracles is condemned to perform twelve nearly impossible tasks as penance (referred to as Labors)

No less than this great hero did Emathion succumb
For none other could overcome this great king
Such a man was my own renowned brethren

By not departing for King Priam's holy city
I would undoubtedly dishonor my enviable lineage
Zeus sprung on my revered paternal side
And maternally linked to the great god Oceanus[47]

For how could I stand idle and witness from afar?
As the very lands of my kinsmen is besieged by Argos
Attributed to delightful Helen's departure from Sparta[48]
Following Paris for the beaches of Troy

And though I have alternative to live a happier life
With an incomparable wife and children to rear
And wondrous lands with abundant riches
Any man on earth would envy such an existence

Though I am handsome and none can compare
And no man on Earth could stake such a claim
For my beauty is spoken all across the Aegean[49]
And my prowess at arms equals my delightful countenance

But such divine gifts are but futile in comparison
To the pursuit of eternal glory and fame
For struggle and sacrifices I choose to endure
Rather than embracing the ignominies of shame

That abstaining from this conflict would assuredly bring

---

[47] one of the Titans; personification of all oceans
[48] Helen was the most beautiful woman in the world and a daughter of Zeus; she abandons her husband Menelaus (King of Sparta) for Paris (prince of Troy), thereby commencing the Trojan War
[49] a sea that lies between Greece and Troy

To the dishonor of my heralded lineage
At the abandonment of my distressed kinsmen
Woeful be that sad day if this were to transpire!"

And the great goddess of the Dawn
Falls to her knees beating her breast
In agony over her beloved son's unwelcomed words
As he was determined to depart for Troy

And even these entreaties of the goddess
Could not dissuade lionhearted Memnon
From sailing for perpetual honor and glory
For this is his due at the Trojan citadel

And the stout son of the goddess, in all his bravery
And in deep reverence to his heroic lineage
Resolutely makes his selfless determination
To lead his men to the walls of Ilium

And after mother and son share candid moment
Golden Eos departs for the sacred halls of Olympus
Her heart burdened by the fate of her son
And the sufferings that he would undoubtedly endure

And great Memnon continues his preparations
To sail the expanse of Poseidon's domain
En route to his ancestral Trojan homelands
Determined to do what he may for the Dardanian resistance

Shortly after all Aethiopian battalions are assembled
As the sea faring vessels are swiftly prepared
And provisions dutifully allocated amongst the massive fleet
In anticipation for the treacherous journey to Troy

And who are the great conquerors of vast Aethiopia
To accompany great Memnon, king amongst kings?

- 13 -

Allegiance owed to you no less from Agathon Aknatides
Prince of the famed Nubian nation

These ancient peoples favored by Artemis[50]
Renowned for their hunting and archery skills
Also included in your company is great Tanutamen[51]
The stout hearted King of the Axumites

Excellent horsemen whose homelands stretched
South of Thebes into the holy city of Matara
One would be remiss to not mention famed Ergamenes[52]
The great Kushian general and commander

Whose fame came about as a young boy
When he dared to slay a great Aethiopian lion
As it leapt to devour his infant brother
The great beast's mane a testament to his prowess

The Meroitian prince Aithops too joins the expedition[53]
Richest amongst monarchs of the Aethiopian lands
And dear cousin to great Memnon Tithonides
His awesome might in battle unmatched

Accordingly such a tremendous mortal was paired
With the magnificent princess Eridia
Her mother was glorious Pandia,[54] daughter of Zeus
Thus an incomparable man was betroth to a magnificent wife

---

[50] daughter of Zeus; sister of Apollo
[51] commander in Aethiopian army; king of Axum, kingdom adjacent to Aethiopia in northeast Africa
[52] captain in Aethiopian army; lord of the realms of Kush, territory between Aethiopia and Thebes
[53] captain in Aethiopian army; prince of Meroe, a nation located northwest of Aethiopia; cousin of Memnon
[54] daughter of Zeus and Selene (goddess of the moon)

Such are the men included in the Aethiopian contingent
Eager to attain great honor for their tremendous exploits
And encounter the fearsome armies of Atreus' sons
Their pedigree unparalleled as they stand assembled

And before mighty Memnon addresses his vast armies
He turns to the array of famous commanders and generals
And peers directly into the eyes of each of these men
Offering to each a steely and unflinching glare

And the son of the goddess is pleased by what he sees
His most trusted comrades respond resolutely
As Memnon witnesses sheer will and determination
That all bravely would accompany him, even to death

And great Memnon then turns to the massive gathering
And he begins to address his devoted subjects
"Brave Aethiopians! Honored by the Olympians themselves!
Your prowess at arms is known throughout the world!

A peaceful existence we enjoy from foreign invaders
For none dare to besiege our lands for fear of annihilation!
And no mortal is brave enough to venture to our realms
Since great Perseus,[55] the brave hearted son of Lord Zeus

As he departed Argos for our lovely shores
In search of adventure in our wondrous abode
The son of great Zeus sets forth in heroic fashion
Risking life and limb to save the lovely Andromeda[56]

Actions unlike those of our contingent of men
As we leisurely dawdle as timid spectators from afar
And cavort in our supple and blessed lands

---

[55] son of Zeus; slayer of the Gorgon Medusa
[56] Aethiopian princess; wife of Perseus

As others actively seek honor and fame in abundance

We must cease inaction, my beloved and brave comrades!
For no longer shall we stand idle in worldly conflicts
As it is improper for a great nation such as ours
To abstain from matters deemed considerable by Zeus

Our absence from the Great War is even more pronounced
For the besieged Trojans are our own kinsmen!
Shame on us if we refrain from fighting in this war!
For our two cities are ancestrally connected to Dardanus

And thus by honor we are obligated to intervene
And though the Achaean forces may be great in sheer size
And their captains may be the hardiest of warriors
We too are men whom can wield the dreaded lance

And our reputation as swordsmen is unmatched!
For we pursue the enemy relentlessly as he flees in chaos!
And many times have we performed the awful dance of war
Much to the chagrin of our unfortunate and vanquished foes

And long though the voyage to holy Ilium may be
And the varied perils of the sea be fearsome
And our departure may anger many Olympians
We shall ultimately triumph in our heroic endeavors"

And the men all cheered the high spirited words
That came forth from the son of the goddess
For they are inspired to do battle with the Argives
And offer succor to the war weary Trojan armies

And proper sacrifices are swiftly made to the Olympians
As venison is duly slaughtered and libations are dedicated
And prayers to father Zeus, Apollo, and Artemis the huntress
Gray eyed Athena and Queen Hera too included

As fervent sacrifices are made to appease Ares the war god
For his gluttonous thirst is satiated only by spillage of blood
And to Aphrodite, Hephaestus,[57] and wily Hermes
With much allocated to trident bearing Poseidon

Ravisher of ships and men alike that dare to traverse the seas
For only the strong endure Earthshaker's treacherous domain
This most feared Olympian, himself a son of strong Cronus
That ghastly lord of Queen Rhea[58] whom deemed it fit

To devour all of his helpless progeny one by one
And subsequently the Titan is compelled to disgorge each
Through a stratagem designed by Gaia[59]
For her will is to overthrow her haughty son

So that great Zeus could proceed as ruler of the universe
And though the thunder lord was strongest by far of all
Poseidon is offered the choicest Aethiopian mutton
And libations flow freely for the Trident Bearer[60]

Such honors were given to the lord of the Sea
As the son of the goddess sought safe passage
Through the treacherous waters of the sea
With purpose to arrive safely to the beaches of Troy

And although great Memnon was keenly aware
That gray bearded Poseidon supported the Achaeans
He could not be cognizant of the magnitude
That this reason alone would stand as a great impediment

---

[57] son of Zeus and Hera; god of fire and forge
[58] wife of Cronus; queen of the Titans; mother of Zeus, Poseidon, Hera, and Hades
[59] the mother of Cronus and the Titans; personification of the earth
[60] another reference to Poseidon

To a timely arrival to Priam's glorious citadel
Though the Olympians loved Memnon immensely
As evident in his physical appearance and prowess at arms
The son of the goddess blessed in all earthly attributes

And in spite of his love for the venerable Aethiopian king
Conflicted Poseidon makes the arduous choice
To leave great Memnon and his comrades
To the awful mercy of the treacherous seas

In hopes of dissuading Eos' peerless son
To abandon his indomitable campaign
And thereby allow Achilles to sack stubborn Troy
Honoring the entreaties of Nerenian[61]Thetis

Memnon's supposition is that Poseidon's affections
Accorded to him and his magnificent lineage
As well as his bountiful offerings to the great sea god
Were sufficient to appease Cronus' mighty son

And the lord of the wide ranging oceans
Not absolute in opposition to the descendants of Tros
At times throughout the conflict on the Dardanian beaches
Interceded on behalf of besieged Trojans

Aeneas Anchises' son was a benefactor
As he faced fierce Diomedes son of Tydeus
Blessed by Athena to rule the battlefield that faithful day
Best by far on the Idaean[62] plains

Thus Tydeus' son Diomedes ravaged the Trojan armies
Killing its brave men and pillaging at will
Driving the Dardanian rank and file to flight

---

[61] another reference to Nereus, father of the Nereids
[62] reference to lands adjacent to Mount Ida (located near Troy)

As he was supported by Zeus's gray eyed daughter

Lion-hearted Aeneas espied Diomedes' work
And intervened to stop his onslaught
Matched against both Tydeus' son and Athena
Overmuch for Aphrodite's brave son

Accordingly Aeneas was wounded
And his companion Pandarus[63] slain
But Aphrodite's son was gratefully saved
By great Poseidon's unexpected act of adoration

And although the horses of Tros were taken
By Pallas[64] supported Diomedes
Aeneas was returned to the Trojan citadel
Brief respite from sorrowful war

Thus Poseidon's rejection of Memnon's entreaties
Determined after heavy and careful deliberations
Caused the son of the goddess and his men
Meritless distress and awful strife

Affliction not apportioned solely to the Aethiopian
Contingent alone, as word of Memnon's departure arrives
To the blessed realms of Libya, swiftly dispersed by Ossa[65]
To the chagrin of a powerful Queen of those lands

Her famed love for the venerable son of the goddess
Unrequited after countless entreaties

---

[63] famed Trojan archer; son of Lycaon; broke truce between Greeks and Trojans when he wounds Menelaus with one of his arrows

[64] another reference to Athena; Pallas was a childhood companion of Athena whom she killed in a dispute

[65] goddess of rumor

And so her anguished heart suffers endlessly
Despite the multitude of gifts and offerings to great Memnon

Gold, silver, and many other precious metals
As well as varied oxen, plentiful sheep, and exotic birds
All brought to the son of the goddess in a relentless effort
To win his unyielding and devoted affections

The queen of Libya even commits paternal betrayals
Disclosing the elicit plans of her father
As he contemplated declaring war against Eos' son
And annihilation to his peoples and wondrous lands

She sends her emissaries covertly to Aethiopia
Forewarning Memnon of her father's evil plot
And foil the Libyan monarch's ambitious goals
Averting unbearable catastrophe and sufferings

And grateful is Memnon for Cyrene's loyalty
The son of the goddess makes her supreme ruler
After vanquishing her father's vast armies
And establishing dominion over the Libyan realms

And the ravishing Cyrene would effortlessly forego
Her undisputed sovereignty over holy Libya
For the love of the redoubtable Memnon
As she is overcome by his beauty and nobility

And now word of his departure to Troy
In defense of the beleaguered Scaean Gates
As he is dutifully and ancestrally bound to do
Renews agony in the heart of the Libyan queen

She swiftly calls to her handmaiden Ilionae
Her wise counselor and most trusted companion
And loveliest of Cyrene's childhood playmates

Both venerable women born on the same day

And the Libyan queen begins, "Oh Ilionae!
My sweet sister and dearest companion!
Once again my heart endures amorous torment!
That tremendous son of Eos stirs it so

For I have loved only him since first glimpse
For he is the handsomest man in the entire world!
And none could deny his beauty is unrivaled
As only his prowess and godlike virtue are of equal

And though many kings in these splendid lands
All famed and brave men honored by Olympus
Incessantly pursue betrothal only unto me
None I can love as I do the king of Aethiopia

And now he determines it best to defend holy Ilium
To match his strength against those haughty Argives
As they aspire to topple King Priam's city
For the sake of the luckless Spartan king

His lovely wife follows the Trojan prince
Overcome by his youth and enticing presence
She abandons her home and marital vows
So pleasing are the men descended from divine Dardanus

I myself similarly overwhelmed by his progeny
And now I wish to no longer live!
No desire do I have to partake of earthly joys!
For I exist only to serve my lord Memnon"

And the saddened Ilionae answers Cyrene's lament,
"My dear sister, do not despair!
For your joy is my own heart's joy
And your pain is unequivocally my own!

And if you descend to dark Tartarus[66]
I too cease to breathe the fresh air
And to walk the expanse of our lush countryside
For your life and mine are inseparably intertwined

Will you listen to my desperate entreaties?
Are you willing to heed my concerned advice?
Seldom have I made request of you, oh great Queen!
But now I am obligated to do so

And though you have on many an occasion
Adamantly petitioned the son of the goddess
To be your husband and beget a powerful union!
Yet that steel hearted man has been steadfast in his refusals

I now seek allowance to depart for holy Aethiopia
And beseech its great King in a kneeling posture
To reconsider his brave decision and forego
The treacherous pathway to the shores of Ilium

And in the alternative remain in our lovely lands
And continue his undisputed reign over the territories
So that the fires of passion that burn in your heart
May still have hopes of an imminent matrimony"

And the great Queen of Libya sullenly replies,
"Oh Ilionae, what you propose in your infinite love for me
Are undoubtedly the desires of my unquenched heart
And the unchecked infatuation that I must endure

For even as the son of the goddess ignores agonizing pleas
And departs to oppose the Argives, nary a thought of me
His remaining in Aethiopia is my preference

---

[66] another reference to the underworld, the land of the dead ruled
by Hades

Even if he continually withholds his stubborn love

So my sweet sister, do as you will
For my love for beautiful Memnon remains undeterred
And by the grace of the Olympian gods
Our wishes will prevail upon the son of the goddess"

Accordingly Ilionae swiftly travels to Memnon's realms
Departing the comforts of prosperous Libya
For she is determined is to convince the son of the goddess
To abandon his campaign to assist Priam's peoples

Queen Cyrene's handmaiden and close confidante
At last arrives in holy Aethiopia without a moment to spare
As she rushes to the palatial abode of Tithonus' son
While Memnon and his contingent are readying to set sail

And Ilionae meekly seeks audience of the Aethiopian king
She offers her request first to Meroitian Aithops
Memnon's own beloved cousin and comrade
A mighty man renowned for his comeliness

Lovely Ilionae swiftly presents her case to Aithops
In supplication she asks him to intervene
And assist in persuading the resolve of famed Memnon
And save the life of the love stricken Libyan queen

The tears flow freely from her lovely visage
As she beats her breasts in awful agony
For the fate of the sorrowful Cyrene is certain
If the son of the goddess rebuffs her pleas

Gentle Aithops pities their sad plight
And without delay he takes Ilionae to his cousin
The regal voice of the son of the goddess discernable
As the Aethiopian king supervises the final preparations

And Ilionae immediately hurls herself to the earth
Pleading on behalf of Libyan Cyrene
She reminds him of her sacrifices made in love
And of the Libyan queen's unadulterated loyalties

Ilionae implores the son of the goddess to abandon his plans
And retract his allegiance to besieged Troy
To remain on the lovely Aethiopian continent
And to continue his undisputed and prosperous reign

And though the son of the goddess pities her dilemma
And expresses his high regard for the Libyan queen
He nonetheless denies Ilionae's poignant petition
Offering his heartfelt compassion while doing so

Distressed Ilionae returns to the Libyan citadel
Reluctantly she delivers the response of Memnon
To the chagrin of the heartbroken Cyrene
Resigning the Libyan queen to her untimely demise

So begins Cyrene, "That hard hearted son of the goddess
Has plainly and concisely made his intentions clear
For he loves me no more than he loves the Argives
And lacks gratitude for my sacrifices on his behalf!

Ostracized by kin for aiding that redoubtable man!
In a contrived effort to acquire his affections
And now I must perish for the lack of this love
For all hope is lost of my passions being appeased"

And with these words lovely Cyrene enters her chambers
Ignoring the heartfelt pleas of her chambermaids
And the entreaties of her loyal and saddened subjects
As they begged her to reconsider her decision

But the Libyan queen refuses to change her stance

Listlessly she walks toward her bed in an emotionless state
And orders the doors to be tightly barred shut
Never to again appear before her beloved peoples

And the beautiful and heartbroken Cyrene
Takes a jeweled sword into her soft hands
And slowly plunges the blade deep into her bosom
Disengaging herself from the miseries of her unrequited love

And the demise of the great Libyan queen spreads swiftly
To all realms and across all kingdoms on earth
Even as far as the golden halls of divine Olympus
As all mourn the sorrowful death of lovely Cyrene

And upon receiving word of these distressing events
Memnon is saddened by the death of the Libyan queen
And the son of the goddess acknowledges her legacy
As he promptly issues commandment to honor Cyrene

A constant vigil be held throughout all Aethiopia
As remembrance to the great Libyan queen
And testament to her devotion and symbol of her legacy
Forbidding the eternal fires from ever being extinguished

Such is the charge of the son of the goddess
For his piety is equaled by his famed beauty
And after these arrangements are made
Great Memnon orders his armies to prepare for departure

And so the Aethiopian flags are duly hoisted
As the vessels are provisioned with victuals and necessaries
And the brave and adventure-lusting men of Aethiopia
Set sail into the abyss of Poseidon's vast realm

II. Echidna at Thebes

Boreas, the northern wind, calm and content
As the day he assumed the stallion's visage
And begat Erichthonius' illustrious colts
A breed matchless in both beauty and speed

Such is the disposition of the deity as the Aethiopian fleet
Traverse the vast and wide ocean
And all the elements are at ease, and if had remained such
Great Memnon would swiftly reach the Trojan beaches

But Nereus' swift footed daughter Thetis
Immensely concerned for the sake of her own son
Myrmidon Achilles, ravisher of the Trojan armies
That awful man, more like a plague!

She swiftly goes to the steward of the northern wind
And although he is brother unto great Memnon
Boreas is hopelessly envious of Eos' unequalled love
For her absolute favorite amongst all her progeny

On her knees the daughter of Nereus beseeches the wind god
With absolute certainty of the likelihood
That she could persuade moody Boreas to cause mischief
And in a jealous fit turn against his famed brother

And Thetis begins to offer her pleas to him,
"Boreas, you know why I appear suddenly in your presence
For I stand here before you as a supplicant
Beholden to what you decide, as is your prerogative

My requests are dictated by a mother's love for her son
That magnificent man, reared by Peleus in rocky Phthia
And I am woefully shackled to my immortal sorrow!
As his path has been chosen as ordained by the pitiless Fates

And imminently close looms his unfortunate death!

As his fate is intertwined with that of a mighty man
More like an exalted god than an ordinary mortal
Namely, I speak of great Memnon Tithonides

The son of the goddess now makes his trek across the seas
As he and his brave comrades are steadfastly bound for Troy
To offer succor to Priam and his Dardanians
And his arrival brings about the demise of my beloved son!

And though I know in my heart it shall be so
For no deity or mortal can defy the shears of cruel Atropos[67]
As she discriminately cuts the thread of life
At the apportioned second in the continuum of time

Such is the lot of an immortal parent of a mortal child!
For I shall have to endure the loss of my darling favorite!
But in hopes of prolonging his life
And to enjoy his last precious remaining moments

I pray you do my biddings, just this once!
And delay my unendurable agony and pain
By making great Memnon's voyage abroad
An arduous task that others shall eternally speak of

Although he is peerless and loved by the gods
Evident in his beauty and great hearted prowess
And born of the same wondrous goddess as yourself
He is nonetheless a scourge to me and to those whom I adore

And equally an annoyance to yourself and your brothers
For it is known throughout the realm of Olympus
That Eos the rosy fingered goddess of the dawn
Loves incomparable Memnon above all other offspring

---

[67] the eldest of the Fates

And so I implore you to stir up your winds
And cause the Aethiopian vessels to set off course
Send those brave men to some far away realm
And thwart him from reaching the Scaean Gates"

And thus swift-footed daughter of Nereus states her case
Thereby setting anew a fiery sibling rivalry
And Boreas readily assents to the request of Thetis daughter
As he swiftly causes his winds to violently gust

Determined is Boreas to cause troubles for his brother
As a gathering tempest is divinely conjured
By the provoked god as he takes steady aim
At the Aethiopians ships to appease his envious heart

And as great Memnon and his men are resting in tow
A Nubian archer named Briteus is suddenly propelled
Violently out of the seafaring vessel
As the north wind abruptly changes it course

And the scales of fortune suddenly tilted against Memnon
Disturbing the tranquil voyage of the son of the goddess
As moody Boreas and his northern winds assaults
The Aethiopian fleet, obliging the entreaties of Thetis

And the men all frantically clutch parts of the vessels
As great Memnon takes a hold the reins of the helm
Navigating against the sudden rush of the abounding waters
As his trusty comrades all manage to endure Boreas' assault

And witnessing his handiwork and its lack of success
And the brave defiance of Memnon and his comrades
Angry Boreas seeks the assistance of his windy brothers
To break the will of mighty Aethiopian monarch

"Notus and Eurus, I implore you to assist me![68]
For we finally have that brother of ours at a disadvantage
He whom commands the lion's share of our mother's love!
Leaving the rest of her brood malnourished of affection

Superior though he may be in his appearance
And in prowess, manifested in his tremendous feats at arms
We should not lack for adulations from our mother, nor
Should we stand idly by as he is beneficiary at our expense

So let us join our powerful and wild winds
And divert Memnon and his devoted comrades
From his stated mission of arriving at holy Ilium
As bulwark to the besieged peoples of Priam

And thus earn further honor and divine praise
Contributing to the pride and vainglory of our mother
As she boasts of his fame and accolades
To the denigration of the rest of her progeny"

And both Notus and turbulent Eurus alike
Acquiescing with the words of their brother
For both windy deities felt maternal neglect, and
Accordingly assent as accomplices in the assault of Memnon

And both the powerful east and southern winds
Along with their enraged brother Boreas
Bombard the vessels of their famed brother
Thereby appeasing their long standing sibling envies

And such was the lot of distressed Memnon
One mighty mortal against three determined gods
As the vessels at last give way to the divine siege
And the fleet is scattered throughout the seas

---

[68] the gods of the south and eastern winds

And great Memnon conjures a roar as loud as thunder
Rallying his men to stand strong and firm
Against the raging assault of the furious winds
Thus redoubtable Memnon exhorts his men to endure

And the son of the goddess then shouts in defiance
Provoked by the immense anger that assembled within him
"My brothers, we born of the same goddess mother
Nurtured and suckled by the same breasts

And yet you decided to assault me so!
As I head to Troy for the sake of my forbears
To provide succor to a besieged nation
Attacked by Olympian supported aggressors

By father Zeus! Your assault is out of full envy of me!
I ask what offense have I ever offered to you?
In my quest to seek honor and fame
And advance our heralded shared lineage

It is now your ill intent to cause me despair!
In spite of our shared maternal link
But my will shall never bend to your aggressions
So cease your meddling and return to your divine duties!"

Then Boreas answers great Memnon Tithonides,
"Brother, refrain from your audacious speech
For you above all else have been honored
While the rest of us are continually neglected

Unable to obtain our mother's commendations
All rewarded to a single issue instead of divided equally
And one is honored above all others in the family
While the remainder are deemed inferior

Now is your opportunity to suffer strife my brother!

And experience the unendurable pain
That the rest of iridescent Eos' brood
Are eternally fated to suffer because of you

Your handsome visage and pleasant demeanor
Brave and stout is your spirit and heart
And your prowess at arms undisputed
Unmatched are you at wielding the lance

Yet none of these attributes shall avail you now
As you face opposition from our wild winds
For many a brave hero has succumb to them
And today you shall have a similar destiny"

After this proclamation by Boreas is delivered
The conflict between brave Memnon and his brothers ensues
As the north, east, and southern winds intensify the assault
While the Aethiopian king defiantly refuses to relent

And a tug of war between powerful forces continues
Akin to the ordeal between Laelaps and the vixen[69]
Also known as the Teumessian fox in many realms
A terror for those lands the monster ravaged

For it could never be destroyed nor captured
As the vixen was matched against Laelaps[70]
Magical hound destined to catch all it pursues
Thus an impossible back and forth commences

Similarly both sides are in a virtual deadlock
And though the son of the goddess is outnumbered
He alone matched against his three immortal brethren

---

[69] a gigantic fox destined to never be apprehended by either gods or mortals
[70] a dog destined to always capture whatever prey it hunted

His spirit refuses to acquiescence to the ill spirited plot

And the conflict is witnessed in horror by a sorrowful Eos
And the dawn goddess looks on with maternal concerns
As her beloved son battles the windy deluge
Created by his brothers at the behest of Thetis

And Eos swiftly goes to the lovely Graces[71]
Aglaea, Euphrosyne, and Thalia
Three beautiful and delightful goddesses
Desired by many amongst the ranks of the immortals

And rosy fingered Eos, goddess of the dawn
Fully aware of the propensities of her windy sons
And their wild affections for the lusty Graces
Makes her plea to those three wondrous goddesses

To engage Boreas, Notus, and Eurus
And distract them from their evil intentions
And provide respite for seafaring Memnon
For she so adored her and Tithonus' revered son

"Lovely goddesses, I come to you under extreme duress!
Compelled to witness a quarrel between my sons
Slyly provoked by the sea nymph[72] Thetis
As a familial bond is forever shattered!

And moreover, unwarranted is the enmity
Of the winds against their renowned brother
For he is regal, and yet remains the most humble of men
And his purity of heart is unmatched by any

Boreas, Notus, and blustery Eurus

---

[71] goddesses of charm; attendants of Aphrodite
[72] female nature deities

Began this awful strife against my darling favorite
As a result of biased and misplaced perceptions
Breaking the very heart that beats within these breasts!

So now I seek your assistance in ending this struggle
For my sons have long had desires for you
And would cease this needless bickering
For eagerly they would be in your delightful company"

And the Graces readily obey radiant Eos
As they swiftly appear before Boreas
And before Notus and blustery Eurus alike
Thus causing all three to be diverted from their task

And from their troublemaking intentions derived from envy
To spite their incomparable brother
As lustful desires now become priority
And the assault of great Memnon an afterthought

And so Eos is able to dispel of the conflict
And swiftly stint the familial strife
As the son of the goddess and his besieged comrades
Survive their harrowing ordeal against the winds

And although some vessels are needlessly destroyed
As good and loyal men are lost in the calamity
Nonetheless the brave and hardy Aethiopian contingent
Survive as they wash along the shores of Thebes[73]

That magnificent and divinely blessed citadel
And the city of great Dionysus' conception[74]
When thunder lord Zeus visited lovely Semele[75]

---

[73] city near Egypt

[74] god of wine; son of Zeus

[75] mortal mother of Dionysus; a princess of Thebes

In her chamber, intent on an enamored act

And thus begat a great god to a mortal woman
And she is forever hated by Queen Hera
Who tempted the gullible princess
To make an ill fated request of her divine lover

And sorrowfully to her own demise
Semele requests to behold the mighty thunderbolt[76]
Weaponry used by Cronus' son as supreme ruler
Overmuch for a mere mortal to fully witness

As Semele perishes before the radiance of the thunderbolt
Incinerated by its intense calefaction
To the dismay of the saddened Olympian
As the wine god is orphaned prior to his glorious birth

And Memnon is afforded refuge in the city of Semele
The wondrous nation of the famed Seven Gates
Bountiful in its riches and excesses in much better times
Though none would know this by its current state of affairs

For misfortune and strife are abundantly present in the city
And the hapless people of Thebes are beset
By an ancient and fearsome creature
Namely Echidna, mother of all earthly fiends[77]

Half nymph in her upper torso, half serpent below
Mate of the monstrous Typhon[78]
And sworn enemy to the great Olympian gods
Now eternally confined to the pillars of Aetna[79]

---

[76] indestructible weapon of Zeus
[77] daughter of Ceto and Phorcys (sea deities); mother to many of
the monsters in Greek mythology
[78] son of Gaia (earth) and Tartarus (personification of hell)

Echidna, wholly enraged at the Theban peoples
And inflicts massive ailing from famine and awful drought
As ordained by the monstrous deity
For her insane fury runs unchecked

Unabated are the sufferings of the ancient Theban citadel
A blood debt owed for the perceived untimely slaying
Of Echidna's beloved daughter at the hands of Oedipus[80]
As the ill fated man made his journey to the ancient city

Invoking insatiable and uncontrollable sadness in Echidna
A monstrous mother surviving her offspring
But this was not the first time she has suffered
The loss of one of her ill begotten children

For her monstrous progeny includes the Lernaean Hydra[81]
The scourge of many poisonous heads
Each one destroyed swiftly replaced twice
Thus an impossible foe to subdue

The fiendish Hydra persist until mighty Heracles
As he endlessly suffered in his Labors
Destroyed the venomous beastly fiend
By cauterizing the destroyed roots

And too she anguishes over the destruction of the Chimera[82]
Part lion, goat, and venomous serpent
Fire breathing and fearsome to behold

---

[79] after defeat at the hands of Zeus, Typhon is trapped inside Mt. Aetna

[80] reference to the Sphinx; daughter of Echidna and Typhon; body of a lioness, wings of an eagle, face of a woman

[81] serpent guardian of the entrance to the underworld at the lake near Lerna

[82] fire breathing monster that ravaged the country of Lycia

Another gruesome bane upon humankind

Unstoppable until matched against mighty Bellerophon[83]
Supported by Pegasus, the winged steed[84]
Although matched against the fire belching hellion
Overcomes its fury as ordained by the Fates

And it would be folly not to mention
The beastly Crommyonian Sow[85]
Spawn of fire breathing Typhon and the serpent nymph[86]
Ravager of the lands which its name was derived

Until the redoubtable Theseus[87] from far off Athens[88]
In pity of the of Crommyon nation
Dutifully destroys the gluttonous sow
Forever a testament to his mighty prowess

Such were her brood destroyed by heroes
The children of Typhon overcome one by one
But the loss of her darling favorite in Thebes
Overmuch for Echidna to simply disregard

Thus the people of Oedipus[89] face her awful wrath
And death and sorrow is rampant in these lands
To Theban mothers, fathers, and children alike
To appease the anger of the serpent nymph

---

[83] Corinthian prince whom settled in Lycia; grandfather of Glaucus
(a Lycian prince and Trojan ally)
[84] winged horse; offspring of Poseidon and Medusa
[85] a gigantic wild pig
[86] another reference to Echidna
[87] son of Poseidon; founder of Athens
[88] city in Greece named for Athena, goddess of wisdom
[89] king of Thebes; fulfilled a tragic prophecy of slaying his father
and marrying his mother; kills the Sphinx as he travels to Thebes

Theban excesses in the past wholly abundant
For the city was rich in precious earthly metals
And the croplands blessed by the Olympian gods
Now all utterly diminished by Echidna's rage

And those unfortunately caught in her pathway
Ruthlessly slaughtered and devoured
Cattle, sow, and mortal alike
Destroyed with reckless impunity

Such was the undertaking of the monstrous Echidna
And the forlorn Thebans offer numerous libations
Finally acknowledged by pitying Apollo of Delphi
As he replies to their entreaties through his famed oracle

And counsels Thebes of the arrival of a mighty hero
To rid the holy lands of its strife
And that this savior was goddess born
The most handsome and pious man alive

And the Theban emissaries rejoice at the prophesy
In hopes that their awful plight would soon be resolved
For well versed are they of Memnon Tithonides' greatness
As foretold in all realms around the world

And now the prophecy was brought to fruition
When Memnon's contingent washed along the Theban coast
To the delight of a heartened King Polybus[90]
And to the zealously overjoyed Theban peoples

And as the son of the goddess and his men make approach
To the seven fold gates of lofty Thebes
Unbeknownst to them the sad plight of its inhabitants
As they humbly request succor from the benevolent king

---

[90] king of Thebes

For many of their necessaries were displaced or destroyed
During the melee with the north, east, and southern winds
And though the great Aethiopian king survives
He and his venerable comrades are now in disarray

And the son of the goddess makes his entreaties
For supplies and provisions to replenish the vessels
And enable his armies to forge ahead to Pergamus[91]
And confront the invading Argives in full force

To the solace of all the Dardanians!
Mercilessly ravaged by the deadly lance of the Myrmidon[92]
A respite for the peoples of besieged Troy
Nearly thwarted by a stratagem of Thetis

And so the forlorn King of Thebes makes his reply,
"Great Memnon, you are welcomed to these bereaved lands!
And your presence is most pleasing to my wearied eyes!
And to those all assembled in the Theban court

There was a time the riches of these lands were unparalleled
And all of Thebes never lacked for any necessity
Our magnificent halls cloaked in gold and silver
Rivaling the palatial abode of the gods and goddesses

But we have in some manner offended the Olympians
For the wealth of the city is swiftly diminished
As a scourge has been sent upon our homeland
And the foul Echidna destroys crops and irrigation

That monster conjointly assails our helpless nation!
And many brave Thebans ventured forth in opposition
With haughty promises of liberating holy Thebes

---

[91] another reference to Troy
[92] another reference to Achilles and his armies from Phthia

Each hoping to expel the monster from our lands

Yet none return home after the hellish encounter
As she senselessly destroys our women and men
All because she feels aggrieved at one of our own
Namely the downtrodden and unfortunate Oedipus

For the Theban monarch overcame the fiendish Sphinx[93]
As she assaulted all those whom traversed our lovely lands
Compelling those whom she hopelessly encountered
To answer her tricky riddles or be wholly devoured

Such a gruesome fate for any to suffer!
And these actions continued unabated for many years
For many rightfully feared the terrible Sphinx
And Thebes was isolated until the exploits of Oedipus

And now the Fates have smiled upon us again!
For your arrival brings our besieged nation hope
As your renown and bravery are famed throughout the world
And your feats at arms are admired in all earthly realms

Great Memnon, I offer to you whatever you desire
Anything that these lands are able to provide to you
My only request is that you exert your awesome strength
And mercifully free us from the mate of Typhon"

And the solemn Memnon patiently stands by
And listens to the entreaties of the Theban monarch
The son of the goddess is sympathetic to his dilemma
And is resolved to encounter the vicious Echidna

And the son of the goddess answers King Polybus,

---

[93] daughter of Echidna and Typhon; body of a lioness, wings of an eagle, face of a woman

"Gentle king, your words stir my heart!
Long has your lands suffered this injustice
For the serpent nymph is relentless in her enterprise!

And long lasting are the troubles of the Theban peoples
This citadel once the crown jewel of the world
And its gates the envy of all earthly realms
Now it languishes in waste and utter ruins!

Despair no longer, my friend Polybus!
For me and my brave comrades
Shall do all that is in our dominion
And as father Zeus judges as fitting

To rid your kingdom of this pestilence
To the delight of all those aggrieved by Echidna
And restore golden Thebes to its past prominence
Allowing your peoples to once again prosper"

And lion hearted Memnon solemnly promises assistance
And to rid the holy lands of its fiendish enemy
Namely Echidna, the mother of all monsters
No matter how daunting the task would prove to be

And king Polybus welcomes the Aethiopian armies
Offering to them all his worldly possessions
Confident is he that the son of the goddess would overcome
The serpent nymph and free Thebes from her bondage

And a great feast is prepared for the heroic men
With the finest wines and meats offered
As all of Thebes exuberantly rejoices
In revelry, honoring mighty Memnon and his comrades

And before any partake of the wondrous banquet
A young lamb is duly offered to the Olympians

As sacrifice in beseeching divine assistance
Solicitations of accomplishing a successful conclusion

And the Aethiopians and Thebans retire to slumber
As hunger and thirst are wholly satiated
And all anticipate the coming day and what it brings
As the son of the goddess prepares for an epic duel

And all arise in the first strokes of day break
The Aethiopian contingent eagerly makes preparations
All exhorting one another to battle to the uttermost
As Theban guides lead them to the lair of Echidna

And Memnon takes aside a selection of his commanders
While the remainder of his armies remain nearby
Trustworthy and courageous men are all those present
For each fought in many battles alongside Eos' brave son

And so great Memnon and his contingent
The best by far amongst mortal men
Forged in hardy steel and brutal war
And thoroughly primed for honor and glory

Swiftly take up arms and ready the encampment
As they prepare to do battle with the mother of all monsters
Anticipating assault from the dangerous serpent nymph
As she arises from her deep and cavernous abode

And the cunning Echidna espies them from afar
And plots the demise of the Aethiopian king
But first she waits until the cover of night
When Helios[94] has completed his journey across the skies

For the stratagem was to commence her attack

---

[94] god of the son; brother of Eos; uncle of Memnon

And employ lethargy as an accomplice
After the men have supped and relax guard
Surprising the Aethiopian contingent as they slumbered

Such was the plan of the serpent nymph
Unbeknownst to the famed son of Eos
As he and his loyal men lay in wait
Anticipating the advance of Typhon's mate

Bewildered they are that the monster had yet to appear
For she often emerges in her siege of Thebes
Destroying untold croplands and laying waste
Without fear of retaliation for her horrid actions

Yet the Aethiopian contingent continue to remain on guard
Ready to unsheathe sword at a moment's notice
As the hours of the day slowly past away in oblivion
And nightfall stubbornly arrives in Thebes

And then the Aethiopian men slowly begin to relax vigil
As false confidence creeps slowly into their minds
Convinced the serpent nymph has abandoned her campaign
Fearful of opposing the formidable son of the goddess

And so they foolishly lay down heavy helmets and lances
And audaciously set down their swords and shields
As they allow their heavy eyelids to shutter
And begin reposing tired limbs and weary bodies

And all this does not go unnoticed by the serpent nymph
As an opportune moment to assail her foe arises
And so Echidna swiftly rises at the eve of midnight
And deftly attacks the resting Aethiopian band

And some of the men nearest to Echidna
Are suddenly awakened from dormant sleep

And swiftly reach for their still weaponry
Determined to face a deceptive and terrifying opponent

And the serpent nymph gnashes her gruesome teeth
And from the depths of her coiled body emits a growl
Her piercing shriek shaking the very gates of Thebes
A chilling sound to all those within earshot

Who first did awful Echidna vanquish?
Mighty Cerces, [95]the great champion in the dance of war
Is first to meet with the monstrous deity
And although distinguished in battles with mortals

He effortlessly succumbs to the serpent nymph
As a grain of wheat is overcome by stone
Bending in submission to its overwhelming strength
So falls brave Cerces son of Laelops[96]

Next to fall victim to Echidna is swift footed Laopis[97]
Bravely he meets the serpent nymph without flinching
As he attempts to battle the monstrous hag with his sword
But in the end suffers a dismal and deadly fate

As prophesied shortly after his renowned birth
A joy to both of his delighted parents
His concerned mother suddenly awakened by a nightmare
That her son would perish in gruesome manner

Far away from the lovely shores of Aethiopia
At the hands of a fiendish ancient deity
And though she attempted to prevent Laopis' departure

---

[95] Aethiopian commander
[96] Aethiopian commander; Laelops is a close comrade of Emathion and is also slain by Heracles
[97] Aethiopian commander, brother of Tanutamen

She is unsuccessful in her enterprise, for none can defy fate

And next the lion hearted Aimpthos[98] encounters Echidna
As he hastily takes up his mighty lance
And aims it at her body with intent to pierce the scaly coils
Of the hellion's thick and impenetrable dermal

But the tough skin of the serpent nymph
Survives the encroachment of the ill fated weapon
It barely breaches the hideous hide
And destroys the lance of mighty Aimpthos

Preceding the destruction of that mighty man
A mortal versus an awesome monster
As Echidna is overmuch in the unequal struggle
And she effortlessly slaughters another Aethiopian captain

And the havoc ensues left and right
As the raging Echidna exerts her will with impunity
The serpent nymph rebuffs without much difficulty
The onslaught of the Aethiopian assault

Her slaughter apparent from the trail of gore
As the severed limbs of mighty men are scattered about
On the bloody ground in the pathway of the raging fiend
For the massacre of the Aethiopian contingent is her intent

But there is one man, best by far of all assembled
For great Memnon is determined to cease the slaughter
Alarmed by the gruesome handiwork of the serpent nymph
As that mighty man readies his huge lance and shield

The son of the goddess swiftly makes his advance
Heartbroken at the demise of his comrades

---

[98] Aethiopian commander

And at the callous manner in which they all perish
Brave Memnon is set on revenge against pitiless Echidna

And the monstrous serpent nymph roars mightily
"Son of the goddess, Memnon Tithonides
Dare you present challenge to me?
I, an awesome force that even the Olympians abhor!

And though you possess divine characteristics
Stout-hearted king of wondrous Aethiopia!
Of courage, strength, and incredible prowess
And beauty – none is your equal on earth

What makes you confident that you can match Echidna?
And oppose my edict that holy Thebes suffers?
For the losses that I have needlessly endured
At the hands of one of their own heroes

Though strong and brave you undoubtedly are
Not even your tremendous strength is enough
To thwart my intentions upon cursed Thebes
Nor shall you prevent my verdict from coming to fruition

Until my thirst for revenge has been assuaged
For the ferocity of my rage no mortal can withstand
And though you have different designs
You shall not defeat me as you imagine"

And the son of the goddess defiantly answers her,
"Vengeful Echidna, mother of all scourges
Your unjust torments shall end this instance
The Theban people unfairly aggrieved

Punished as a result of an heroic act
As wily Oedipus in his travels bound for Thebes

The son of Laius[99] flees his childhood home of Corinth
In a futile effort to escape an unfortunate fate

Unknowingly he fulfills his awful destiny!
By first slaying his estranged birth sire
As both met at a crossing not too far from these holy lands
And next entering into unholy maternal matrimony!

But well before this unthinkable and heinous act
Laius' son is accosted by the dreaded Sphinx
And with evil intent she poses a sly query
Confident the Theban would be unable to answer

She salivates at what she believes to be her next meal
But to no avail! Oedipus solves the complicated puzzle
To the utter dismay of the monstrous beast
And she takes her own life to the delight of Thebes

And now you torment the citadel in her stead
An even crueler substitute than the Sphinx
As you lash the flesh with your forked tongue
Terrorizing those that venture into your pathway

And powerful force though you may be
The time of your awful monstrosities
And your merciless and cruel assaults
Shall end to the delight of the Theban nation"

And with these words Memnon takes up his mighty lance
Heavy for a tenfold men to handle

---

[99] a past king of Thebes; it was foretold that he would bear a son
(Oedipus) whom would slay him and marry his wife; after
fathering Oedipus, he orders the infant to be abandoned at a nearby
mountain; infant Oedipus is found by a shepherd and subsequently
adopted by the king and queen of Corinth

But light in his magnificent hands
And with all his might he flings it at the bane of Thebes

With resolute intentions of inflicting a dolorous wound
Upon the body of the ancient scourge
And end her brutality against his brave countrymen
By conquering and subduing the monstrous hag

And the hungry weapon pierces the bosom of Echidna
Entering deeply into her horrid breasts
Those which succored her monstrous progeny
Each an indomitable pestilence to mankind

And she screeches in awful agony from the gash
A consequence of the lodged Aethiopian dart
As the searing pain reverberates throughout her body
Never before experienced by the monstrous deity

And the son of the goddess, aware of his advantage
Unsheathes his sparkling jeweled sword
And swiftly advances upon the wounded creature
Determined to end her unfortunate life

And the once haughty serpent nymph
Now utterly cognizant of her fragile mortality
Begins to plead to the son of the goddess for her life
Requesting forbearance from imminent slaying

And Memnon Tithonides, the righteous warrior
A man unparalleled in piety and purity of heart
Adhering to his own moral and humane virtue
Is thus prevented from killing the serpent nymph

And so the son of the goddess spares the life of Echidna
But first makes her swear an irrevocable promise

Indelibly upon the dark river Styx[100]
A holy oath even the Olympians are bound to obey

To forever cease her assault of holy Thebes
And to depart the lands of the gentle King Polybus
As great Memnon banishes the monster to her cavernous lair
Never to again return to the lands of Semele

Accordingly the awful Echidna begrudgingly yields
Because her foe is by far mightier than she
And the serpent nymph barely escapes with her own life
Due to the mercy of Eos' benevolent son

She swiftly flees the scene of her atrocities
As murky blood seeps from her grievous wound
Pierced by the might of the Aethiopian weapon
The scourge no longer afflicts the land of Oedipus

And thus the terrors of the serpent nymph are abated
At the hands of the heroic Memnon Tithonides
The salvation of the besieged Theban people!
As the son of the goddess attains a magnificent feat of arms

And those brave men depart the ferocious Echidna
Fulfilling the covenant with Polybus and his subjects
By ending the horrors of the fiendish deity
As mighty Memnon is forever endeared to holy Thebes

---

[100] river in the underworld; sacred to the immortals

III. The Nereids

And as the glorious Aethiopian contingent
Triumphantly returns to the Theban citadel
An exuberant and joyous King Polybus
On bended knee greets the son of the goddess

"Great Memnon, pride of the goddess Dawn!
And equally the greatest benefactor of Thebes
For we offer our everlasting homage and fealty
On a whim, at your beck and call!

Forever indebted to the divine lands of Aethiopia
Shall unequivocally be Thebes and her grateful peoples
Our alliance fortified and enduring in perpetuity
For your strenuous acts in releasing us from subjugation

As the monster is put to flight by your mighty lance!
And she escapes the wrath of your magnificent sword
No longer does she prosper in causing strife and pain
In her savage revenge for the demise of the fiendish Sphinx

And Thebes shall once more be a bountiful metropolis!
As we fearlessly open our once shuttered sevenfold gates
Welcoming all peoples with open hearts and arms
Plentiful in our hospitality as is our ancient custom

And though you are now duty bound to depart for Ilium
And to intervene in the greatest of mortal warfare
We pray that you and your brave comrades
Grant allowance so we may show our immense appreciation

And in the morn you shall have all requisite provisions
The best that these lands can provide
And we shall ardently replenish your ravaged fleets
Meager recompense for your incomparable feat of arms"

And the son of the goddess makes his grateful reply,

"Good King Polybus, our friendship is cemented
As Aethiopians and Thebans exchange fervent vows
And two greatest of nations eternally bound to one another

How could one not offer succor to holy Thebes?
For your great metropolis is divinely favored
The beginnings of the great god Dionysus
And nurturer of many heroes and famed heroines

So what I and my comrades have undertaken
When we made covenant to encounter the serpent nymph
Any honorable man would undertake the same task
And accordingly the Olympians accede to our great triumph

So let us honor the immortals in our upcoming revelry
As the banishment of Echidna is due to Olympus' blessings
And let our sacrifices and potent offerings
Encourage them to favor our future endeavors"

And with these words the valiant son of the goddess
Along with King Polybus and all within the grand hall
Lift their golden cups offering sincerest libations
As they fervently beseech the commendations of Olympus

And so the peoples of Thebes joyously celebrate
The departure of the monstrous scourge from their lands
And readily partake of the great feast that was prepared
In honor of godlike Aethiopian monarch

And the brave comrades of the son of the goddess are feted
And honored like gods amongst mortals
A show of gratitude from the delighted Theban nation
At last allowed to once more flourish as before

And furthering the generous display of gratitude
For the splendid victory of the son of the goddess

The Theban king duly commands the Theban stone cutters
Men renowned for their extraordinary skills in masonry

To commence the construction of a massive monument
A colossus forged in strong sandstones and quartzite[101]
A magnificent structure befitting the son of the goddess
Commemorating the triumph of mighty Memnon Tithonides

Fortified to withstand the elements of wind and rain
An eternal memorial for future generations to behold
And though King Polybus considers this gesture unequal
Nonetheless sanctions the erection of the colossus

And after the jubilation and merriment abates
The Aethiopian king dutifully recalls the task at hand
And swiftly commands that the vessels be provisioned
And that all preparations are made for impending departure

The fleet is handsomely restored and reinforced
As the Aethiopian contingent are once more rejuvenated
As sights are set once again for the Trojan shore
Aspirations of relieving Priam's citadel of its occupation

And due sacrifices are offered to honor the Olympians
As an auspicious departure from Thebes is sought
And father Zeus nods in acquiescence to the entreaties
By commanding the seas and winds to remain calm

To the utter dismay of silver footed Thetis the sea nymph
As she is unable to quiet her persistent torment
For maternal concerns ravage her restless thoughts
And thus continues plotting against the son of the goddess

---

[101] reference to the Colossi of Memnon, two massive statues
overlooking the Nile River in ancient Thebes (modern day Egypt)

And so the daughter of Nereus calls to her exalted kin
Commencing a council to express her concerns
And to seek out the assistance of her lovely sisters
The fifty daughters of the old man of the sea[102]

First to come is Actaea, Agave, Amathia, and Amphinome,
Amphithoe, Amphitrite,[103]Apseudes, Arethusa
Next Asia, Autonoe, Beroe, Callianassa, Callianira, and
Lovely Calypso,[104]Ceto, Clio, Clymene, Cranto, Creneis

Then Cydippe, Cymo, and lusty Cymatolege,Cymodoce,
Cymothoe, Deiopea, Dero, and sly Dexamene,Dione, Doris,
Doto, Drymo, Dynamene, Eione, and delightful Ephyra,
Erato, Eucrante, Eudore, Eulimene, Eumolpe, Eunice

Then came Eupompe, Eurydice,Evagore, Evarne, Galene,
Galatea, and inquisitive Glauce, Glauconome, Halie,
Halimede, Hipponoe, Hippothoe, and amorous Iaera,
Ianassa, Ianeira, Ione, Iphianassa, Laomedeia

Next came Leiagore, Leucothoe, Ligea, Limnoria,
Lycorias, Lysianassa, Maera, Melite, Menippe,
Nausithoe, Neaera, Nemertes, Neomeris, Nesaea,
Neso, Opis, Orithyia, Panopea, Pasithea,

And finally comes lovely Pherusa,Phyllodoce,
Plexaure, Ploto, Polynome, Pontomedusa,
Wily Pontoporeia, Poulunoe, Pronoe, Proto, Protomedeia,
Psamathe, Sao,Speio, Thaleia, Themisto, Thoe, and Xantho

---

[102] the Nereids; daughters of Nereus and sisters of Thetis
[103] queen of the Sea; wife of Poseidon
[104] in the *Odyssey*, as Odysseus attempts to return to his homelands
in Ithaca after departing Troy, he is washed ashore on her island
and engages in a romantic relationship with the goddess

Accordingly her magnificent siblings gathered in support
Of Thetis' plan to further delay the planned arrival
Of the son of the goddess to the Scaean Gates
In a concerted effort to prolong the life of her beloved son

And the forlorn Thetis speaks to the gathering,
"My sisters, fully aware are you of my immense sufferings!
For no mother should know the awful pain
Attributed to the demise of her beloved child!

As I now sadly stand before you on behalf of this brave man
That stubborn son of Peleus born in the Phthian foothills
Woefully is he now fettered to an unfortunate destiny!
His fate ordained even before his decision is settled upon

Such misfortune apportioned to my beloved son!
And his dreadful fate in the hands of the son of the goddess
As Memnon cruelly persists in his voyage to Troy
Eos' son determined to abet his ancestral kinsmen

Hardened is his resolve to endure across Poseidon's realm
To offer succor to King Priam and his famed allies
In dire straits by the exploits of Myrmidon Achilles
For none other alive can withstand him in awful battle

As so I beg you all to hear my painful plea!
And to defer my own inconsolable losses
By offering an impediment to those resolute Aethiopians
And thus delay their impending approach to holy Ilium

Proffering enticements to those brave and sea faring men
So that they choose to abide in these lovely isles
And to remain here for an elongated period of time
Thereby postponing the awful fate of swift footed Achilles"

And a teary eyed Thetis implores her sympathetic sisters

To distract great Memnon and his famed commanders
And thus allow the scourge of Troy[105] and its peoples
Continuance to ruthlessly ravage that city of King Priam

And the lovely Nereids delightfully set about the task
With dual purposes in mind as they venture forth
Making preparations to enrapture Memnon and his comrades
And to appease the entreaties of Thetis

And thus quenching their own lustful desires
For the Aethiopian contingent were men of renown
Second to none in virtue, physical attributes, and prowess
With the handsome son of the goddess being most coveted

And thus the stratagem is devised, unbeknownst to Memnon
As he and his comrades effortlessly navigate their vessels
For lord Poseidon allots them favorable waters
And all aboard the ships envision a swift arrival to Troy

And within a short time Memnon espies buoyant isles ahead
Mindful that it was necessary for the fleet to resupply
And replenish what was rightfully expended
The son of the goddess commands the vessels to disembark

And the Aethiopian ships set anchor to the exotic lands
Tranquil and soothing its plains appear upon initial sight
With wondrous and colorful flowers and varied lotus
A momentary respite from the rough and wild seas

Also visible are many species of birds and pheasant
Along with clear lakes and lush streams
Plentiful are the sheep and large oxen
Roaming freely about the lush and green countryside

---

[105] another reference to Achilles

The son of the goddess, satisfied that all necessaries
Could be acquired from these wondrous realms
Dictates that the island be further surveyed
As he apportions the task to brave Sthephios[106] and his men

While the others remain amongst the docked vessels
To gather necessary victuals and replenishments
In preparation for the phase of the journey ahead
For the sumptuous isles offered varied provisions

Meanwhile Sthephios and his loyal contingent
Begin inspecting the expanse of the remarkable province
Suddenly and with both amorous and deceptive intentions
A band of Nereus' daughters make approach towards them

And Sthephios and his men gaze at the lovely goddesses
As divine effervescence illuminates where they stand
And the stunning deities seductively encircles them
While simultaneously admiring their Aethiopian beauty

First to address them was lovely Ianassa
"Oh sea wearied men forged in steel
After your heroic battle with a vicious monster
Namely she who bore the cunning Sphinx

The defeat of the serpent nymph known in all realms
Of your handsome king wholly subduing Typhon's mate
As word of your exploits travels swiftly and far reaching
For the salvation of Thebes again traverses the Aegean!

And now by fortune you arrive to our palatial isles
To the delight of myself and my assembled sisters
For we most desire to be in your company

---

[106] Aethiopian commander; brother of Agathon, king of Nubia,
lands adjacent to Aethiopia

To consort with men descended from mighty Zeus himself

Allow us to properly acknowledge your coveted presence
For you are most certainly in need of rest and respite
And we shall cater to all of your bountiful needs
As deserving of such tremendous men of distinction

As we stand ready commanded to serve your desires
To ensure during your sojourn that you lack for nothing
For we request that you accept our entreaty
To feast and delight in our divine presence"

And those godlike men effortlessly acquiesce
As they accept the hospitality of the daughters of Nereus
Offered at the instigation of Thetis silver foot
The cunning daughter of the ancient deity of the Sea

And so the rest of the Nereids that accompany Ianassa
Takes the hand of a willing Aethiopian captain
And dutifully escorts him to the magnificent palace
Itself surrounded by alluring flowers, streams, and animals

And the delighted Nereids swiftly disarm their mates
As the magnificent Aethiopian armor is left at the gates
And all enter that wondrous abode, fit for an Olympian
Anticipating gaiety and amusements assuredly to transpire

First the men of Memnon are abundantly feted
Partaking of wines, venison, and lush fruits
As the daughters of Nereus entertains their companions
Indulging them with the lustful delights desired by the flesh

As Sthephios and his contingent are hopelessly seduced
By the delights of the alluring sea goddesses
Upon the insistence of Nereus' wily daughter
As the overwhelmed men neglect their apportioned task

And all of this was unbeknownst to their magnificent king
As Eos born Memnon stands by the vessels
Awaiting the return of those sent to survey the foreign lands
For the son of the goddess is unaware of Thetis' trickery

And after many untold hours elapse without nary a sighting
Nor sighting of Sthephios and his accompaniment
The son of the goddess becomes quite concerned
And prepares an expedition to discover their whereabouts

Led by himself and his trusty cousin brave Aithops
As the rest of the men remain to guard the ships
While the others hastily arm in preparation for battle
As each takes up lance, sword, shield, and helmet

And after they are properly armed for war
The son of the goddess and his chosen men
Resolutely advance in search of Sthephios and the others
In awe of the astounding sights of the island along the way

As Sthephios and the others witnessed much earlier that day
And suddenly Memnon espies a massive golden palace
And recognizes the Aethiopian armor near the entrance
As the shields and swords lay quietly as though abandoned

And so the son of the goddess prepares the men for combat
For he could not fathom that Sthephios willingly disarmed
And therefore Memnon supposes they were assaulted
And held captive within the walls of the impressive structure

And great Memnon draws his famed sword
As he leads the men into the wondrous yet unknown abode
And his loyal comrades follow closely at his heels
And they are alertly prepared to attack at a moment's notice

And as they continue towards the magnificent compound

A sudden brilliant light illuminates the area nearby
As a sweet intoxicating aroma fills the air
And at once Memnon becomes aware of a divine presence

And suddenly a staid deity appears before him and his men
Regally bedecked in her ambrosial and flowing robes
Her permeating beauty and grace wholly incomparable
A wondrous sight to behold by those lusty men

Though unflappable stood the Aethiopian contingent
Nonetheless are awestruck by the lovely immortal
As the goddess singularly lavishes all her attention
On great Memnon as she delivers her presentation

"Son of the goddess, I come before you amicably
And to offer answers to your burning inquiries
For your brave and trusty men are well founded
As they comfortably lodge with my indulgent sisters

I am called the Amphitrite the Nereid
And I count myself a child of the Old man of the Sea
And no less wife to blue haired Poseidon
The trident bearing ruler of all aquatic realms

My sisters and I offer hospitality to you
And to your men, as you are most welcomed here!
To freely partake of the riches offered by these lands
And of anything else you may too desire

I implore you to relax your strenuous vigilance
And to loosen your powerful grip of the lance
For you shall not find war in these realms
So grant me leave to remove your tunic and breastplate"

And with these honeyed and subtle words

The Queen of the Sea[107] gently takes the strong hand
Of Memnon and leads him to the majestic palace
And his men obediently emulate their famed king

And as they enter the extravagant dwellings
Servants swiftly provide refreshments and other fare
And subsequently bathe them in steamy saunas
To the delight of the sea faring Aethiopian men

And thus delayed are their ambitious pursuits of Troy
Undertaken to defend the homelands of King Priam
And dually drive away the haughty Achaeans
From the ravaged and besieged Dardanian kingdom

Too deferred are the attainments of immeasurable glory
So that future generations would forever remember
As the son of the goddess traverse the treacherous seas
Enumerating the legend of Memnon and his glorious armies

Eternal accolades nearly derailed by the plot of Thetis
As the Aethiopian contingent are attended by her sisters
Without difficulty they are seduced by divine wiles
As even the hardiest of mortals succumb to their will

And those brave men are provided desired victuals
From the extravagant excesses offered by the sisters
And additionally amorous advances are conferred upon them
By the lusty goddesses, themselves fiercely desired by many

In the halls of Olympus as well as throughout earthly realms
One such instance being that of the lovely Galatea
She tirelessly sought by the Cyclops Polyphemus[108]

---

[107] another reference to Amphitrite
[108] a one-eyed Cyclops; son of Poseidon; antagonist of Odysseus in
the *Odyssey*

A monstrous being is tortuously enamored

Of a ravishing goddess whom scorns her admirer
As Polyphemus offers many potent gifts
And eternally pursues his unattainable prize
All for naught and as he is forever rejected

This same Galatea sleeps in the arms
Of brave Axumian Tanutamen, great ally
To the son of the goddess born Memnon
As divine conquest is freely given by the daughter of Nereus

And the lovely and much coveted Iphianassa
Heralded sister of Thetis swift foot
Passes her time idly with the redoubtable Aithops
Lieutenant to his famed and heroic cousin

And himself renowned throughout all realms of Aethiopia
A youthful yet deadly warrior in awful battle
Accordingly he is paired with an immaculate goddess
As both enjoy the company of one another

And as the Aethiopian men are thoroughly entertained
None other than lovely Amphitrite herself
Regal spouse to the brother of mighty Zeus
Seeks the love of the incomparable son of the goddess

Partly in accordance with the mandate of silver footed Thetis
But also due in part to her strong affections for Memnon
By far the most handsome amongst mortal men
As lust is set afire within the heart of the Queen of the Sea

And thus Amphitrite desires to lay with great Memnon
And make him her paramour, in violation of her vows
A marital covenant made a long time ago near the peaks
Of the exalted and heralded Mount Olympus

As a youthful Poseidon, conqueror of mighty Cronus[109]
Pursues the loveliest of Nereus' daughters
The blue haired Olympian presents many bountiful gifts
In exchange for an eternal bond of fidelity

Amphitrite refuses the offerings from the neophyte sea lord
Steadfast is her resistance to the proposals of Poseidon
And only upon the concerned paternal advice of Nereus
Does lovely Amphitrite reluctantly yield to him

Forging an uneasy and tenuous alliance
Between the lineal descendants of Pontus[110]
And the powerful subduers of the Titans[111]
Thus cementing the Olympians undisputed supremacy

And accordingly Poseidon is matched
With the loveliest goddess of the Sea
His sought after prize decisively claimed
And unchallenged is his reign of the aquatic realms

But marital vows are many times betrayed
As lusty Poseidon came to love many
One of his conquests being the ravishing Medusa[112]
Preceding her monstrous transformation

---

[109] Poseidon assisted Zeus in defeating his father Cronus and the Titans
[110] personification of the sea
[111] deities that reigned prior to the ascendance of the Olympians; sons and daughters of Gaia and Uranus
[112] monstrous Gorgon with snake-like hair; all whom beheld her was instantly transformed into stone; Medusa was once a beautiful woman until she offended Athena by having a tryst with Poseidon in one of Athena's temples; as a consequence she is transformed by the goddess into monster

Also loved by the great lord of the Sea
No less than Aethra, [113]progenitor of great Theseus
Begotten by her subsequent to lying with Poseidon
On the Sphairian island off the coast of Athens

And thus with a guiltless conscious, Amphitrite approaches
The handsome son of the goddess and articulates
In no uncertain terms her passions towards him
Without alluding to her matrimonial state

The great goddess of the sea makes her solicitations,
"Memnon, transcendence of the goddess Eos
Long have I beheld your marvelous countenance
A wondrous compliment to your well muscled physique

Paralleled only by your prowess at arms
Most gifted are you of all the demigods by far
For none can deny you possess all of the attractive traits
That woman both divine and mortal desire

For is this not the very reason for the demise of Cyrene?
The unfortunate Libyan queen dwelling in dark Erebus[114]
A forlorn subject of Hades[115] in his cavernous realms
Never to again partake of the bright sunlit world

As a result of your refusal of her piteous entreaties
Her amorous desires for you unrequited
She suffered the same torment as I now endure
A queen and a goddess beholden to one impeccable man!

And now I, like the Libyan queen, offer my unflinching love
And willingly succumb to whatever you decree

---

[113] queen of Athens

[114] another reference to the underworld

[115] lord of the underworld and of the dead; son of Cronus

For I beg of you to have mercy upon this wretched deity!
And allow me to wholeheartedly quench my passions

And to grant to you whatever you should long for
As you are the one I chose as my coveted lover
So I beseech you not to break my enraptured heart!
And partake of the pleasures that I shall offer to you alone"

And Great Memnon replies to the anxious goddess
"Lovely Amphitrite, wife to the great Sea god himself
Your entreaties are humbly acknowledged
And I would be remiss to refuse your request

But in adhering to my own morality
And not to offer offense to the mighty Olympians
By fornicating with an immortal goddess
However tempting your lustful advances may be

For such actions are not pleasing to mighty Zeus
His wrath I fear more than anything in the world!
For he is invincible when he wields his bolts
Destroying anything that obstructs his will

For such was the misfortune of the venerable Anchises
Shortly after he copulates with the divine Aphrodite
The forbidden union produces a mighty hero
And elicits the fury of the son of Cronus

He takes up the mighty thunderbolt with ease
Hurls it from the heights of Olympus in a rage
It swiftly strikes the son of Capys[116]near the Idaean plains
It's awful force crippling the famed Dardanian monarch

And though no longer able to pursue adventures

---

[116] son of Assaracus, grandfather of Aeneas

Nor further fame and glorious accolades
Nonetheless the lover of Aphrodite is grateful
That he escapes alive from the wrath of Zeus

Furthermore another mighty son of Cronus lurks
An unspeakable offense to him if I acquiesce to your request
For Poseidon Earthshaker is feared by all mortals
As his huge trident is foil for many seafarers

The lord of the wide ranging oceans
Would undoubtedly be thoroughly vexed
And all of Hades shall speak of his retribution
If I were to gaze upon the body of his beloved Queen"

And so Memnon resists the overtures of Amphitrite
As she despondently turns away from Eos' son
Her heavy heart is battered by his measured rejection
As her overwhelming temptation is temporarily refuted

And while the daughter of Nereus is saddened
Concurrently admires the resolve of the son of the goddess
And this esteems him more so to the wife of Poseidon
And thus furthering the depth of her love for him

And while her sisters fulfill their amorous desires
With the handsome and lusty men of Aethiopian fleet
Amphitrite fruitlessly continues her pursuit of Memnon
By offering all manners of gifts to him

In a concerted effort to win his unyielding love
She first presents him with a silver cropped lance
With delightful engravings depicting his lineage
For the goddess is well aware of his penchant for arms

This wondrous gift is followed by many others

Including a golden cup from Hesperia[117]
Far off mystical lands near the abode of Atlas[118]
As he shoulders the weight of the earth as punishment

A bequest befitting the redoubtable son of the goddess
And Amphitrite's efforts are not lost upon Memnon
As he graciously accepts these divine gifts
But persists in his refusals of her passionate entreaties

But the amorous daughter of Nereus
Remains steadfastly against capitulating to these refusals
Although her overtures consistently rebuffed
And her longings for the son of Eos are unbearable

And as the son of the goddess unaccompanied
Ventures forth into the forests in search of wood and lumber
For reinforcement of the vessels are his aims
For purpose of persisting in his quest for the Trojan citadel

The Queen of the Sea suddenly appears before him
The goddess is extravagantly clothed and beautiful
As the Olympians would see her in all her splendor
Her erotic scent is reminiscent of the orchids on the island

Her striking physique is visible through her celestial robes
And her soft and supple skin enticing to the eyes
The intent of the lusty daughter of Nereus abundantly clear
For she aspires to seduce the handsome son of Tithonus

---

[117] land of mystical gardens in the far western corner of the world;
akin to the biblical Garden of Eden
[118] Atlas (one of the Titans) held the entire world on his shoulders
as punishment from Zeus for taking sides   against the Olympians
in war

Gazing longingly at him, the sea goddess begins,
"The cold Aethiopian stones must be your beginnings!
False is the legend of your being the son of that radiant Eos!
For you have cruelly refused both my love and splendid gifts

Without a care for how this affects sad Amphitrite!
As I stand before you heartbroken and at your mercy!
A saddened goddess before a dispassionate man
For now I long to be some mortal woman in Aethiopia

Or a Thessalian princess bedecked in golden robes!
At least I would be able to end this eternal misery
And my life may mercifully reach its terminus
In the same manner as the unfortunate Libyan queen

Never again to gaze into the bright rays of the sun!
As she choose to end her finite and awful existence!
Freeing herself from the bondage of love unrequited
She now dwells painlessly in the sanctuary of dark Erebus

But the Fates apportion immortality to sad Amphitrite
As my parents preceded the reign of the Olympians
And my grandsire himself the personification of the Sea
And so wretchedly I must consider other alternatives

And accordingly I now compel you to accept my love!
Even if this is not what you willfully desire
Take me as you would take your own wedded wife
Without fear of the repercussions of obeying my command"

And with this the lovely Amphitrite slowly disrobes
Revealing her naked body to the son of the goddess
As she compels mighty Memnon to lay with her
In direct violation of her matrimonial vows

And a torn Memnon responds to her emotional edict,

"Glorious wife of great Poseidon, it hardly behooves me
To take you into my arms and assuage your pangs of love
And thus offend the fearsome Poseidon Earthshaker

And yet you compel me to perform this unthinkable act!
As is your own divine prerogative
Knowing full well the strife that will undoubtedly arise
Between myself and the lord of the Sea"

And so in spite of his deep reservations to the contrary
Memnon acquiesces to the command of the Sea queen
As was her right and her due as an immortal goddess
For the desires of Amphitrite are beyond her divine control

And the son of Eos reluctantly quenches her passions
As Amphitrite so desperately petitioned him to do
And in the process incurs the wrath of the Trident Bearer
Though this not his preference, nor what he sought

And so the incomparable men of the Aethiopian armies
Hopelessly subjected to the stratagem of Thetis
For on its face deemed a successful enterprise
As Memnon is held captive on the isles as Amphitrite's lover

And while all of these events are in motion
An indignant and troubled Eos espies all
And her anger towards Thetis is uncontrollable
As she swiftly proceeds to Olympus to make complaint

And magnificent Eos is greeted by none other than Zeus
He that possesses the mighty and invincible thunderbolt
And thus was more powerful than all in sum
As he was on the eve of Cronus' demise

And Eos kneels before the lord of the Olympians
And pleads with him in a subdued and humble tone,

"Oh great Zeus, irresistible Aegis bearer
As you have professed to care for my needs, hear my plight!

My incomparable darling favourite, brave Memnon
Besieged on all fronts by his irresistible enemies
This magnificent man, whom has always honored the gods
As no mortal on earth has nor shall before

Since the morn that I bore him to Tithonus
That faithful day on the Aethiopian plains
A delight to both me and my lordly husband
His unparalleled beauty evident from his beginnings

And well I knew even then of his unfortunate fate
A selfless path chosen by a courageous man
And though a mother is compelled to suffer from this choice
Must I stand aside while she acts untamed?

I speak of silver footed Thetis, the delight of Nereus
While her dreaded progeny awful Achilles
A scourge to the Trojans and Dardanians
Continues in his brutal siege of holy Ilium

The daughter of Nereus has already intervened once before
Causing a quarrel amongst my offspring
Unleashing endless sufferings for my beloved Memnon
From the fatal animus of his windy brethren

And next she employs seduction and submission
As her unscrupulous weapons of choice
Conspiring to prevent the redoubtable Aethiopian contingent
From reaching the shores of far away Troy

In resistance to your very own divine edict
That great Memnon shall achieve glory everlasting
As rightfully due to a man of such stature and prowess

An eternal testament to his incomparable existence

And so I make request that you force the Nereid
To cease her meddling in the affairs of my son
And to contain our conflict within the walls of Olympus
Or I shall be compelled to confront her aggressions"

And thus rosy fingered Eos implores
Great Zeus as he stands majestically on his throne
And the son of Cronus is sympathetic to her complaints
And accordingly responds by summoning Hermes

The renowned messenger of high Olympus
With his famously winged sandals
Cunning Hermes swiftly arrives before his glorious father
And stands in silence as Great Zeus articulates his will

"Hermes, I desire that you go to Thetis without delay
And tell her that I desire her to cease her activities
In opposition to great Memnon and his comrades
Undertaken on behalf of her son the Myrmidon

As he relentless attacks that city I so love
And the peoples of the good king Priam unjustifiably suffer
Staggering losses of many brave and courageous men
And splendid sons at the hands of ruthless Achilles"

And so Zeus sends his messenger to order Thetis to desist
Her transgressions against the Aethiopian king
And Cronus conquering Zeus also mandates
That lovely Amphitrite release her incomparable hostage

And Hermes swiftly departs the golden halls of Olympus
And makes his way to the abode of Thetis
He instantly arrives to her seaside estate
And upon greeting Thetis, glorious Hermes begins earnestly,

"Daughter of Nereus, I come with an edict from father Zeus
The mighty cloud gatherer and ruler of us all
His divine will is that you immediately cease your conflict
With the venerable son of the goddess dawn

Although your actions are derived from maternal concerns
And Aegis bearing Zeus holds you in high regard
His divine will shall not be thwarted by any
And thus you must yield to his commandments"

In response a distraught Thetis beats her breasts in sorrow
As her interventions are conclusively extinguished
And accordingly the Fates would no longer be delayed
As the liberation of great Memnon and his men is imminent

And next Hermes proceeds to the fruitful isles
Where the glorious daughters of Nereus are engrossed
Delighting the brave and lusty comrades of Memnon
And the cunning messenger finds a love stricken Amphitrite

And the son of Zeus swiftly delivers his message,
"Sea queen, this matter requires your prompt attention
For the son of Cronus seeks your full compliance
For none can defy the will of mighty Zeus

So take heed and do as the Cloud gatherer commands
Though in strong contradiction to your own designs
For your affections for Memnon are famously known
Yet you still must release him from your commandment"

And Hermes makes known to her the verdict of Zeus
Much to the chagrin of the Queen of the Sea
For she had grown quite fond of the son of the goddess
And dreaded to be deprived of his pleasing presence

And the tormented goddess makes her response,

"Son of Maia,[119] your speech is hardly welcomed here!
For I so love and adore the mighty Aethiopian king!
And my preference is to be his wedded wife in perpetuity

And yet this shall never be so during my existence!
For the lord of us all sees fit to deprive me of my delight!
Unendurable shall be the loss of his company to me
For none – god or mortal – equals the son of the goddess"

And Amphitrite feels immeasurable pain in her heart
For she truly loved that incomparable man
But all must yield to the will of mighty Zeus
And thus she reluctantly rescinds dominion over Memnon

And the swift footed Hermes then goes to Eos' son
As he stands longingly near the shores of the sandy isles
Helplessly peering out into the expanse of the oceans
For he is divinely compelled against his will to idle there

The son of the goddess takes notice of Hermes' presence
And accordingly Memnon gives his full attention to the god
As a glimmer of hope begins to renew his dampened spirits
That the intervention of Olympus would end his captivity

And so the illustrious son of Maia addresses the forlorn hero,
"Son of the goddess, why dawdle as if in a fanciful dream?
While your Trojan kinsmen suffer at the hands of Achilles?
Do you now abhor achieving fame and everlasting glory?

Or have you grown weary of adventure and risk?
I see that your famed Aethiopian courage now fails you
And you covet the desires of the flesh afforded by these isles
While Ilium falls before the might of the Achaeans"

---

[119] mother of Hermes; eldest of the Pleiades (daughters of the titan Atlas)

And the son of the goddess replies to these inquiries
"Glorious son of Zeus, why ask of my sad plight?
For my predicament is well known in the halls of Olympus
As I have been compelled into the bed of the Sea queen [120]

And without option I must obey her divine commandments
For she is the daughter of old Nereus, an immortal goddess
Contrary to my own designs of departing these lands forever
As my own desires are to set oars to the seas without haste"

And wily Hermes makes his reply to the words of Eos' son,
"Courageous Memnon, loved by lord Zeus himself!
No longer fear the wrath of lovely Amphitrite
For the Thunderlord warrants your swift embarkation

And all must obey the commands of father Zeus
So order your men to make the necessary preparations
And swiftly depart these realms without further delay
After making due offerings to honor the Olympians"

And so the messenger of Zeus exhorts the Aethiopian king
To gather his loyal comrades and board the regal vessels
And to set sail for the besieged city of Tros
For the Sea queen would no longer present obstacle

To the sheer delight of city sacking Memnon!
For this was what the son of the goddess wanted most
To cross the Aegean and arrive to the famed Scaean Gates
And assist in repelling the fierce Achaean assault

And to offer respite to his desperate kinsmen
And forever endear himself to a grateful nation
And although his own mortality is at risk as a result
Eternal honor and greatness takes precedence

---

[120] another reference to Amphitrite

And so Hermes departs after delivering his father's edict
As the son of the goddess immediately readies for departure
Commanding his men to make the appropriate preparations
As the vessels are replenished for the journey ahead

And a heartbroken Amphitrite suddenly appears before them
And gingerly takes Memnon aside for a private moment
To make a final request of him as he takes leave of her
In an attempt to assuage any acrimonies he may possess

"My love, though your departure is utterly displeasing
I offer my sincerest regrets for any perceived offenses
And beg your pardon for my impassioned transgressions
For my actions were derived from unassailable affections"

And empathetic Memnon answers the Queen of the Sea,
"Amphitrite, forever shall I hold you dear to my heart
For your hospitalities offered to me and my comrades
And never before have men been so feted by goddesses

How could I bear ill will against Nerenian Amphitrite?
And your actions undertaken out of love and not malice
And now we depart one another under auspicious accords
For there is no enmity in me against you"

And with these words Memnon takes her into his arms
As a tearful Amphitrite poignantly embraces him
And beseeches the son of the goddess to remember
Their union, though more short lived than she desired

And so great Memnon and his men set oars to the water
As they are bound for the Trojan citadel full speed ahead!
And the Aethiopian contingent continues its epic quest
Nary a thought of potential perils yet to be endured

IV. Chrysaor

As the Aethiopian vessels venture forth along the ocean
And into the tenuous grasp of the wide ranging seas
That spiteful cousin unto isolated Phthonus[121]
Namely Ossa, her vile and ill begotten words

Spread swiftly to the great Earthshaker himself
Interrupting the lord of the Sea as he reposes
Regarding the infidelity of his beloved wedded wife
And of the mighty man for whom she shattered marital vows

And upon receiving the salacious propaganda
The son of Cronus becomes uncontrollably enraged
His wrath and fury is so palpable
That the very ocean itself reverberates beneath his feet

And Poseidon hastily plots his retribution
As he indignantly assigns blame for the affair to Memnon
Although his sought after vindication is wholly unwarranted
Resolute is Earthshaker in exacting his misguided revenge

For the noble and righteous Memnon Tithonides
More godlike than a mere mortal, initially
Resists the advances of the lusty Queen of the Sea
In an effort to avoid offending the fearsome lord of the sea

Until he is compelled by Amphitrite to do her bidding
For the son of the goddess is unable to refuse divine orders
As all mortals are bound to dutifully follow
The divine mandate of the immortal deities

And such is the sole justification that compelled
Eos' son to become the consort of the daughter of Nereus
As the son of the goddess is coerced into the illicit affair
In spite of wisely knowing the repercussions of these actions

---

[121] god of envy

Namely that Poseidon would be furious at the union
And now these fears come to fruition as the son of Cronus
Lay out his plans to harass the famed Aethiopian king
With his divine arsenal fully unleashed at his disposal

And though the lord of the tumultuous seas himself
So loved that magnificent son of Eos and Tithonus
For Memnon is always the foremost in his offerings to him
The perceived indiscretions are overmuch to pardon

And even though the lusty Poseidon had many lovers
And accordingly possessed no basis for his ill feelings
The trident bearing god could not bear the tortuous thoughts
Of his chosen mate in the arms of another

And so an envious and spiteful Earthshaker
Takes up his indestructible and feared trident
And strikes the oceans with all of his might
As he whips the currents into a chaotic frenzy

And the otherwise tranquil ebb and flow of the waves
Violently changes course upon the insistence of Earthshaker
As the waters near the ships of great Memnon erupt
Intent upon the destruction of the Aethiopian vessels

And as the son of the goddess and his loyal men
Navigate the lofty vessels atop the calm waves of the sea
Eagerly anticipating arrival to the far away shores of Troy
The intense force of Poseidon's fury is unleashed upon them

And Memnon is confounded by these sudden events
As he and his comrades are assaulted without warning
And the angry waters begin to violently crest
Threatening to engulf the ships and all those aboard them

And though many are tossed in aquatic conflagration

Those brave men remain resolute in their survival
As they courageously battle the hostile elements
And great Memnon exhorts them with rousing words

"My great Aethiopian comrades, stand firm!
For we are more like stone than ordinary men!
Having endured much without bending, and we shall
Encounter yet far worse dangers apportioned to us by fate!

For glory and everlasting fame are not effortlessly attainable
And much shall we suffer in our quest for honor
For the Olympians bless only the strong and unyielding
As lesser men disintegrate into utter obscurity!

I implore you all to remain resolute in our endeavor!
And we shall not be moved by the ferocity of the sea!
For there is no doubt that Earthshaker has abandoned us
And is determined to force us to cease our enterprise

Our foremost intentions of reaching the Scaean Gates
And provide succor to our besieged Dardanian brethren
By engaging the haughty Achaeans in war and strife
As we wield the fatal lance and forged cold steel

But we shall set foot upon Troy's sandy beaches
And enter that golden citadel ruled by the good king Priam
And future generations shall speak of the mighty exploits
Of our fearless contingent from a long time ago"

And thus Memnon Tithonides speaks stirringly to his men
Lifting their dejected and overwhelmed spirits
His heartened comrades persists in the intense struggle
As the turbulent sea continues its furious eruption

And what should have destroyed the besieged fleet
Is bravely endured by the mighty Aethiopian men

To the total dismay of the trident bearing god
Furthering his rage and resolve to continue the assault

For in the mind of the angered son of Cronus
Existed a wicked plot to devastate the son of the goddess
And his loyal men for the perceived affront of Memnon
By steering them to the lands of a hungry fiend

And so Poseidon intensifies his powerful aggression
Assuaging his pain from the matrimonial betrayal
Distraught that he no longer possesses the love of his wife
As the ravishing Amphitrite chose mighty Memnon instead

And thus righteous Memnon is compelled to tolerate
Immortal displeasure in abundant and excessive force
As his lot is cast upon the golden scales of Zeus[122]
And unfortunately sinks low to the hallowed ground

And the Aethiopian contingent continues on
Bravely battling the extreme and dangerous elements
Though nature is often the consummate victor
In futile battles against sad mortals

And shortly thereafter the battered vessels crash ashore
Sorrowful lands long abandoned and dreaded by humanity
As Lord Poseidon's rage is mercifully abated
And divine rationality starts to set in

As the men of great Memnon are at last afforded respite!
From that great god's awesome demonstrations
And the barren lands are thoroughly welcoming to them
A symbol of escape from the treacherous seas

---

[122] reference to divine scales of Zeus used to determine the fate
mankind

They swiftly make approach towards the desolate land
And though uninhabited and sparsely populated, it seemed
An incarnation of a Garden of Hesperia to the sea weary men
After the harrowing ordeal versus the lord of the Sea

And the Aethiopian fleet rejoices as they dock the ships
After surviving the sustained divine onslaught
As fading hopes are again restored and renewed
And once declining ambitions are tenuously intact

And after the vessels are tethered and secured
The son of the goddess privily gathers the men
A council of his generals and most trusted commanders
To ascertain how best to regroup and again set sail

For arriving to Troy remained the plan of great Memnon
And to intervene in the dispute famed throughout the world
Partaking of the epic battles along banks of the Scamander
Though powerful forces opposed this lofty goal

And at the conclusion of their candid deliberations
And upon the recommendations of his wise advisors
It is unanimously and conclusively determined
That the barren lands be thoroughly explored

For its potential to offer much needed provisions
And to obtain the necessary and sought after victuals
To reinforce the storm battered Aethiopian vessels
And replenish the massive armies of Memnon

And accordingly Eos' son sends chosen captains
Men of great character and of brave stock
To survey the isolated and barren lands
Though they appeared inhospitable and uninhabitable

Unaware they were of the misfortune concocted

By the Earthshaking lord of the Sea
An unjustified punishment meted by Poseidon
In response to lovely Amphitrite loving Eos' son

For on the far end of this desolate terrain
Stationed remotely in the wide reaches of the ocean
Dwelled a viciously hideous creature
With constant cravings of mortal flesh to satiate

And a boundless appetite perpetually unappeased
Afflicted with this condition since his inception
As the monstrous Chrysaor[123] awaits his prey
For the scent of mankind lingers tantalizing close

A fearsome and gigantic being is the son of Medusa!
As he undisputedly rules the sad and distant lands
That the son of the goddess and his faithful comrades
Lucklessly set upon as they escape the fury of the Sea lord[124]

The dreaded monster is brother unto Pegasus
The winged horse tamed by Bellerophon
An indispensable ally against the Chimera
As the hero king triumphed over his evil foe

Chrysaor's accursed birth itself a result of an act of violence
As both the fiend and Pegasus are simultaneously born
When Zeus sired Perseus slew the dreaded Gorgon
Medusa, for the sake of the Aethiopian princess[125]

His aim to recover the head of the Gorgon
And employ as a weapon to liberate the lovely Andromeda
The son of Danaë[126] deftly takes up the forged sickle

---

[123] son of Medusa the Gorgon; monstrous cannibal
[124] reference to Poseidon
[125] another reference to Andromeda

And accomplishes his goal of slaying the horrid Medusa

And thus two siblings spring forth
From the severed neck of the slain Gorgon
One bright, the other dark and dreadful
Linked only through familial pedigree

Perseus then swiftly ventures forth to lovely Aethiopia
And finds solemn Andromeda as she does selfless penance
Subsequent to boastful proclamations of Queen Cassiopeia[127]
That her beauty is greater than those of the Nereids

A foolish charge from the reckless queen!
Thus confining her daughter to an unjustifiable death
And the princess is shackled along the Aethiopian shores
For the uninvited appearance of Cetus the sea monster

Sent in anger by the trident bearing Poseidon
For the affront offered to the lovely daughters of Nereus
And Cetus hungrily approaches the forlorn Andromeda
For its desired repast is the lovely Aethiopian princess

And as the sea monster makes attempt to devour its prey
The son of Zeus unveils the head of the Gorgon
Thus transforming the beast into inanimate stone
Forever a testament to his magnificent exploits

Occurrences precipitating beginnings of the ravenous giant
And events preceding the arrival of Memnon and his men

---

[126] mother of Perseus; daughter of Acrisius of Argos; the Oracle at
Delphi prophesied that Acrisius would be slain by his grandson;
after being impregnated by Zeus, Acrisius condemns Danaë and
the infant Perseus to be cast into the sea in a wooden chest for
purposes of preventing his own death
[127] queen of Aethiopia

Upon the dreaded wastelands of the fiend Chrysaor
His vicious intent to entrap men unaware of his existence

And so the ravenous son of Medusa looms in secrecy
Awaiting the Aethiopian men to approach his lair
With a goal of appeasing his ancient hunger
Accelerated, considering the quality of quarry

And by a stratagem he plots to apprehend
And to assuage his monstrous delights
By setting out all manner of venison and wines
And fruits, treats, and other victuals

To lure the Aethiopian contingent into his trap
And accost the men as they partake of the delightful meal
Reveling in his cannibalistic banquet
And appeasing his ancient longings for human carcass

And all of this is unknown to the son of the goddess
As he selects brave Aeocles[128] to lead a contingent
And disperse about the unknown lands
To determine potential risks and benefits of its exploration

And thus the mighty son of Emathion is charged
He along with the other brave and fearless men
All of noble birth and magnificent lineage
The best by far amongst earthly mortals

And Aeocles readily obeys the commandments
Of the son of the goddess as he gathers his men
And they swiftly commence the mission without delay
While the others stand back to set up camp near the shores

And Aeocles along with his trusty comrades

---

[128] Aethiopian captain; son of Emathion; nephew of Memnon

Begin arming themselves as if readying for war
Cloaking themselves in breastplates and bright tunics
And taking into their hands the Aethiopian made steel

As they venture forth surveying the gloomy lands
And many strange and sickening sights are witnessed
Articles of clothing and weapons are strewn about
As if abandoned in terror by panicked masters

So too observed by the bewildered and concerned men
Fragments of bone scattered throughout the pathways
A gruesome admixture of human and beastly remains
As if both were gluttonously devoured simultaneously

To the horror of Aeocles and all those present
And each man tightens his grasp on the trusty lance
And alertly grips the pommel of the sword
Prepared to encounter the perpetrator of the cruel handiwork

And they cautiously continue the dark journey
As bright Helios begins his routine descent
And the lurking shadows fearlessly make appearance
Creating a landscape for the eerie silhouette

Of mangled bones, marrows, and sinews
And the high rising foliage with its twisted bark
Forming nightmarish contours upon the dusty earth
As the rays of the sun continue to dissipate

Yet the brave men venture onward in spite of these images
And within a short distance arrive upon a dry riverbed
Where the cooling waters once flowed freely and unabated
Now a distant memoir of the abandoned province

And just as the Aethiopian contingent cross a dry riverbed
An intoxicating aroma fills their nostrils

The smells of roasted lambs and pheasant
And fruits, wines, and other refreshments

And slightly ahead redoubtable Aeocles spots these items
Laid out in the midst of a dry and desolate field
And though the area is unusually quiet
Aeocles and his men are enthralled by the feast

For they are extremely parched and famished
From the earlier ordeal versus Earthshaker
And from traversing the barren expansive plot
Accordingly the men are obliged to assuage their hunger

And they swiftly disarm from their bulky attire
Removing strong breastplates and laying down heavy shields
And before partaking of the sumptuous meal before them
They offer prayers and thanks to the merciful Olympians

Pouring libations to almighty Zeus and the others
As was due to the powerful immortal deities
For the perceived salvation provided to those weary men
For they were oblivious to what lay ahead for them

And so these mighty men are observed by the giant
As they indulge themselves near his devious ambush
The men delighted after their arduous journey
To freely partake of the deadly enticements of Chrysaor

And as Aeocles and the others replenish themselves
Monstrous Chrysaor makes his fatal maneuvers
And is successful in trapping the unsuspecting men
Within his hidden device beneath the hallow earth

A deep and uninviting domicile for strangers
In which no escape could be found
And so a surprised Aeocles and his men

Are hopelessly imprisoned to their utter despair!

Then huge Chrysaor swiftly reaches into the abode
A feat that no other earthly creature could accomplish
And swiftly the giant corrals the unlucky Drasops[129]
Then promptly begins to gorge himself on that mighty man

A Meroitian horseman and companion unto great Aithops
The famed Drasops renowned for his equine skills
As none in Aethiopia could prevail against him in the race
For the Meroitian was a favorite of the god Hermes

His skills now useless against the immovable Chrysaor
As the horrified men swiftly reach for weaponry
Determined to recover a beloved and respected comrade, and
To commence the counter attack against the fiendish giant

Alas, the sword and lance are of no avail!
Against the fierce brother of Pegasus, intent upon his prey
And thus came the end of Aethiopian Drasops
A sad mortal matched against a monstrous scourge

Unfortunate too is the lusty Eithicros[130]
As he suffers a fate similar to Drasops
The Axumian captain bravely endeavors to battle the son of
Medusa, yet is thoroughly overwhelmed from inception

And Aeocles along with the other ambushed men
Recognizing they were engaged in an unequal battle
Matched against an irresistible force of nature
Hastily flee to the corners of the cavernous trap

---

[129] comrade of Aithops; born in the same hour as the Meroitian prince
[130] distant relative of Tanutamen

The monstrous giant attempts temporarily frustrated
As a result of the cunning maneuver of those besieged men
And Chrysaor is thwarted from further indulging his appetite
For his huge hands are unable to grip any of them

And so the men of Aeocles nimbly retreat
Assembled in peripheral corners of the dungeon
In an effort to defer the strenuous intent of the cannibal
And delay their seemingly inevitable demise

And so Chrysaor, recessed in his onslaught
Determines it best to cease his assault of those shocked men
Confident is he in partaking of subsequent meals
As the Aethiopian men are hopelessly confined

And so momentarily the cravings of the giant are appeased
As Chrysaor gradually withdraws from the accursed area
To the relief of Aeocles and the others
As they are permitted to regroup from the abrupt onslaught

And Aeocles turns to address his awestruck comrades
"Great men of mighty Memnon, do not be despondent!
Nor let the grief at the demise of our brothers overcome you!
For our hour of descent to Tartarus has yet arrived

And we shall soon see the Trojan capital we now seek
For we are descended from the Olympians themselves!
And even if we all perish in our commendable aims
We shall slay this loathsome giant plaguing mankind!

Resolved in the knowledge that a stronger avenger awaits
For our great king Memnon shall surely overcome this beast
So for now we shall prepare for the fiend's next attack
And by the grace of Zeus we shall endure as best as we may"

The brave Aeocles speaks these encouraging words

Renewing hope within the spirits of his battered men
That revenge would be soon be theirs when the giant lay
Dead, as they are rescued by the son of the goddess

Meanwhile Memnon Tithonides patiently awaits the return
Of his well endeared lieutenant and the other men
Prior to commanding his godlike men to proceed
Deeper into the dark and unknown terrains

But a great goddess, concerned for the mighty hero
Hastily goes to the venerable son of the goddess
As he was unaware of the daunting challenge that lay ahead
Accordingly Artemis seeks out Memnon to forewarn him

For the goddess knew well the precarious danger
Posed by Chrysaor to the Aethiopian contingent
And of the ancient cravings plaguing Medusa's spawn
That he would undoubtedly satiate through his stratagem

And the daughter of Zeus suddenly appears before the
Aethiopian king to offer her candid advice to him
Of Chrysaor's schemes and ill willed intentions, for
Artemis intended for Memnon to end the hideous practice

And so the huntress goddess[131] speaks to brave Memnon
And only he, peerless amongst mortals
Hears Artemis as she articulates her urgent message
"Son of the goddess, divine Memnon Tithonides

Beloved of the gods upon high Olympus
Take heed, an ancient danger lurks nearby
For on this isolated province lies a fatal obstruction
To your much anticipated arrival to the Trojan citadel

---

[131] another reference to Artemis

For herein lies the behemoth and horrid Chrysaor
A child of no less than the snaked haired Medusa
Brought forth as the Gorgon is overcome by the son of Zeus
For the love of an Aethiopian princess

The hideous cannibal is left alone to appease his appetite
Preying on storm ravaged men lost in the tumultuous seas
Those lucklessly tossed into the dark abyss of these lands
To be devoured by a ruthless and craven giant

By trickery and deceit he lures potential quarry
His victims unfortunately perish as the vicious cycle
Continues, for even as we speak, Chrysaor eagerly awaits
On the far end of these gloomy lands for your presence

Alas, trusty Aeocles and the others are now in peril
Entrapped within a dungeon crafted by Chrysaor the giant
Famished men overcome by need for sustenance
As they were enticed by venison and wines laid out

And even more fearsome beyond his abnormal proportions
Is the stubbornly impenetrable dermal of Chrysaor
Resistant to the cold steel of mortal weaponry
A useful weapon that is maternally inherited

Thus presenting an untenable predicament
In thwarting the gruesome designs of the giant
As the son of Medusa is armed with a crucial advantage
When facing his overwhelmed adversaries

Those whom dare to have the courage and resolve
And seek to resist the will of Chrysaor
Unknowing that battle with the fiend is futile
For the giant is immune to their desperate assault

But in these cold lands there abounds

A natural antidote to Chrysaor's concealed asset
Obscure to the inferiority of mortal vision
Thus making the perennial almost impossible to discover

Bur readily discernable by divine eyesight
Not far from these barren fields you shall find what you seek
For the herb is bright amidst this darkened background
Its coloring appears red, then yellow, then turquoise

Constantly shifting its illumination to avoid detection
Furthering the advantage held by Chrysaor
But now you are equipped with precious knowledge
To locate and utilize the much coveted plant

Son of the goddess, go forth and find the perennial!
This herb must be affixed to your Aethiopian weaponry
And thus nullify the tremendous advantage of Chrysaor
His sole repellant from being vanquished by any"

And after conferring with the son of the goddess
Huntress Artemis departs as suddenly as she appeared
Her primary intended mission is effectuated
For godlike Memnon is now prepared to defeat his adversary

And so the son of the goddess and his loyal comrades
Begin their intense search for the prized herbs
Sorely needed for war against the horrid Chrysaor
In an effort to attain the liberty of his trapped men

As they are hopelessly imperiled at the mercy of the giant
While Chrysaor sleeps peacefully, digesting his meal
The terrible son of Medusa savoring his gruesome banquet
With intentions of further satisfying his subsequent cravings

Meanwhile stout-hearted Aeocles continues to urge his men
To remain determined, though ravaged those brave men are

And the Aethiopian commanders' words wholly unnecessary
For the men in his company are descended from Zeus

And thus are prepared to face subsequent attacks
And to defend each other against the awful giant
As they alertly await huge Chrysaor to make his approach
Resolute that Pegasus' brother sorely earn his next meal

And shortly thereafter a loud and thunderous bellow is heard
And the very earth beneath the men violently shakes
Signaling the dreaded approach of the hungry behemoth
As he relishes thoughts of fulfilling his cravings

Swiftly mighty Aeocles and his brave companions
Reach for swords, shields, and Aethiopian lances
And assemble in battle formations within the constricted pit
Readying themselves for the coming assault of Chrysaor

And the giant obliges as he reaches deep into the dungeon
His arm met by a thrust from the lance of brave Aeocles
As Emathion's son next takes his sword and attacks the giant
While the others hastily follow suit against the fiend

Futile is the attempt to slay the impenetrable Chrysaor
For he is armed with skin like wrought armor
And the cold steel is unsatisfactorily deflected by his hide
As it harmlessly bounces to earth after missing its target

After the initial and wholly unsuccessful onslaught
A self assured Chrysaor launches his own fatal offensive
And woeful is the retribution that the giant renders!
His overwhelming response a display of blood and gore!

Whom did the giant ravenously devour in his fiendish rage?
First Oeneor, then redoubtable Adrasius
Two stout cousins reared together in a serene Kushian city

These two heroes often competing with each other

For one was skilled at the bow and arrow
While Oeneor was acclaimed for his swordplay
And as such neither could defeat the other
In the field that either thoroughly excelled in

Yet none of the other youth in their lush homelands
Could match to the prowess of the blessed cousins
And accordingly selected to accompany the grand contingent
To the pride and delight of their family and peers

And as both brave men attack the abhorrent giant
They find to their utter dismay that weapons be of no avail
As Chrysaor's dermal predictably affords him protection
For lances and swords of mortal are useless against him

And the courage of the two cousins is for naught
As both suffer the same desolate fate
Against a heartless and ravenously hungry monster
Eager is Chrysaor to devour his vanquished quarry

As he savors the flesh of Oeneor and unfortunate Adrasius
And thus appease his unnatural and enormous appetite
The cannibal quickly indulges without delay
And then callously tosses aside the bones of the cousins

Aeocles and his battle heartened men, though horrified
By the inhumane treatment of the remains of their comrades
And by the brutality of the assailment of the giant
Nonetheless continue on against the indefensible

Next to face the deadly and provoked Chrysaor
A famed Nubian archer called Peplios[132]

---

[132] brother-in-law of Agathon

Deftly takes up his bow and quiver of arrows
And takes deadly aim at the body of the fiend

Great Peplios launches his indomitable arrow
Not a miss! The dart strikes the intended target
And what would assuredly bring death to another victim
Is dismally unsuccessful versus the hide of Chrysaor

And as Peplios the archer takes up another arrow
Intent again upon the destruction of the giant
He is unfortunately not given another opportunity
As the son of Medusa snatches him from the pit

And devours yet another brave Aethiopian champion
As the unlucky Peplios meets his awful fate that day
Needlessly destroyed by the hands of the raging Chrysaor
As the fiend is wholly determined to end more lives

For the sake of his overwhelming cravings
As well as due to his unjustifiable annoyance and anger
At the defiance and resistance of his Aethiopian foes
To thwart his apparent cannibalistic intentions

And although the son of Medusa is awesome to behold
And possesses a devilish and fearsome countenance
And survival versus him appeared to be an impossible task
Aeocles and his men still bravely stand their ground

All while the woeful subjects of Memnon are suffering
Trapped in the pit and unequally matched against Chrysaor
Continuing to fight to save their imperiled lives
As required by their exalted and famed bloodlines

The son of the goddess and his concerned companions

Relentlessly search for the necessary herb
That would assist in vanquishing his gruesome opponent
While the reckless carnage of the giant continues

And as the battle against Chrysaor rages on
The son of the goddess and his trusty men
Galvanized by love and concern for besieged brethren
At last locate the majestic and elusive perennial

Not far from where Aeocles and the others are entrapped
In a nearby cave the herb hides itself
Flashing its varied and shimmering colors
And then suddenly camouflages itself in the darkness

For it did not desire to be discovered
And avoided detection by any and all costs
As revealed by the huntress goddess Artemis
In her immense love for the son of the goddess

Redoubtable Memnon lies in wait for the perennial
To again reveal itself to him and his men
And as the herb illuminates deep turquoise
Then abruptly changes to a ruby red hew

And at that moment the son of Eos clutches the coveted herb
And rips the roots out from underneath the hardened ground
As the once resistant and stubborn perennial
Succumbs to the might of the godlike son of Eos

And Memnon affixes the subdued seedling to his lance
And the remainder on his sparkling bejeweled sword
In preparation for his impending conflict with Chrysaor
To conclusively end the cannibalistic practices of the giant

Swiftly the son of the goddess seeks his besieged comrades
As he eagerly anticipates confronting the awful giant

Unaware was the self aggrandizing and arrogant Chrysaor
That a powerful demigod sought him out for battle

Peerless Memnon Tithonides, Echidna conqueror!
Resolute is the son of the goddess
To put an end to the terrorization of his comrades
And rescue his men from the clutches of the giant

And as they sally forth in search of the spawn of Medusa
More of Memnon's beloved comrades are slaughtered
Yet despite their predicament they still keep faith
That great Memnon would rescue them from awful Chrysaor

Such are the hopeful thoughts of the besieged men
As Chrysaor continues his onslaught against them
The fiendish giant seeks their utter demise
To satiate his yearnings for more human flesh

And as mighty Memnon continues his quickened search
They espy the same mangled bones and human remains
Marrows, sinews, and the dark bloodstained ground
Witnessed earlier by Aeocles and his contingent of men

And they are equally appalled by the inhumane sight!
And concern for their companions increases ten fold
And thus they hasten the search for Aeocles and the others
A renewed sense of urgency after the gruesome sighting

And shortly thereafter the son of Eos makes approach
To the dungeon where his stricken comrades are trapped
And engaged in struggle versus the seemingly indestructible
Chrysaor, just as he takes brave Aeocles into his fatal grip

To the horror of great Memnon and his contingent!
As they espy the remains of fallen and devoured companions
Beloved comrades and allies since the earlier days of youth

The spectacle provokes the anger of the son of the goddess!

And a furious Memnon loudly shouts out to Chrysaor
"Monstrous giant, forever shame shall be upon thee!
For your gruesome practices and horrid actions
Bringing sadness and dread alike to innocent men!

As the unsuspecting victims, men of high honor
And of distinct and divine bloodlines
Are slain due to your cannibalistic thirst
An affliction suffered since your unwanted birth

But an end shall now be made of this habit
For I shall not forbear this inevitable conflict
Nor shall I refrain from attacking to the uttermost
And exact revenge for my aggrieved comrades!"

And with these indignant and forceful words
Great Memnon takes up his heavy lance
And his famed sword in his huge hands
Both outfitted with the magical herb

As commanded by the goddess of the hunt[133]
And the son of the goddess advances against Chrysaor
While his loyal comrades follow their commander in unison
As they take various battle positions opposite the giant

The intent to put an end to this scourge!
And the gigantic and haughty son of Medusa
Confidently ventures towards the men with huge strides
Determined is he to meet the son of the goddess in battle

But unbeknownst to the arrogant giant
Great Memnon Tithonides possesses the ancient knowledge

---

[133] another reference to Artemis

Of the antidote to the survival of awful Chrysaor
As the majestic herb is firmly affixed to the sword and lance

Making the weaponry adequate for the fatal standoff
And thus equalizing the chances of the participants
As the incomparable Memnon presses forward
And commences the clash with his fearsome foe

While the others brandish their bright Aethiopian weaponry
All battle hardened and proven in the ways of war
Poised to support the assault upon the fiendish Chrysaor
The son of the goddess launches his dangerous lance

And the powerful weapon grazes the neck of the Chrysaor
Instantly murky blood spews from the open gash
And had not the giant instinctively swerved
The deadly missile would have assuredly killed him

Thus the giant barely escapes with his forsaken life
And the son of Medusa's heart begins to pound incessantly
As the blood from the wound inflicted by fierce Memnon
For no one has ever come so close to destroying him

A swift jolt of mortality encompasses a bewildered Chrysaor
For the giant never before experienced unendurable pain
Nor the dark blood which flowed from the gash
Accordingly he pauses as sudden shock sets in

And after this brief abeyance from the deadly encounter
Chrysaor begins to understand that the son of the goddess
Possessed the forbidden knowledge of the magical herb
No doubt through the intervention of a divine god or goddess

For the giant sees that his demise is the intent of Olympus
And Chrysaor becomes angered by this revelation
Resentful the gigantic being is at the Olympians

Intensifying the giant's resolve to fight to the bitter end

And the stubborn Chrysaor attempts to corral the son of Eos
In a final effort to avoid his imminent doom
And before the giant could grasp redoubtable Memnon
The son of the goddess maneuvers his hardened sword

And with a single stroke from the cold Aethiopian steel
Severs the hand of the desperate Chrysaor
The appendage falls with a loud thud to the ground
As the fiendish giant bellows in uncontrollable agony

So effortlessly did the Aethiopian sword penetrate
The behemoth's hide, once thought impervious to assault
Thus affording the continuation of his horrid practices
And now his dead limb lies near the remains of his victims

Trepidation palpable in the mind of overwhelmed Chrysaor
As what he supposed to be impossible materializing
Mortal weaponry hewing his gigantic body to pieces
As his overdue and imminent death looms

And the son of the goddess further presses his advantage
Piercing the belly of the giant, the power of the herb
Exposing the weaknesses of the son of Medusa
As a subdued Chrysaor is leveled to the cold earth

And a previously unvanquished adversary
Is no match for the son of the goddess
As he brandishes the indestructible Aethiopian sword
To the delight of Aeocles and the trapped men

And the triumphant Memnon Tithonides shouts to his foe
"Giant, will you now yield and save your imperiled life?
And refrain from your hideous practices
Returning to the decent norms of humanity?

For mercy is freely given if sincerely requested
And atonement made for your multiple offenses
Beginning with refuting your cannibalistic savagery
Offensive to both the immortal gods and mankind alike

For this practice must come to an immediate and eternal end
And though you have already lost limb from my swordplay
There is a chance yet of hope and redemption
Wretched though your predicament now appears"

And thus the son of the goddess makes request of his foe
For his pure heart would not willingly slay
Any living being, giant or mortal
If atonement could readily be achieved

But the insubordinate Chrysaor
Undaunted even in the face of his demise
Remains stubbornly recalcitrant in his response
Defying the will of the Memnon Tithonides

And so the giant musters all of his remaining strength
Directing his gigantic proportions in a desperate attempt
As the monstrous Chrysaor lunges at Memnon
Determined to make a final stand, foolhardy indeed!

An ill fated decision by the doomed Chrysaor!
To the woeful detriment of the overmatched giant
For his opponent was by far more powerful than he
Divinely favored and greatly loved by the Olympians

And so came the end of awful Chrysaor
As mighty Memnon wields his fearsome sword
Dealing a dolorous stroke to the lamentable giant
As his comrades encourages their peerless leader

And so the reign of the monstrous offspring of the Gorgon

At long last comes to a fortunate and absolute end!
As the son of the goddess attains yet more glory
And avenge the deaths of his beloved comrades

V. The Abduction of Triton

And by the grace of merciful father Zeus
As he is perched on his throne high above earthly realms
Brandishing the powerful thunderbolt as the lighting flashes
And keeping a keen watch over the realms of mankind

The lands once ruled by the cannibalistic giant are liberated!
And sunlight is restored to the desolate fields
As the once besieged flowers, foliage, and animate beings
Wholly embrace a new and more magnanimous monarch

And Aeocles and the others trapped in Chrysaor's pit
On the brink of imminent death at the hands of the fiend
As they bravely battled the once invincible son of Medusa
Are rescued and happily greeted by welcoming comrades

And remains of those that did not survive the ordeal
Are gathered and interred as befitting their ranks
And funeral rites are administered to these brave men
With many tears and reminiscing of much happier times

And a sad Memnon issues orders to construct a pyre
As well as a marker to commemorate his beloved comrades
So that future generations would forever remember
The sacrifices made by them as they battled a deadly foe

Accordingly the famed Nubian archer Peplios
And Kushian Oeneor along with his cousin Adrasius
And the Axumian commander brave Eithicros
Along with the horse taming Drasops from beautiful Meroe

Each afforded proper remembrances by their godlike king
And faithful friend, for heart stricken is sad Memnon
As he was unable to rescue his beloved comrades
And thereby alter their misfortunes ordained by the fates

And as the redoubtable Memnon prepares to depart
The liberated lands of Chrysaor, and continue onward
A spiteful yet powerful goddess espies this from afar
And anxiety slowly creeps into her embittered heart

As Hera keeps close vigilance of the Aethiopian contingent
For her eyes sees all things of grave concern to her
And the wife of great Zeus is provoked
As a great threat to her beloved Achaeans draws closer

For the queen of the Olympians is keenly aware
In her divine knowledge that were Memnon to arrive at Troy
His incomparable prowess at wielding the lance and sword
Inevitably would inflict havoc upon the armies of Argos

Shortly upon reaching the shores of holy Pergamus
And disembarking from the Aethiopian vessels
Thus expediting the death of the dreaded Myrmidon
And provide reprieve to the peoples of holy Troy

Hera too knew that invincible Cloud Gatherer,[134] her mate
Commanded Thetis the silver footed daughter of Nereus
To abstain from further conflict with the son of the goddess
At the heartfelt request of the radiant Eos

Subsequently after the goddess of dawn approached Zeus
In all of her iridescent and brilliant splendor
Bedazzling is the golden goddess as she beseeches him
And the son of Cronus readily capitulates to her request

For great Zeus so adored redoubtable Memnon
For his purity of heart and pious nature
And for his potent and bountiful offerings
Accordingly the son of the Dawn is honored by Olympians

---

[134] another reference to Zeus

Thereby Zeus' edict to Thetis is effortlessly delivered
To the dismay of a saddened and subdued Thetis
For the sea nymph was too loved by the Thunder lord,[135] and
Assumed that his affections would override Eos' request

But it became quite apparent to the mother of Achilles
That Eos and her peerless son were too endeared to Zeus
And possessed the coveted blessings of Cronus' mighty son
Even more so than the line of the Old Man of the Sea[136]

And the queen of Olympus in her limitless enmity
And determination to cause strife for the son of the goddess
Plots against the revered Memnon and his loyal men
For her sole purpose is to bring more anguish to Troy

By devising a stratagem to prevent their arrival to Ilium
And allow more death and sorrow to envelope the city
As the Dardanian plains become a washed in blood and gore
While Achilles ravages the Trojan armies unchecked

Divine punishment for Paris' slight to the powerful goddess
That woeful day he chose Cytherean[137] Aphrodite
Over Hera and Pallas Athena as loveliest of the three
An ill advised judgment causing immeasurable suffering

Thus Hera was determined to seek retribution
And so the Queen of Olympus appears before great Memnon
In his dreams as he peacefully slumbers
Shortly after his deadly confrontation with Chrysaor

As the Aethiopian contingent regroups and replenishes
Abiding for a final evening on the dreaded lands of the giant

---

[135] another reference to Zeus
[136] another reference to Nereus
[137] Cythera or Cypris were lands sacred to Aphrodite

As those brave men repose before an exodus to the seas
Again heading for the once bright citadel of Troy

Meanwhile Hera disguises herself in the likeness of Eos, that
Radiant goddess who provides light after the dark of night
The Olympian queen falsely parades as a concerned parent
Intent upon protecting the interests of her offspring

Under this guise Hera appears before a slumbering Memnon
"My son, your magnificent beauty and fame is well known
Throughout the expanse of the entire world
As you pursue justly deserved glory in the lands of Dardanus

Yet you have been deterred in your awesome quest
Redirected by a cunning plot of the daughter of Nereus
For the purposes of facing the monstrous Echidna
A task undertaken by you for the sake of Thebes

And then a preoccupation with Nereus' lovely daughters
Too at the behest of Thetis silver foot
And to partake in an unprovoked dalliance
As commanded by the lovely Queen of the Sea

To lay with her in disfavor of trident bearing Poseidon
And thus engendering the anger of the Earthshaking god
As he plots your demise at the hands of gigantic Chrysaor
The terrors of the behemoth conclusively terminated

But now I desire your safe and unabated passage
To holy Ilium without further divine incidence
And this my son can be only be achieved
Through relatively difficult and somewhat evasive means

By seeking to capture the elusive Triton[138]

---

[138] son of Poseidon; messenger of the sea

The swift herald of trident bearing Poseidon
A trusty messenger of the haughty seas
As he bears the trident of the great Sea god himself

For he alone knows the least treacherous pathway
To your coveted and most desired destination
That sorrowful and piteous domicile of Helen
For much acclaimed is the beauty of the Spartan queen

As she graces the bed of the fortunate prince Paris
To the utter dismay of the Spartan Menelaus
And a quarrel between two love stricken men
Thus creates conflict between two mighty nations

And the Trojans anxiously await your arrival
For your lance is rightfully abhorred by the Achaeans
As you wreck havoc amongst the Argive ranks
For none shall be able to withstand your awesome fury

But first you must apprehend that wily herald
And by sheer force you must corral that sea deity
By compelling Triton to reveal all secrets that he possesses
And knowledge that concerns you and your loyal armies

Triton's presence is rarely pronounced to the world
For it is his nature to banter about undetected
As he freely traverses the expanse of the wide ranging seas
Without a care nor worry of ever being accosted

But the sea herald leaves an unmistakable trail
As he effortlessly glides along the aquatic estates
And few possess this divine knowledge and wisdom
The key to the whereabouts of the evasive Triton

For not far from where you now stand
Lies an abandoned and desolate island

Its only occupants are the green foliage and wilderness
Densely populated with shrubbery and brush

Here is where you and your brave men should encamp
As you await the appearance of swift Triton
And his merry procession as it traverses the waters
For such is his distraction to ensure he remains undetected

Keep watch for the colorful appearance of the hippocampi[139]
Sea horses traversing in a graceful sway
These majestic creatures of the limitless and blue seas
Constantly accompany the procession of the sea herald

And once you espy the presence of these hippocampi
As you lay in wait for the joyful herald
His broad shoulders barnacled with bright sea shells
Capture that son of Poseidon and compel submission"

And so Hera misadvises the son of the goddess
Ill will and intentions her primary ambition
For the purposes of further inflaming the raw passions
And anger of the sea god Poseidon Earthshaker

As he already held the son of Eos in high disfavor
For following the explicit commands of his queen
As Amphitrite desired the peerless Aethiopian king
To lie in her divine chambers as her preferred consort

And Queen Hera knew in her malicious and plotting heart
The inevitable abduction of Triton the sea messenger
Beloved son and confidante of Lord Poseidon
Would thoroughly and utterly vex the Sea god

Engendering yet more troubles for the son of the goddess

---

[139] sea horse-like creatures

And his loyal men as they continue their voyage
In hopes of swiftly reaching Pergamus without further
Molestation, such are the aspirations of the son of Eos

Confident that Thunder lord Zeus loved him
And accordingly bless continuance of the quest without
Further incidence, sanctioning a speedy arrival to the Troy
Under the divine auspices of the great Olympian king

Affirmed by the night time visit from his beloved mother
For the son of the goddess supposed the dream to be sincere
And upon waking from his justly deserved slumber
Memnon makes swift preparations to confront the sea herald

And so Hera's stratagem is firmly planted
As the peerless Memnon is roused to accost wily Triton
And the son of the goddess swiftly commands his men
To set about their unseemly task ahead

And forcibly take hold of the messenger of the seas
In an effort to discover a pathway of least resistance to Troy
Impervious to the perils of Poseidon's vast domain
And at long last encounter a glorious destiny abroad

And so the Aethiopian contingent change course of the ships
By navigating the vessels to the meager island
Covered in heavy foliage, forests, and leafage
But otherwise abandoned in the midst of the seas

And the son of the goddess gives further orders
To place the ships on the far side of the isles
Cloaking the vessels behind the heavy green vegetation
So that none approaching would be able to discover them

And after this uncomplicated task is accomplished
The son of the goddess commands a select group of captains

To accompany him for the upcoming ambush
As they camouflage while awaiting the approach of Triton

And before Eos' son and those chosen for the mission
Conceal themselves beneath the dense foliage of the isles
Great Memnon leaves the command of the others to Aithops
With orders to keep a close watch of the Aethiopian vessels

And so they lie in secrecy amidst the thick forests
Awaiting the presence of the hippocampi
And the delightful procession of the glorious sea horses
An indication of the proximity of the sea herald Triton

And so Memnon and the others patiently stand still
And after a short while their endurance is justly rewarded
As a sudden and joyful contingent arrives from the seas
Encompassing lovely nymphs and wondrous tropical pisces

And other sea deities joyously playing their trumpets
As much merriment is made near the isolated isles
Also in tow as anticipated are the glorious hippocampi
As they bestrode in various bright and delightful colors

Some green, aqua blue, and bright crimson
And shimmering emerald, beige, and gold
Sparkling coral, amethyst, and deep olive
Dark cerulean, midnight, and many other astonishing shades

And at last making appearance is Triton himself
Dashing is the son of Poseidon in physical presence
Possessing the upper torso of a splendidly handsome youth
And the lower body of a maritime pisces

His countenance is distinguishable with ease, as he carries
The indestructible trident of the seas in hand, venturing
Forthwith the decree of Poseidon, his aim to pass by

Undetected while attention is diverted to his procession

And so the vigilant son of the goddess
Whose tremendous physical prowess is famed
Hastily restrains the astonished sea herald
And forcibly overwhelms Triton through his sheer might

And the bewildered messenger of Poseidon offers resistance
For never before has Triton been taken against his will
As he vigorously struggles against his powerful assailant
But his effort is for naught against the strength of Memnon

The herald of the oceans violated as never before
As the accompanying sea nymphs give alarm
To the chagrin of all inhabitants of Poseidon's realms
At the abduction of their beloved and revered Triton

And so great Memnon, divinely deceived
Keeps a tight grip on the herald of the Sea lord
And gently speaks to Triton in sympathetic words,
"Messenger to Poseidon, please be still

For my intent is not malicious or in ill will
Evil plotting is assuredly not the basis for our encounter
As we are harmless and sea ravaged men from Aethiopia
And battle hardened descendants of lord Zeus himself

Our motivations lay towards the Trojan plains
To defend the sacred homelands of our kin
The besieged descendants of ancient Dardanus
As they encounter the brutal and haughty Achaeans

And we set sail from our realms for this sole purpose
For divinely favored are we in all human attributes
Embarking from the majestic Aethiopian shores
And homelands of proud and beautiful people

- 111 -

And shortly after I and my comrades depart our blessed isles
Some Olympian maliciously ordained strife
No doubt a divine supporter of the Argives
In an effort to prevent us from reaching Troy

First a confrontation planned with a monstrous being
As she ravaged the hallowed lands of Thebes
Echidna, the matriarch of all worldly scourges
And the terrors of her offspring are well known by all

We mercifully escape the clutches of Typhon's mate
And as byproduct we compel the serpent nymph to flee
Abandoning her campaign against the good King Polybus
Forever she is banned from the city of the sevenfold gate

Next we are seduced by the lovely Nereids
At the behest of Thetis the silver footed daughter of Nereus
As we become paramours of those delightful goddesses
And nearly fall prey to Thetis' attempt to thwart our mission

As we are released at the urgings of Zeus Cloud Gatherer
And thus set about once again on course for holy Ilium
But earthshaking Poseidon, whom is your own progenitor
Becomes angered by my obedience to Queen Amphitrite

And now I unwillingly become engaged in an awful struggle
Opposite the son of Cronus, against my own sincerest wishes
And as consequence we are scattered about the seas
And battered by the rage of the furious waters

Finally given respite on the shores of Chrysaor's realm
Furloughed in the desolate lands of the cannibal
Indeed appropriate repose for our perceived transgressions
The Sea lord determined to destroy me and my comrades

And we are confronted by the ravenous behemoth

Indeed a loathsome and gigantic opponent
He lays ambush to my unsuspecting and innocent men
And destroys several of them, best by far amongst mortals!

And then savagely devours our beloved comrades
These horrid actions bringing abysmal suffering and pain
To us all, as these esteemed men forfeit their lives to a fiend
And now we dually mourn and commemorate their feats

Impenetrable was Chrysaor's hide as he perpetuated his will
Until the merciful daughter of Leto[140]
Reveals the antidote to defeating the giant
And we are permitted retribution against the son of Medusa

Blessed by the Olympians to withstand his monstrous assault
And mercifully endure Chrysaor's inhumane appetite
Fortunate are we in the slaying of Medusa's offspring
As father Zeus sanctions success for our company

And now my divine mother descends from the heavens
In her concern for the sufferings of my comrades and I
Splendid is she in her iridescent and sparkling robes
Revealing herself to me as she appears before the Olympians

And in a dream she offers candid counsel to me
As to avoid more conflict with enraged Poseidon
As well as the other Olympians whom support the Achaeans
By seeking these isolated isles in the midst of the seas

And to solicit your ancient knowledge as to the best course
And swiftest pathway across the ocean to holy Ilium
That city surrounded by divinely constructed walls
So that we can be of assistance to our besieged kinsmen

---

[140] mother of Apollo and Artemis; daughter of the titans Coeus and
Phoebe

And so upon the advice of my beloved mother
I have sought your presence so far away from my homelands
On this remote parcel deep within the abyss of the sea
Where my comrades and I are momentarily encamped

In our longing for arrival upon the Trojan shores
We continue to remain resolute in our convictions
And high is our anticipation of the coming battles
Only to commence upon your cherished guidance

And so my lord Triton, herald of the wide ranging seas
I beseech you to have mercy upon guiltless men!
Sea weary and divinely tested contingent we be
Request enlightenment on the course of least resistance

To our desired destination of holy Ilium
And we shall be eternally indebted to your service
And our offerings shall be abundant to your noblesse
For we are men of divine and illustrious stock"

And thus the son of the goddess
Makes humble entreaty to Poseidon's herald
In hopes of persuading Triton to acquiesce
And to allay his concerns resulting from his detention

And a mischievous Triton sees an opportunity
For exacting dual aims of attaining freedom and retaliation
The messenger swiftly devised a plan to trick Memnon
By falsely assisting the son of the goddess and his comrades

And misdirecting redoubtable Memnon and his contingent
Leading them further away from the shores of Troy
Into the unknowns of more dangerous and foreign lands
In lieu of the intended destination of the Aethiopian fleet

And wily Triton makes his reply to the Aethiopian monarch,

"Memnon Tithonides, handsomest of earthly men!
Your might at arms is unrivalled
And your lofty exploits known throughout the world

Your humble request of me is minimal
In comparison to your heralded eminence
And your well deserved honor and fame
Most pleasing even to the lord of Olympus himself

It would be my greatest privilege
To assist you as you make your way to Troy
By presenting an unchallenged course through the seas
As you have needlessly suffered in your journeys

First matched against fearsome Echidna
Though your awesome strength compels her to succumb
And abandon her unjustified siege of Thebes
Typhon's mate compelled to swear the holy oath of Styx

Her sacred promises to refrain from further atrocities
And crimes committed against the Theban nation
To spite the hopeless peoples of sad Oedipus
For his fatal rebuff of the cunning Sphinx

And your dalliance with the lovely Nereids
Acquiring the eternal adulations of Amphitrite
An act widely known in the realm of the seas
As its Queen bestows her favors upon the son of Eos

And I would be remiss not to mention your recent encounter
Versus the hideous offspring of the hated Gorgon Medusa
As Chrysaor lusts for the flesh of vulnerable men
His practice ended at the hands of the son of the goddess

And yet further glory you shall attain in the lands of Priam
Your name forever endeared to future generations

And thus I wholeheartedly reveal to you, great Memnon
A speedy pathway to Ilium across the realms of Poseidon

You must first voyage west through the Aegean straits
And navigate your vessels along waters in opposite direction
And though this may appear contrary to logic
For the Scaean Gates lie due east of these remote isles

The waterways of least resistance within proximity
Near the majestic coast of the far away Thessaly[141]
And there lies an eastern path free of peril
And this shall led you to your desired destination

To the salvation of the besieged Trojans!
Much anticipated your glorious arrival shall be
And an imperiled nation shall soon thunderously clamor!
As the mighty Aethiopian fleet makes it anticipated landing

And so I counsel you, son of the goddess
To closely follow my careful directive without deviation
As well as to swiftly release me and my alarmed contingent
So we may proceed in delivering Poseidon's decree"

And a delighted Memnon rejoices at these words
As hopes are renewed upon the words of the sea messenger
And without delay he releases his hold of cunning Triton
To the relief of both the sea herald and his delegation

Mighty Memnon readily acquiesces to the herald's request
Deceived by his concealed trickery and falsehoods
As the son of Poseidon makes his way back into the seas
Satisfied that revenge is exacted upon the son of the goddess

And the adjoining sea nymphs, Pisces, and tropical fishes

---

[141] lands north of Aethiopia and west of Troy

As well as the other sea deities in his divine company
Elated at the momentous return of the herald of the sea
From the dominion of the mighty Aethiopian monarch

Joining the procession in unison are the hippocampi
Too joyous at the return of their beloved master
Contentment abounds in the hearts of the majestic creatures
As they prepare to reconvene escorting the sea lord's herald

And the trek begins anew upon the orders of Triton
Anxious are the participants to revive the procession
Boundless revelry amidst the expanse of nothingness
And a resumption of the paramount task at hand

Sense of urgency too assumed by the Aethiopian men
And accordingly the son of the goddess gathers his comrades
Revealing to them the route as dictated by Triton
As they contemplate the veracity of the herald's suggestion

And it is swiftly decided that they would follow the advice
And thus prepared to depart the isolated isles
And its dense forests, foliage and woodlands
As the Aethiopian contingent is due west towards Thessaly

And a young lamb is selected from the herd
The best amongst the many of the Aethiopian stables
And fervent prayers are offered to the Olympians
As due sacrifices are made to honor those powerful deities

And the son of the goddess and his men board the vessels
As they fearlessly enter the unpredictable seas
The magnificent ships are guided into the waiting waters
As all are hopeful that this latest excursion is without peril

And the winds gently fill the Aethiopian sails
An early indication of divine auspices and blessings

Rewarding them for the bountiful sacrifices offered
And hopes of reaching the Dardanian plains are apparent

So begins the latest journey across the wide ocean
As Triton's guidance appears to be genuine and sincere
For the son of the goddess has no reason to disbelieve
The false words of the mischievous messenger of Poseidon

And the expectations of the men gradually begin to rise
Optimistic thoughts of encountering the Achaean armies
Testing their famed mettle against the might of the Argives
And honoring their heralded and divine lineage

And what marvelous sights are witnessed as they traverse the
Ocean and cross the calm and peaceful seas?
Yet more hippocampi, dolphins, and varied aquatic species
Frolicking near the surface of the steady ships

And the sea creatures are too interested in what they see
For rarely witnessed is the likes of mortal men
And the gentle spectators courageous venture to the vessels
Amicably interacting with the Aethiopian contingent

A respite for the sea wearied men from their travails
And a diversion from the monotony of the waters
And from the constant sounds of the paddling oars
Affording them a temporary and rare state of bliss

And as the mighty fleet witnesses the wonders of the sea
Trident Bearer Poseidon receives salacious hearsay
Of Triton's abduction at the mighty hands of the son of Eos
His newly minted rival and increasingly bitter foe

And Poseidon angrily devises more troubles
For mighty Memnon and his fleet
Due to this latest slight by the son of Eos

For the Sea lord is unaware of the deceits of Hera

And suddenly the rage of Poseidon is manifest
As the alarmed elements dutifully respond
For yet again that mighty sea god brandishes his fearsome
Trident, rousing his allies of the treacherous seas

And once more the encumbered son of the goddess
Is compelled to endure the resentment of indignant Poseidon
Offended at both the perceived violations of his spouse
Aggravated by the bold affront to his beloved herald

And although wily Triton had done his part
In creating mischief for the famed Aethiopian monarch
By intentionally misdirecting the son of the goddess
And sending the vessels far off path from besieged Troy

A thoroughly enraged Poseidon is intent upon violating
And destroying the sea faring Aethiopian vessels
As he tosses the waters and provokes the fierce winds
Yet the stalwart men remain resolute in their determination

As again battle lines are drawn in a struggle amidst the seas
The wills of Poseidon and mighty Memnon are pulled taut
In yet another confrontation between two immovable forces
As the son of the goddess and his comrades fight for survival

And so the unflappable Memnon Tithonides exhorts his men
As each reaches for various parts of the strong vessels
Portions of the ships refurbished from previous damage
Reinforced with components from the lands of Chrysaor

And while these godlike men are able to save themselves
Such is not the case for the various livestock
As lambs, pheasants, and others amongst the other herds
And carefully preserved victuals and other necessaries

Blatantly and needlessly tossed into the ocean
And transformed into fodder for the scavengers of the seas
According to the scripted plans of the son of Cronus
As Earthshaker continues to violently wield his trident

And gradually the well fortified vessels begin to give way
To the incessant onslaught of the forces of nature
As parts fracture from the storm battered ships
Succumbing to the fury of the lord of the Sea

And all of this is observed by a concerned Eos
As her beloved son fearlessly endures the wrath of Poseidon
Unjustly persecuted due to the manipulations of Hera
As she assumed the likeness of the rosy fingered goddess

And provoked great Memnon to accost the sea herald
Restraining the wily deity against his will
This affront coupled with the reluctant act
Of obeying the command of a lustful Amphitrite

Queen of the Sea, who loved Memnon immensely
And thus consummates her passionate desires
By compelling that mighty man to lay with her
As the rest of the Aethiopian contingent obliges her sisters

Precipitating the extreme response of the fierce Earthshaker
As he yet again conjures an aquatic conflagration
Poised to once and for all destroy redoubtable Memnon
As an example to those whom the Sea lord deems a foe

Precipitating the intervention of the rosy fingered goddess
For she is resolved to assuage her son's wrongful suffering
And so Eos duly appeals to another of her offspring

Namely Zephyrus, the glorious western winds[142]

For no hostility existed between the wind deity and his
Sibling, though his blustery brothers bitterly opposed
Memnon, as animosities abounds within Boreas, Notus, and
Eurus, a continuation of familial strife inspired by envy

Yet gentle Zephyrus did not share the same feelings as the
Others, for that god is inclined to maternal obedience
And much more apt to assist his besieged brother
Antagonistic to the aims of his windy brethren

And Eos swiftly summons Zephyrus to her abode,
"Oh westerly wind deity, my beloved son
Dutifully subservient you are to the wishes of your mother
And once again I beseech you for assistance

For your brave brother Memnon is distressed
As never before since that wondrous day I bore him
To redoubtable Tithonus on the Aethiopian shores
To the sheer joy of both myself and the entire world!

For his unparalleled beauty and delightful countenance
And wisdom, genial spirit, and proclivity for righteousness
Apparent since his much revered adolescence
And this golden child is much loved by the Olympians

Best amongst his peers from a tender age
And thought his mighty man could resign himself
To a peaceful existence with a dutiful and lovely wife
And beautiful daughters along with powerful sons

As his divine and magnificent lineage is widely dispersed

---

[142] son of Eos; brother to Memnon; brother to Boreas, Notus, and
Eurus (the north, south, and east winds)

Across the wondrous and beautiful lands of Aethiopia
Forever honored and remembered for his just reign
Instead that courageous man chooses an alternative destiny

And he sets sail for the shores of holy Ilium
To assist his kin against the haughty Achaeans
In defense of the threatened Trojan citadel
For he is not dissuaded by impending perils

As he dutifully departs for the Scaean Gates
His intentions commendable as the vessels advance to Troy
And now a mighty man is precluded from his goals
As he is opposed by spiteful gods and goddesses

Even as we converse, the Trident Bearer rages on
Angered by the satiation of his wife's uncontrollable urges
As her lust and love for the handsome king of Aethiopia
Commence fatal conflict amidst the wide ranging seas

And wily Hera, the queen of golden Olympus
In her unjustified haste to satisfy old grudges
And to assist the Achaeans relentless onslaught
Furthering the savagery of the irresistible Myrmidon

She plots against your brother in an effort to dupe him
By fabricating my unique likeness
And encouraging Memnon to seek out Triton
And forcefully hold the god against his wishes

And incomparable Memnon is deceived by the plot
As he effortlessly captures the herald of Poseidon
And immensely offends the furious lord of the Sea
As he stirs the elements into a frenzy against Memnon

And so now your brother unjustly suffers, as he
Bravely endures the awesome power of the enraged deity

Therefore I require your swift and immediate assistance
I beseech you to steer the Aethiopian band safely ashore

And deftly guide the Aethiopian vessels with your winds
Safely away from the torrents of the disturbed ocean
As they are violently shaken by the will of Lord Poseidon
And allow respite to come to those sea ravaged men"

And trusty Zephyrus readily obeys his beloved mother
Directing his winds to fill the sails of the vessels
Intervening in conflict between the Memnon and Poseidon,
Offering sustenance and support to the Aethiopian men

The western winds guides the ships away from the storms
Into less hostile and more hospitable territories
Near the calming waters on the shores of Thessaly
And the fatal threats against them are temporarily abated

And thus the merciful Zephyrus guides his grateful brother
And his equally thankful and relieved comrades
To safe haven away from the fury of Poseidon
Zephyrus' actions undertaken with a sincere heart

As the ships are washed ashore a remote province
Whose sovereign is a beautiful and ravishing goddess[143]
The expanse of these lands dominated by a wide lake
With cooling waters and springs befitting the divine

And the Aethiopian vessels capsize along its banks
Providing refuge to the son of the goddess and his men
The piteous Aethiopian contingent, absent of guilt and fault
Unjustly persecuted by the hostile lord of the aquatic realms

And so the rosy fingered goddess of the Dawn

---

[143] reference to Bolbe, a Thessalian lake goddess

With the assistance of her son the western wind
Intervenes successfully in the divine struggle
And the cruel will of Poseidon's is briefly thwarted

VI. The Isles of Bolbe

Bewildered by the prodigious turn of events
After yet another harrowing ordeal versus Earthshaker
Grateful is the battered Aethiopian contingent for its survival
Though hopelessly shipwrecked in strange and foreign lands

As they escape the fury of the Sea lord's might
And the dangerous currents that emanated from his trident
For lesser men would have readily succumb
Matched against such an awesome opponent as Poseidon

And the Aethiopian men lay exhausted near the shores
A familiar landscape since the joyous initial departure
From their lush and beautiful Aethiopian homelands
Realms honored above all others by the Olympians

And as the godlike men rested upon the pitying beaches
 Recovering from their near fatal encounter
A band of Naiads[144] make approach near where they lay
And begin amusing themselves with leisure and recreation

Carelessly these beautiful deities frolic, naïve to strife
For eternal merriment and play is their preoccupation
And curiosity and wonder intrigues their virgin minds
For never before had these delightful goddesses beheld men

Unversed in the ways of mortals are the water deities
Though they heard many anecdotes reciting tales of both
Contemporary heroes and of great men of days long past
And delightful narratives of conquering kings and queens

These Limnades,[145] inhabitants of the unmolested land
Pleasant subjects of a just and ravishing monarch
Thessalian Bolbe,[146] a goddess unmatched in beauty

---

[144] water nymphs
[145] another reference to a Naiad

And in her splendid mannerism, grace, and famed virtue

The wondrous goddess herself a daughter of Tethys
And of her adoring husband Oceanus Uranides
And though the god amongst the ranks of the mighty Titans
Nonetheless wisely he refrains from conflict with Olympus

And thus that god is cherished by father Zeus
Revered is Oceanus above all other ancient deities
Accordingly his descendants are held in divine favor
And permitted to continue residency in their beloved seas

Accordingly lovely Bolbe is granted her aquatic domain
Replete with tropical fruits, trees, and exotic animals
To rule as the goddess deemed fit and proper
As she is attended to by her loyal and faithful subjects

And these same subjects now deliberate amongst themselves
To ascertain the best course of action in the atypical situation
As never before had they been in such a predicament
For they had a decision to make amongst two choices

Whether to simply evade the strange and destitute men
And not provide the much coveted victuals and refreshments
Permitting the damaged vessels to become deteriorated
And thus neglect their harassed and desolate visitors

Or in the alternative display genuine kindness and mercy
And rescue the strangers, welcoming them as guests
Providing venison, wines, and other desired fare
And demonstrate the magnanimous extent of their hospitality

Without undue delay the Naiads choose to assist the men

---

[146] lake goddess in Thessaly; daughter of Oceanus (personification
of the sea) and Tethys (sea goddess)

As they cautiously approach the son of the goddess and his
Weakened comrades, for they were deprived of the
Necessaries of life, and accordingly languish by the sea

And though the men are rugged and wild to behold
For such is the appearance of men after fatal struggle
Each are offered fresh drink and scrumptious foods
And clothing to cover their bare and chiseled bodies

And the pleasant goddesses abide with them as they recover
Humming sensual melodies to relax the men while others
Frolic and dance to amuse their guests, as Memnon and
His comrades assuage their ravenous hunger and thirst

And once the meal is thoroughly consumed and digested
Each Naiad gently takes the hand of a restored man
And leading him along the pathway to a palatial estate
The abode itself magnificently adorned in gold and silver

The brilliance of the structure illuminates the islands
For the wondrous residence was befitting an Olympian
Bedecked throughout in diamonds and other precious earths
An immaculate compliment to the serene and peaceful lands

As great Memnon and his comrades make the effortless jaunt
Accompanied by the gracious and lovely Naiads
As they lead the Aethiopian men to their exalted queen
For she sojourns within the walls of her palace

And the goddesses swiftly unbar the pearl gates
Inviting the men to enter the wondrous compound
And great Memnon is the first to cross the threshold
Followed closely by his trusty and brave companions

And as they enter the great hall of the residence
A large and magnificent lion strides before them

And regally approaches the men with confident steps
Its sheer size intimidating even to the bravest of them

And a cautious Memnon slowly draws his sword
Preparing to meet assault from the feline
And as the great lion make its approach to Eos' son
The ravishing Bolbe suddenly appears before all assembled

The lovely goddess walks to the lion and gently strokes him
And the beast kneels in reverence to the daughter of Oceanus
Purring gently as she caresses its great golden mane
To the awe and amazement of the Aethiopian contingent

And the escorting Naiads present their assemblage to Bolbe
Providing an introduction to their magnificent queen
And the goddess is intrigued by the presence of the men
Though ragged and tattered in appearance they were

And so lovely Bolbe makes inquiry of her battered guests,
"Piteous men who have washed upon my far away shores
With the appearance of vagrants sorely in need of succor
After an ordeal with the unforgiving elements of the seas

For cruel is the journey of fragile and delicate mortals
Ordained to Tartarus after the threads of life are severed
Such appeared to be the destiny of you unfortunate men!
Deterred mercifully through intervention of my servants

As my Naiads took pity upon your desolate condition
Fetching you from the sandy beaches of my lands
And providing you with the necessaries of existence
Bread, fresh water, and other conferred ancillary benefits

And as due repayment for the hospitality shown
I simply require your truthful and full disclosure
Of whom you are and of your origins?

And what faraway nation you venture from?

Enlightenment of your ancestral lineage
And from what lands are you derived
For only men of divine stock could endure as you have
Though unfortunate thus far your journey appears"

And the son of the goddess stands before all present
For purposes of addressing Bolbe and her loyal subjects
Pleasing in appearance and in his regal stature
As he readily obliges the request of the lake goddess

"Queen Bolbe, wholeheartedly shall I reveal our identity
For your merciful band of Naiads graciously rescued us
My comrades and I are from the lovely lands of Aethiopia
A wondrous kingdom immensely blessed by the Olympians

And I count myself honored to be the ruler of these realms
Eternally abundant with game, fish, and plentiful herds
And lovely women gifted with wisdom and grace
With brave and hardy men as worthy companions

And our wondrous abode provides all that is desired
As the croplands and wheat are readily harvested
And the riverbeds are never dry nor desolate
And none dare to invade our holy lands

Nor accost our magnificent and envied citadel
For our armies are feared in all earthly realms
And provocation of our anger is ill advised
For the Aethiopian lance does not cease until it pierces flesh

And now we stand in supplication before you great goddess!
As we barely escaped the wrath of Poseidon Earthshaker
And are eternally grateful to your largesse
Provided by you and your delightful contingent of Limnades

For I and my comrades have been unjustifiably assaulted
Ever since we left our beloved Aethiopian shores
Tossed about the expanse of the wide ranging oceans
Compelled to encounter the unforeseen forces of the seas

And yet still our spirits remain strong and unbroken
And our resolve steadfastly and wholly intact
And now I shall convey to you the horrible tales of sad men
And recount the piteous details of our misadventures

Well intentioned were our primary motivations
As we prepared our vessels for the grand voyage
Hastily we put oars to waters without delay
Leaving our beloved and other things familiar to us

To defend holy Troy from the onslaught of the Atreus' sons
And provide succor to the homelands of our kin
The besieged and hopelessly encircled Dardanians
As they encounter the haughty Achaeans

And as we set sail from lovely Aethiopia for this purpose
Departing that magnificent realm of prosperity
Homeland of a proud and beautiful people
Divinely favored in all human attributes

I and my loyal comrades ran afoul of the Fates
As some Olympian maliciously ordained
Our inevitable confrontation with a monstrous deity
The fearsome Echidna, scourge of holy Thebes

That fiend saddened over the demise of her beloved child
Slain by the unfortunate Theban Oedipus
I speak of the wily Sphinx, a curse to unsuspecting travelers
As they are forced to answer the riddles of the monster

And succumbing to the beast if unsuccessful in response

A woeful fate for the many of her luckless victims
Until she met the redoubtable Oedipus
Putting an end to the monstrous practice

And so the matronly and enraged Echidna
Relentlessly tormented the Theban peoples
And by the grace of the Olympians
I and my brave men discouraged her gruesome goals

By expelling Typhon's mate from the seven gates
As she swears an oath before the river Styx
And Echidna forfeits her cavernous and dark abode
Forever banished from the city of Dionysus

To the delight of the good King Polybus and his court
As the gates of the city are now open to the outside world
And we are honored like the Olympians themselves
As an ancient alliance between our nations is renewed

And as we set forth once more for the Dardanian plains
And before we dare set our vessels to the seas
Potent sacrifice are made in honor of the immortals
Unfortunately to no avail, as our troubles are multiplied

Apprehended at the behest of the Nereid Thetis
By her lovely siblings on a deserted parcel of land
Compelled to become paramours of those goddesses
A lusty diversion as we are held against our will

For the Queen of the Sea herself commanded me to be
Her lover, in violation of her matrimonial vows
And my goddess mother empathizes with our plight
And pleads our case to the son of Cronus himself

And Zeus is merciful as we are released upon his command
We again we set our ships on course for holy Ilium

But a provoked Poseidon has other plans for our contingent
Angered by my obedience to Amphitrite's commands

And as struggle ensues against the furious Lord of the Sea
As our glorious contingent is violently tossed and scattered
And mercilessly battered by the rage of the waters
Finally afforded respite in the horrid lands of Chrysaor

A loathsome and frightening opponent indeed!
As the fiend brings sufferings to me and my men
Devouring our beloved and courageous comrades
For his monstrous hide is impenetrable to our weaponry

This fatal fact revealed by the huntress goddess
As she guides us to the magical and vibrant herb
Its existence unbeknownst to the minds of mortals
Exposing the vulnerability of the son of Medusa

And so blessed by the Olympians, we are able to withstand
Chrysaor's monstrous rage and appetite
And after this ordeal, upon the supposed advice of my
Mother, the goddess of the bright and radiant dawn

We apprehend the messenger of the wide seas
As he and his merry cavalcade traverse the waters
Conveying the irresistible will of Poseidon Earthshaker
Delightful scenery to our sea weary eyes

And so after taking hold of the venerable sea god
As he bore the regal symbol of the Lord of the Sea
We are provided what we seek from Triton the herald
And the son of Poseidon continues on in his journeys

But all is for naught as we subsequently discover
For the appearance of my goddess mother is a hoax
A stratagem by the biased queen of Olympus

As Hera's misleading counsel is exposed as false revelation

Her vicious aims to provoke Poseidon Earthshaker
By tricking me and my comrades to capture his herald
Under the ruse that Triton would provide a safe pathway
And allow us to proceed unmolested to Troy

Furthermore, a mischievous Triton makes folly for us
As he plots to frustrate our approach to the Scaean Gates
By misdirecting our deceived Aethiopian vessels
Thereby causing the ships to sail opposite the Idaean plains

And to our dismay this ordeal would be further compounded
For we are again ferociously ambushed by Trident Bearer
As Poseidon is vexed at the apprehension of his loyal herald
And by his perceived offenses against him by our company

Unceremoniously we are tossed and assaulted by the seas
Thoroughly punished for our perceived transgressions
And for my violation of the liberties of Triton
As I readily succumb to the successful plot of Hera

And by the grace of my beloved mother
We are mercifully washed ashore upon your lands
As your Naiads display kindness to our piteous band, and
Though ravished in body, we are unconquered in resolve"

And with his response the redoubtable son of the goddess
Kneels before the ravishing Bolbe and offers a gift
A wondrous urn crafted in indestructible ceramic
Recovered from the liberated lands of the defeated Chrysaor

And an offering of gratitude to the daughter of Oceanus
Inlaid with gold at the periphery of the marvelous pottery
A gift truly befitting the awed lake goddess
For the astonishing token itself is a rarity

And so moved within her heart is Bolbe
Both by the misfortune of the Aethiopian contingent
And by the magnanimity of the son of the goddess
The tears begin to freely flow down her lovely countenance

As they gently stain her delicate tunic
And she is accompanied in her lament by her subjects
For they too are overwhelmed by the sad tales of their guests
Pitying the many sufferings suffered by the courageous men

For the plight of great Memnon is known around the world
As far away as the reaches of Atlas' distant realms
To the deep and cantankerous pits of Tartarus
And even to the high heavens of glorious Olympus itself

And the daughter of Oceanus is equally aware
Of the unfortunate and unwarranted tribulation
And the needless sufferings of Memnon at the hands
Of divine forces, those that fear his arrival to Troy

And accordingly he possesses the admiration of Bolbe
In deference to his numerous and famed exploits
And for the bravery of the son of the goddess and his men
As they resolutely make their way to the sad city of Priam

And so lovely Bolbe makes her reply to Memnon,
"Brave men, born of the divine gods themselves
Your luckless travails are well documented
And intimately known by inhabitants of these lands

For how can one not admire your valor?
And the beauty and bravery of the son of the goddess
His fame is known across the expanse of the seas
For he is divinely favored by the lord of Olympus himself

You are most welcome in our splendid lands!

To repose as you deem proper and fit
Any and all necessaries shall be given
And whatever else I can provide within my power

For it is an honor to have your presence here!
As it graces our far away and distant shores
For you are heroes that will be long remembered
As future generations speak of your deeds and exploits"

And without further inquisition or examination of design
Or inquiries in an effort to validate any curiosities
A judgment is made by the lake goddess
To faithfully cultivate the men to excellent health

And the benevolent lake goddess, Thessalian Bolbe
Her heart bursting with empathy for them
As she is moved by the courage of her Aethiopian guests
And fascinated by their many perilous adventures

Without hesitation offers unadulterated hospitality
Promising to fulfill the desires of the famed men
And restore strength and vigor to the Aethiopian armies
Attempting to ameliorating any prior injustices and wrongs

And so the lovely daughter of Oceanus
Orders her servants to prepare an elaborate feast
All manner of venison, wines, and delectable fruits
The best her abode could offer the renowned contingent

And much merrymaking is made by all present
Commencing the replenishment of the Aethiopian fleet
And though battered from the onslaught of Trident Bearer
Unbroken is the determination of these godlike men

As in due time the son of the goddess and his comrades
Rejuvenated as strength and vitality swiftly return

For Bolbe provides for her famed guests unconditionally
Lavishing her notable goodwill upon those deserving men

And the lovely lake goddess spares no expense
Ensuring that redoubtable Memnon and his comrades
Are availed of all earthly pleasures coveted by them
That Bolbe's abundant largesse afforded

And so the Aethiopian men sumptuously abide
Partaking of all the daughter of Oceanus bestows upon them
As they are permitted to satiate their whims
And indulge in each and every desire that they possess

Freely engaging in varied sport sanctioned by great Memnon
Including hunting, hawking, and other games of endurance
For within the ranks are many strong and competitive men
As each vie for honors associated with triumph

And the isles of Bolbe offer plenty of game for the hunt
The woodlands bountiful in pheasant, quail, and antelope
And the climate always temperate and tranquil
As the exotic and piquant fruits dangled from the trees

And amidst the rustic activities in the forest
The loyal comrades of the son of the goddess
Amused the captivated servants of Bolbe
By recounting stories of their many sights and adventures

Of the abounding lands and realms they encountered
And of the epic battles in which they notably participated
Matched against both mortal and fiendish foes
And of the seemingly impossible struggles involved

And the lovely and delightful Naiads
Are riveted by their Aethiopian escorts
Never before intermingling with mortals, nor

Partaking of the earthly pleasures between men and women

And the handsome men of Aethiopian contingent
Equally aroused by the beauty of Bolbe's subjects
For the innocence of the Naiads are beguiling to them, and
They readily succumb to frolic with their lovely companions

Such is the daily routine of Memnon and his comrades
As they enjoy the wonders provided by the isles of Bolbe
Duly afforded respite from the arduous journey
Accordingly the sea ravaged men are fully restored

And while they swiftly recover fairness and strength
The son of the goddess stands apart from the rest
His beauty and comeliness apparent to all whom beheld him
For his countenance is striking to mortals and Olympians

And uncontrollable desire overtakes a smitten Bolbe
For Memnon is by far the handsomest of men ever to live
And Bolbe is enamored by his physical attributes
And by the genial disposition of regal son of Eos

And in her immense love for the venerable Memnon
Copious attentiveness is bestowed upon the Aethiopian king
As Bolbe herself attends to him as a servant would a king
Ensuring the comforts of great Memnon are thoroughly met

Her efforts undertaken to display her devotion to him
For the lake goddess hopelessly and passionately loved
That incomparable descendant of Dardanus as none other
And she longed to be his constant companion day and night

And accompaniment to the son of the goddess
As she introduces him the wonders of her isles, and
The majestic Thessalian creatures abound as they saunter
Colorful birds, beasts, and arachnids gather nearby

Also revealed to the son of the goddess by ravishing Bolbe
The various trees and fruit bearing foliage
Never before witnessed by mortal men, for
Lovely in appearance and delectable in taste they are

And the great feline of the daughter of Oceanus
Once causing alarm to the comrades of Memnon
Now banters playfully with the son of the goddess
His love for great Memnon equal to that of Bolbe

As both the incomparable goddess and the epic hero
Traverse the wondrously calm and sandy shores
Engaging in this enterprise for many hours and days
As Bolbe is delighted to be in company of her companion

And as the son of the goddess, upon her request
Recounts his many daring feats and exploits
And of his past battles and recent conflicts
Adventures which endeared him to all realms of the world

Lovely Bolbe stands by attentively in fascination
For delighted is Memnon's ravishing and adoring consort
As she listens to his regal and alluringly grand voice
Enthralled by the heroic tales that came forth from his lips

For the goddess admires his gentleness and humble bravery
And reveres his comeliness and stubborn resolve
And Bolbe's desires are fully awakened by the son of Eos
As she longs to give herself to the Aethiopian monarch

The lake goddess covets to caress his handsome countenance
And peer deeply into eyes as deep as the universe itself
The daughter of Oceanus thoroughly infatuated by Memnon
For his godlike appearance is incomparable

And wholeheartedly she desires to be his lover

For her heart is amorously famished for his affections
As she wishes to make the son of the goddess her spouse
And for him to rule as king of her divine isles

And for her Naiads to take his loyal comrades
As loving mates and lifelong companions
To roam the hills of the sprawling lands
And bear children to their lusty husbands

All of this is in the mind of the daughter of Oceanus
Her wishes that eternal joy abound on her isles
Accomplished if handsome Memnon would succumb to her
For the love pangs of the lake goddess are yet quenched

And so Bolbe makes her poignant entreaties
Professing her eternal devotions to Eos' son
For she had become enraptured by his noblesse
And irrevocably entranced by his unparalleled beauty

Delightful is Bolbe's appearance to both gods and mortals
As many are gently refused after courting the lake goddess
But she freely offers herself to Memnon Tithonides
A goddess desiring the adulations of the famed hero

And the son of the goddess obliges a delighted Bolbe
For she is ravishing in her splendid appearance and grace
And without question, and not under any circumstances
Could great Memnon refuse Bolbe's divine commandment

And so the desires of the daughter of Oceanus are fulfilled
The sensuous caresses of that mighty man wholly quell
The burning desires of Bolbe for the touch of his fingers
As Memnon's sought after love is given to lake goddess

And so too are the Naiads gratefully satisfied
As each is paired with a brave Aethiopian commander

Becoming the faithful consort of their chosen mate
To the delight of the goddesses and the men alike!

As simmering lusts and desires are appeased
Beautiful deities are matched with timeless heroes
And the arrows of Eros[147] are disbursed uninhibited
Unleashing a blissful existence for all on Bolbe's isles

And intentions of embarking for besieged Troy deferred
As pursuit of honor and glory are temporarily forgotten
And the counterbalance to the formidable Argive forces
Preoccupied by the patronage of the ravishing lake goddess

And all this is espied by golden Apollo
The glorious son of Zeus thunderlord and Leto
Conceived the same day as Delian[148] Artemis
And mercy is bestowed by the fledgling isles amidst the seas

As lovely Leto is tormented by spiteful Hera
For consorting with Zeus the great cloud gatherer
And conceiving twin deities from their dalliance
As she is confined to wander the expanse of the world

All earthly realms forbidden to provide refuge to the goddess
Ordained by strict decree of the queen of Olympus
Thereby delaying the birth of the divine twins of Zeus
As piteous Leto is refused the assistance of Eileithyia[149]

At last shelter is afforded by neoteric Delos
The diminutive province not yet firmly rooted

---

[147] god of love; son of Aphrodite; possessed arrows which he shot
into the hearts of unsuspecting victims that made them fall in love
with the first person they saw after being struck
[148] island where Apollo and Artemis were born
[149] goddess of childbirth

As it delicately floats in the wide ranging seas
The isles defiantly offering succor to wearied Leto

And now her incomparable son appears before Memnon
In all his splendor, as he is witnessed in Olympus
Just as Memnon along with his loyal companions
Make preparations to hunt a great boar espied in the forests

The great god is concerned about the jeopardized journey
For Eos' son appears to have abandoned his campaign
Of encountering the haughty Achaeans on the Trojan plains
In his zealous obedience to the beautiful lake goddess

And so shining Apollo says to famed Memnon,
"Son of the goddess, why do you needlessly delay?
Mighty king of Aethiopia, immensely blessed by lord Zeus!
To be unrivaled in beauty and appearance

And unmatched in battle, speech, and comeliness
Befitting a man of your peerless lineage
For your tremendous might is readily proven
As you have overcoming both gods and monsters

Your epic quest for Ilium eagerly undertaken as you set sail
For that unfortunate and besieged city, once the proudest
Of all realms, now menaced by the scourge, I speak of
Thetis son Achilles, as he ravages the Dardanian plains

And one brave man now stands between the sack of Troy
I speak of your cousin, mighty Hector Priamides
Though the day of his fate draws eerily near
For the dreaded Myrmidon is supported by Athena

This event shall arrive to the sheer horror of the Trojans
And utter ruin awaits the sad lands of the good King Priam
As the women and children are carried away to servitude

A consequence to Paris' ill advised judgment!

Son of the goddess, your honor is yet attained!
For though your prowess is globally renowned
And no man alive can withstand your fearsome lance
Your greatest achievement is still yet fulfilled

For your strength is required if Troy is to be salvaged
And under no other scenario can Argive fires be averted
For even the bravery of great Hector alone, woefully
Deficient to overcome the will of two envious goddesses

Even as we speak, Priam awaits your arrival to his land
And the whole of uplifted Ilium has hopes anew
For word of your departure from the lovely Aethiopian lands
Inspires the Trojan battalions against an overwhelming foe

So why do you tarry in the lands of Bolbe?
Away from the battles, and glory that is rightfully yours?
Have you taken ill, or become weary of attaining honor?
Perhaps your glorious name is undeserved"

And the son of the goddess is roused by the great Olympian
The words of Leto's son fresh in his mind
As the urgings for adventure swiftly return to him
And the lust for battle are wholly renewed

As yet again intentions of arriving to holy Ilium are
Firmly set in the mind of the mighty Memnon
And so he swiftly gathers his loyal comrades
And commands them to prepare for immediate departure

Leaving the amazing abode of the daughter of Oceanus
And the tender love that Bolbe readily bestows upon him
As the son of the goddess abandons a life of enchantment
Undoubtedly afforded by the lake goddess and her paradise

And the will of Apollo is made known to distraught Bolbe
As her heart becomes saddened by the imminent separation
Between herself and her beloved Memnon
For she so loved Eos' son like none before nor after him

And she implores him to reconsider his determination
As her heart is enveloped with immense suffering
And tears freely flow down her rosy colored cheeks
As Bolbe beseeches the son of the goddess to abide with her

"Son of the goddess, do not harden your heart towards me!
And desert the immaculate love that we now possess
For I could not bear your abandoning me on these isles
And these wondrous lands would transform into a prison!

As the light of the sun is swiftly enveloped by the darkness
As bright Helios retires his golden chariot for the evening
Similarly my own heart will cease to feel joy, and
Swiftly shall it be overwhelmed by utter melancholy!

Nor can I bear the tribulations you undoubtedly shall suffer
For much you and your comrades have already endured
And yet more troubles devised for you by spiteful deities!
As Olympians adverse to your intent maliciously plot

For your approach feared by both immortals and Achaeans
In especial by the Myrmidon king and his cunning mother
For should you at long last reach the Scaean Gates
And duly greet King Priam and the hopeful Dardanian nation

The tide of the Great War shall swiftly turn in Paris' favor
As Achaeans flee the brave and fierce Aethiopians armies
Led by your mighty lance and glorious shield
The haughty armies of Agamemnon routed as never before!

But your own fate lies near those lofty walls of Pergamus

As the women of Ilium sadly observe catastrophic events
And the greatest of clashes commences between demigods
As the incomparable struggle of the Great War crests

For even as we are exchanging our final farewells
And my Limnades and I marvel at your visage a final time
Mighty Hector, your very own dear cousin
Has sadly fallen to Myrmidon Achilles![150]

For no man has yet withstood the lance of Peleus' son
As he is supported by the mighty Olympians themselves
And his destiny is to inflict enduring pain and torment
Unabated, as he is by far stronger than any in Troy

The Myrmidon stricken by the demise of his cousin[151]
As Patroclus dons the attire of swift Achilles
In an effort to drive off the raging Hector
As he sets fire to the besieged Achaean fleets

And so fortunate Patroclus overcomes Lycian Sarpedon[152]
The irresistible Cloud Gatherer's own beloved son
As he hastens to the defense of the Scaean Gates
And takes up arms besides mighty Aeneas and Hector

Sheer sadness, as a courageous ally of Troy is slain!
By a raging Patroclus as the tides of war turns
And that haughty man dares to present challenge to
Mighty Hector, Troy's source of strength and resilence

A foolhardy tactic by Achilles' cousin indeed!

---

[150] Bolbe reveals the death of Hector to Memnon, as recounted in the *Iliad*

[151] Patroclus, cousin of Achilles, is slain by Hector as he wore the armor of Achilles

[152] king of Lycia; son of Zeus; Trojan ally

For Hector was so much stronger than he
As they battled over the corpse of Sarpedon
At the urging of a bereaved prince Glaucus[153]

And Hector Priamides slaughters the son of Menoetius[154]
His vanquished opponent mistaken for another
Even as victory is effortless accomplished
Truths are made known at the stripping of armor

And so the Myrmidon rages in his anger
Determined to meet Hector Priamides
And destroy the pride of holy Troy
A woeful day indeed for both gods and men!

For the grief stricken Achilles, supported by Athena
Slays a brave man as he defends his besieged homelands
Father, husband, provider, and protector
As he bravely stood before the Scaean gates

A stratagem devised by Pallas Athena
To the dismay of his Dardanian protectorate
Beacon of resistance against the haughty Achaeans
As he is overcome by Thetis' son and a mighty goddess

Such awaits you as your vessels reach the Trojan shores
And as you prepare to advance upon the Argives
For once the flags are raised and the battle cry begins
Many beloved comrades and friends shall you lose"

And so Bolbe attempts to persuade Memnon with her words
In a futile effort to convince the man she loved to remain
And rule her isles as her wedded spouse
And enjoy a long life with her, rearing magnificent progeny

---

[153] cousin of Sarpedon; Lycian commander; Trojan ally
[154] father of Patroclus

And though the words of the lake goddess greatly stirred
The stout heart of the Aethiopian king and his men
The son of the goddess remains resolute in conviction
For the revelation of the death of Hector takes a heavy toll

And thereby great Memnon hardens his resolve to set sail
For the desperation of Troy becomes even more apparent
And though he is grateful to his divine consort for hospitality
The son of the goddess gently takes leave of Bolbe

"Daughter of Oceanus, your words are much acknowledged
And forever shall I be indebted for your kindness
As you rescued my men and I from utter ruin
After our fatal encounter with the lord of the Sea

And for restoring our contingent to full strength
Accomplished wholly by you and your lovely Naiads
As you provided the necessaries of sustenance, and
Welcomed us as equals to partake of the riches of the isles

But your counsel, no doubt offered to me out of love
Nonetheless invokes within me unendurable torment!
For my grief is immeasurable and my heart inconsolable!
As incomparable Hector descends to dark Erebus below

Hopes to reunite with my illustrious kin are extinguished!
As his life is taken from him by the dreaded son of Thetis
As he in his immense bravery confronts the fierce Myrmidon
Confident is his foe, for he is supported by vengeful Athena

Forever the greatness of the horse tamer lost to the world!
His sad fate ordained long ago by the Olympians
As he perishes under the high walls of Pergamus
In defense of the lands that lovingly reared him

And though you offer enticing entreaties
Of dually living a full and long life
And betrothal to a goddess whose beauty is beyond compare
And becoming sire of future heroes and queens

My destiny lies in far away Trojan citadel
For I am duty bound to its defense against the Achaeans
And I shall bravely and willingly accept my own fate
Whatever is shall be! As ordained by the Olympians"

And a love stricken and heartbroken Bolbe
Though her wishes are refused by the son of the goddess
In her infinite love for him offers parting advice
To at last guide the Aethiopian king to the Dardanian realm

"Son of the Goddess, handsomest man alive
And cruelest for not having pity upon me!
For though you depart from me, your hopeless lover
Paramount to my heart is your subsequent safety

So please listen to me, one you once had affections for
Will you now hear my concerned counsel?
For the Earthshaker is still passionately enraged at you
For perceived offenses offered against him

Though misplaced is his unjustified fury
Nonetheless he shall hinder your arrival to Pergamus
Provoking the malicious forces of the dark seas
As Poseidon batters and harasses the Aethiopian fleet

You must avoid the wrath of Lord Poseidon
By discovering a genuine route to Priam's city
For your path to the ancient lands of Dardanus
Lies through the dank halls of deep Tartarus

For in the lifeless realm of dark and gloomy Hades
You must seek counsel from the fallen Hector
Still attired in his battle tunic and breastplate
Though now besmirched with murky and dark blood

As it flows freely from the inflicted wounds
Of the hardened bronze of the Myrmidon's lance
Andromache's[155] beloved spouse forever lost
To the utter deprivation of the fatherless Astyanax[156]

Not far from here lies a gateway to the Elysian Fields[157]
In lands held dear to the great harvest goddess
And once you locate the incomparable son of sad Priam
Seek his counsel as best to proceed in your journeys"

And with these words, a distraught Bolbe embraces Memnon
Knowing she would never again enjoy his presence
And her beautiful Naiads also grieve at the tremendous loss
As the mighty Aethiopian contingent depart the great isles

---

[155] wife of Hector

[156] son of Hector

[157] hallowed lands in the realm of the dead where heroes and
heroines dwelled eternally in bliss as reward for their virtues

VII. Elysian Hector

And so mighty Memnon and his glorious comrades
Dutifully follow the counsel of lovely Bolbe
And set oars to the sea in pursuit of an entrance
To Tartarus, the underworld realm ruled by grim Hades

And heavy of heart they all are at the demise of Hector
For the great Trojan commander is admired for his valor
And for his courageous defense of the besieged city
As he brandished his mighty lance to the utter dismay

Of his foreign adversaries, led by the sons of Atreus
His death a great loss for the peoples of Troy!
Emboldening the Argives in their pursuit to sack the city
And thereby hastening the urgency to reach far away Ilium

And the son of the goddess and his determined men
Swiftly guide the vessels along the frothy seas
In hopes of reaching the ingress to Erebus as described
By the lake goddess, and obtain the counsel of fallen Hector

For an expeditious pathway to the great Dardanian citadel
And thereby avoid the rage of the Trident Bearer
As Earthshaker's anger is still aflame
Against the renowned son of iridescent and radiant Eos

And so by advice given in love by Thessalian Bolbe
The son of the goddess departs west of Attica
For the Eleusinian gateway to Erebus
Accessible through the Pagasaean[158] gulf

At holy Eleusina,[159] dear to the goddess Demeter
An eternal testament to her beloved daughter

---

[158] waterway in Pagasae; lands near Thessaly
[159] site of the Eleusinian Mysteries, rites sacred to Demeter
(goddess of the harvest) ; also known as Eleusis

Hades' intransigent bride lovely Persephone[160]
Abducted by the dark lord to be Queen of the dead[161]

And so epic Memnon and his men arrive to their destination
Unmolested by the fury of the seas
To the sacred rites of the harvest goddess
And dually the entrance to Hades' gloomy realm

And without delay the Aethiopian king and his commanders
Approach the concealed and cavernous entryway
And the son of the Eos commands a select group of men
To accompany him as he descends into the dark underworld

While the rest of the armies remain above at the entrance
To guard the vessels and await the return of their famed king
With orders from the son of the goddess to proceed
Onward to Troy if he should fail to return within reason

And as Memnon and his men draw near the dreadful cavity
They immediately hear agonizing sounds
Wailing, demented howls, and tortured screams
Blood curdling to men of a lesser pedigree

Yet the son of the goddess and his brave comrades
Boldly enter the hellish opening to Erebus
The clank of heavy armor and lances prevalent, and

---

[160] daughter of Zeus and Demeter; wife of Hades

[161] after the abduction of Persephone by Hades, Demeter refuses to allow anything to grow from the earth until her daughter is returned to her; fearing the annihilation of humankind, Zeus orders Hades to return Persephone to Demeter, and Hades promptly obeys his brother's commands; however, Hades ensures the return of Persephone to the realm of the dead by tricking her into eating the seeds of a pomegranate, for the Fates ordained that anyone whom partook of the food of the underworld are eternally confined there

Heightened within the confines of the hollow surroundings

As famed Memnon leads the courageous expedition
As they make their way towards the din of a torrent
The massive deluge emanating a near deafening sound
For the murky waters serve as a sadistic canal

And not far from this desolate and tortured place
Lies the infamous and respected river Styx
The long and winding waterways of the underworld
Its streams dreaded by both gods and mortals alike

And so revered are the ancient banks of the Styx
That the immortal Olympians themselves are held
Accountable by its dreaded and frightening waters
As they pledge sacred oaths and promises

And none are allowed to renege on these covenants
For any god or goddess who dared to violate
Attestations made invoking the grand river of Hades
Undoubtedly would suffer unspeakable retribution

And along these waters the son of the goddess and his men
Fearlessly proceed around the shallow bend
As they further penetrate the cavernous abyss
And the coveted sunlight of Helios becomes faint

And within a short span they reach a deteriorated vessel
As the gaunt ferryman Charon[162]awaits them
His enterprise to escort the forlorn souls of the deceased
And silver coinage is the toll for transport

The token provided by the household of the departed

---

[162] ferryman of Hades whom carried the souls of the deceased
across the river Styx for payment of a coin

And indiscriminate is Charon in whom he ferries
For the young, old, fragile, and strong succumb to death
As grim Thanatos[163] lays permanent claim to their souls

And as the magnificent Memnon and his peerless men
Make approach towards the desolate boat
Requesting safe passage from the ancient ferryman
An astonished Charon bellows his inquiry to them,

"Son of the goddess, peerless Memnon Tithonides!
Has prattle and rumor failed to reach Tartarus
Of your untimely and unfortunate demise?
And this is why you stand before the River Styx?

For you and your comrades bear the markings of the living
As you stand before me tall and strong
And your appearance is that of youth and vigor
As vitality and beauty abounds in your presence

The likes not witnessed since the incomparable Theseus
Though daring, he undertakes a fool hardy task
In attempting to abduct Demeter's daughter
For Persephone is unhappy in the embrace of Hades

And so the hero is punished by lord of the dead
An appendage to the great Stone yonder
To suffer for the latter expanse of time
Until rescued by mighty Heracles during his Labors

Also similar in appearance are you to sad Orpheus[164]
As he ventured into these sad and forlorn lands
For the famed lyrist's wife succumbs to the serpent's bite

---

[163] personification of death
[164] greatest musician of Greek mythology; son of Calliope (one f
the Muses, goddesses of the arts)

As the soul fled her listless and pale body

And shortly thereafter departs for Hades' dark realm
And so the son of Oeagrus[165] too sets forth into the depths of
Tartarus seeking the return of his beloved wife
His own life now devoid of joy and happiness

And as Orpheus makes his descent into the underworld
Melodious harmony he employs as persuasion
As the sad din resonates with all whom he encounters
And even the tri-headed guard dog allows safe passage

And he continues his expedition alongside Acheron[166]
Orpheus' magnificent lyre drawing tears and pity
And none who overheard the ballad could resist
And he is granted an audience before Lord Hades himself

The king of Erebus[167] appears stern and imposing
As he stands within proximity of his reluctant queen
Abducted as a youth from the joyous lands of her mother
Compelled to reign over the realms of her husband

And Persephone is moved by the devotion of Orpheus
Thereby granting him the desires of his heart
And Eurydice[168] departs Tartarus alongside her husband
On the sworn covenant that he would not gaze upon her

Nor glance at her countenance until ascension is complete
And Helios' warm bright rays were felt above surface
But the curious lyrist could not resist temptation
And so unhappy Eurydice is swiftly returned across the Styx

---

[165] father of Orpheus; a Thracian king
[166] another famous river of the underworld
[167] reference to Hades
[168] wife of Orpheus

Such is a sampling of those taking this ill advised sojourn
Into the dreaded halls of the dark son of Cronus[169]
As each are met unexpectedly with grave misfortune
For none can extract earthly merriment from these realms

Son of the goddess, why do you now seek a similar course?
And intermingle with the ranks of the deceased?
An eternally unhappy and dreadful coexistence
Baffling to logic, when the Fates allot you otherwise"

And the son of the goddess answers the gaunt ferryman,
"Wily Charon, Hades' ancient and trusted concierge
Living though we are, we have been stridently challenged
Yet we remain unwearied in our expedition for glory

For we have encountered monstrous adversaries
And seductions of ravishing goddesses
And yet none of these obstacles have prevailed over us
As we continue our rigorous path to the lands of Dardanus

And so through unsolicited divine counsel
We are here to seek the advice of fallen Hector
Incomparable was he in the vicious battlefields of Troy
Succumbing only to intervention of Pallas Athena

The aegis goddess tipping the scales
Drawn taunt between two mighty warriors
One defending his ancestral lands
The other a bloodthirsty fiend in pursuit of gore and blood

As that mighty son of Priam fell to the Myrmidon's lance!
For none can withstand a divinely supported foe
And his soul now wanders amongst the ranks of the dead
To the utter anguish of me and my comrades!

---

[169] reference to Hades

And so now we come as humble supplicants
Requesting safe passage over the mighty Styx
Its eternal waters invoked by the gods and goddesses
As an indestructible safeguard of divine promises

For purpose of consulting with the great prince of sad Troy
I speak of horse taming Hector Priamides
My own revered kinsmen and exalted peer
Taken far too soon from us whom love him immensely"

And with these words from the son of the goddess
The ambivalent Charon assents to Memnon's appeal
Acquiescing to living passengers upon his boat
As he demands the customary coinage as payment

And so peerless Ergamenes steps forth
Providing the aged ferryman with his fare
As the Aethiopian contingent board the vessel
And Charon willingly obliges their entreaties

And after all have assembled within the structure
Charon takes up his narrow wooden paddle
Submerging it deep into the revered river of Hades
Commencing the journey across its murky waters

And immediately horrid visuals are witnessed
Sights reserved only for the recently deceased
First observed is the monstrous Cerberus,[170] the
Guard dog of the underworld, possessing three heads

As he ferociously snarls and drivels
A fearsome beast, as befitting his commission
Ensuring that only the dead enters Tartarus
With the heroic progeny of Zeus being the exception

---

[170] hellish hound of Hades; guards the gates of the underworld

And next the Aethiopian contingent witness the sad plight of
Pirithous,[171] famed monarch of the hardy Lapiths
And companion of Theseus, lusting for Persephone
He sets about in his fruitless goal

Of abducting the daughter of Demeter for a second time
To the dismay of the king of the dead
And so Pirithous is richly punished
As he eternally forfeits his illicit earthly memories

And perhaps the most intimidating sighting by far
Of the figures dwelling in deep Erebus
The horrid and avenging Erinyes[172]
Tisiphone, Megaera, and ruthless Alecto

A trio of snaked haired sisters, whose
Objective to exact revenge upon the wicked
Vengeance purposed since their beginnings
A congenital trait since a triumphant son castrates his sire

That faithful day when Cronus auspiciously challenged
Uranus,[173] at the insistence of mother Earth
Enraged at the imprisonment of her offspring
Employs the sickle bearer as her avenger of choice

And subsequently the contingent approaches Tantalus[174]

---

[171] king of the Lapiths, peoples in Thessaly

[172] goddesses of vengeance; born from the castrated genitals of
Uranus

[173] personification of the heavens; father of the Titans; husband of
Gaea; castrated by his son Cronus, and from his severed testicles
the goddess Aphrodite and the Erinyes emerged

[174] son of Zeus; ancestor of Agamemnon and Menelaus; as
punishment for killing his son Pelops (and attempting to serve as a
meal to the Olympians), he is made to eternally stand in a pool of

As he eternally experiences the pangs of ravishing hunger
And extreme thirst, a just and rightful penance
For his contemptuous meal served to the immortals

As he attempted cannibalizing the great Olympians
By slaying and dismembering his own son
Boiling the remains for an ill planned feast
A fiendish and gruesome meal indeed

And too they see the luckless Sisyphus[175]
Forever confined to retrieving a great stone
For return to the top of the gloomy hills
Only to witness it suddenly fall down again

Punishment for his constant trickeries of the gods
And his foolhardy grandiose of superior intellect
Above that of almighty Zeus the Cloud Gatherer
Thus crafty Sisyphus is subjected to a futile exercise

And after a brief excursion near the Asphodel Meadows[176]
Hade's ferryman continues his dreadful tour
And the Aethiopian contingent witness other unearthly sights
As they make approach to the sought after Elysian Fields

And as Charon guides the vessel closer to its destination
Near the outer edges just past the deep abyss of Erebus
A sudden brightness appears out of the darkness
Signaling that the approach to Elysium is proximate

And before reaching these hallowed lands of the underworld

---

water beneath a fruit tree, but never able to quench his hunger or
thirst
[175] king of Corinth
[176] realms of the underworld reserved for those whom lived their
lives neutrally

Where earthly heroes and brave warriors alike
Eternally dwell in bliss and just respite
The Aethiopian men behold the three judges of Hades

Zeus spawned Rhadamanthus, Minos, and Aeacus[177]
Revered for their wisdom and vast knowledge
And accordingly chosen as overseers of justice for the dead
To mete out sentences to the lately deceased

As anxious and forlorn souls await eternal judgment, many
Slated for damnation for wicked acts committed during life
While few proceed onward to the blessed isles of the Hades'
Lands, and the terminus of Memnon's underworld journey

For at last the golden fields of Elysium are reached
As each of the awed men depart the vessel of Charon
Led by the incomparable Memnon Tithonides
And all bid farewell to the accommodating boatman

As he dutifully pivots the ship of the dead
To return yet again to the entrance of the underworld
With purpose of ferrying the neoteric subjects of Hades
And evermore accumulating silver and gold bullion

And the son of the goddess leads his loyal comrades
Across the wondrous fields, unforeseen by most
For the Elysian realm is reserved for the incomparable
Lesser men barred from these prime lands of the dead

Who did Memnon and his men encounter in these realms?
First Alcmene,[178] the heralded mother of mighty Heracles
This granddaughter of the Aethiopian queen Andromeda
And loved by great Zeus for her beauty and courage

---

[177] three judges of the dead; sons of Zeus
[178] mother of Heracles; queen of Tiryns

Next to greet the Aethiopian contingent is prince Cadmus[179]
Revered son of King Agenor and founder of Thebes
This famed man accomplished much during his reign
Accordingly he is eternally rewarded for his virtues

Too the son of the goddess sees lovely Europa[180]
Appearing as she did the day she was accosted
And carried away by a white bull from her homelands
And taken to the far off islands of remote Crete

And though the inhabitants of the Elysian Fields happily
Greet Memnon and his comrades, and welcome the men
To the blessed isles of the underworld, nothing could prepare
The Aethiopian contingent for the next series of encounters

For not far away stood a familiar figure to them all
Espied by a solemn and empathetic son of the goddess
As the great Queen of Libya suddenly makes her appearance
And all those who beheld her are saddened by her apparition

For she is a revered persona amongst the peoples of the
Hallowed lands,[181] and her love for Memnon is legendary
Unfortunate in her unrequited affections is Queen Cyrene
Sorrowfully compelling the Libyan monarch to end her life

And so the tears flow liberally from all those present, for
Even in death Queen Cyrene covets her beloved Memnon
As she gazes upon the son of the goddess longingly
Desperately extending her soliciting arms for a final embrace

---

[179] first king of Thebes

[180] sister of Cadmus; abducted by Zeus in the form of a white bull
and carried her off to Crete, where she bore to him Minos and
Rhadamanthus

[181] reference to Aethiopia and lands of Africa

And the son of Eos sadly acknowledges her
As he stares deeply into her dark and desolate eyes
For devastated is Memnon by Cyrene's untimely demise
A consequence of his not returning her desperate love

The son of the goddess again offers fervent words
And honors the great Queen amidst the realm of the dead
As its inhabitants overhear his sincere protestations
Forewarning them all of the presence of the living

And the bitter Libyan Queen rebuffs his justifications
For even in piteous death she infers a slight from his words
Thereby refusing to pardon Eos' son for perceived wrongs
And so the jilted Cyrene wanders back to her eternal abode

And her sudden departure invokes dismay in the son of Eos
For he held the great Queen in high regard
And thoroughly lamented her unfortunate death
As the Libyan queen made fervent sacrifices on his behalf

And soon thereafter another sad reunion takes place
As Memnon is approached by his beloved fallen comrades
Those tragically lost in combat with monstrous deities
And ruthless gods and goddesses during the epic journey

Fierce Cerces, Laopis and the incomparable Aimpthos
Sadly overcome during the battle with Echidna
As she menaced the Aethiopian contingent at Thebes
Each proudly refusing to capitulate without struggle

Also present are mighty Drasops, Eithicros, and Oeneor
And fierce Adrasius, along with loyal Peplios
These brave and stout men slain during the fatal conflict
Near the lair of the ravenous giant Chrysaor

As the cannibal scavenged their earthly remains

Indulging in his monstrous delight of human flesh
Unbridled in this unspeakable and horrid practice
Finally ended at the hands of the radiant son of Eos

And even in death these glorious men paid homage
To mighty Memnon as he slowly pass them by
By humbly kneeling before their earthly king
Eternally honoring the great son of the goddess

Loyal as the day they dared to set oars to the sea
And accompany Memnon Tithonides as he ventured to Troy
Now sorrowfully mourned by their surviving comrades!
As the Aethiopian contingent seek consultation with Hector

The son of the goddess and his bereaving men
Though overwhelmed by sheer despair and sadness
After interacting for a final time with fallen companions
Continue forward to fulfill the objective of their mission

And as the son of the goddess and his illustrious comrades
Continue to cross the bright lands of the underworld
Refuge amidst the woeful Hades ruled realms
They suddenly witness a regal apparition

That of Dardanian born Hector Priamides
The great light of the Trojan peoples
Bearing a sad and forlorn look on his countenance
As he beheld the son of the goddess and his contingent

Their kinship originating from mighty Tros
Sons of brothers, one is duly chosen
As a consort of rosy fingered Eos
The other as lord of the richest city in the world[182]

---

[182] reference to Tithonus (father of Memnon) and Priam (father of Hector)

Each begat incomparable sons, divinely blessed
Peerless with the lance and the mighty sword
Intrepid Hector notable for taming war horses
And Memnon for his beauty and formidable skills in battle

Such was the lineage of the these two epic men
As they stood before each other face to face
One from amongst the ranks of the living
And the other an inhabitant behind the gates of Elysium

And with intense sadness, Memnon speaks to his cousin
"Great Hector, beloved above all others in the world!
The ravishing Thessalian goddess forewarned of your
Unfortunate death as I sojourned in her wondrous abode

Wretched now am I and the whole of Ilium!
For we have been deprived of your incomparable
Companionship, as I and my comrades tarry
Satisfying our earthly lusts and abandoning obligation to

Troy, her lofty walls vulnerable to the haughty Achaeans
Led by the heartless Myrmidon, for the sake of Menelaus
As Helen abandons Atreus' son for handsome Paris
And responsibility for its defense was yours alone

And as I made my way across the angry seas
Earthshaker becomes my fearsome adversary
And his fury incites delay from the Scaean Gates
As I and my men are matched against monstrous foes

Meanwhile you encounter that merciless man and Athena
An unenviable task to undertake alone, great though you be!
And so unfortunately we now we have our dreadful reunion!
Instead of joyous childhood recollections

When we both aspired to our outsized destinies, and plans

Meticulously contrived for such lofty expectations
Of greatness consummated by the descendants of Dardanus
So that future generations inevitably speak of our exploits

For uncontroverted in the minds of those concerned with the
Great War, that you and I alone, both alive and full of vigor
Even if we be deprived of the aid of our loyal armies
Would effortlessly repel the Argive advance upon Troy

And haughty Achilles less confident, the son of Telamon[183]
No longer boldly stands amongst the foremost of the ranks
And wily Odysseus[184] would advise the Achaeans to depart
Troy, for much revered is the prowess of our might in battle!

Alas, for this shall no longer to be a conceivable outcome!
As the Fates have ordained a different pathway for us both
And mere mortals must succumb to divine edict, thereby
Sparing the armies of Agamemnon our furious onslaught

And now I humbly come before you seeking your counsel
As best to hasten our arrival to the Trojan citadel
For it has been divinely revealed that only you possess such
Knowledge, so we petition you for the pathway to Ilium"

And Hector solemnly makes reply to brave Memnon
"Son of the goddess, delight of both Aethiopia and Troy!
Though far is the distance between the Idaean plains and the
Shores of your hallowed lands, two nations nonetheless

Are ancestrally allied, and destined are you to a much better
Fate than I, for as long as I was permitted to walk the earth

---

[183] reference to Ajax, king of Salamis and ally of Agamemnon
against the Trojans; one of the best warriors
[184] king of Ithaca and ally of Agamemnon against the Trojans;
principal character of Homer's *Odyssey*

I ceaselessly battled the ruthless and tyrannical Achaeans
Thus averting the untimely fall of Priam's realms

And its woeful submission to cruel Argive rulers
Proud Agamemnon, Tydeus' formidable son Diomedes
And Telemonian Ajax, along with clever Odysseus
All lusting for the famed and expansive Trojan wealth

These mighty and unwelcomed men I hardily withstood
And many others, the very best of far away Argos
Even holding off the fiercest champion of their ranks
The dreaded Achilles and his Myrmidon armies

Supported by Delian[185] Apollo, I managed to rebuff them all
With my glorious lance and famed sword
Well known throughout all earthly realms
As I warded off the multiple assaults of the Achaeans

And shortly thereafter a feud arose
Between the son of Atreus and the Myrmidon
A dispute based upon ego and sheer greed
Causing Thetis' son to withdraw from dreaded battle

And so my comrades and I raged in his unforeseen absence
As no Achaean is able to withstand our onslaught
And we set fires to the very fleets of Agamemnon himself
As the whole of Troy rejoices in its plausible salvation

And the desperate Odysseus, along with Telamonian Ajax
Implore Achilles as commanded by Atreus' son
To rejoin the war efforts and rescue the ships
And the prideful, stubborn man swiftly refuses the request

His burning love for Briseis,[186]a Trojan princess

---

[185] inhabitant of the island Delos, birthplace of Apollo

Impediment to saving the Argive contingent
Instead by the desperate urgings of Patroclus
Sanctions the donning of his armor by his beloved cousin

And again the Myrmidons ride forth into battle
My commanders and I fooled by the stratagem
An Argive guise perpetrated for respite, as the Dardanians
Mistook the son of Menoetius for his much stronger cousin

Like a ferocious bear awakened from a brief hibernation
Returned to the battlefield to appease bloodthirsty Ares
And apprehension spreads hastily amongst the rank and file
Due to the supposed reappearance of the dreaded Achilles

And the tides of battle are swiftly turned, as we are thwarted
From our purpose of burning the Argive ships
Alternatively fleeing in panic to the high walls of our city
As it appears as though great Zeus now favors the Achaeans

And neither Trojan nor ally is spared from the onslaught
As the Olympians grant victory to young Patroclus
And he rages in the blood stained fields of our ancestors
Slaying many beloved captains and their comrades

The Myrmidon's cousin permitted to overcome
Even the exalted children of the divine Olympians
As his lance pierces the breastplate of the Lycian monarch[187]
Mighty Zeus assents to the demise of his own beloved son!

---

[186] cousin of Hector; given to Achilles as a war prize after her capture from Lyrnessus (lands near Troy); she is subsequently taken from Achilles by Agamemnon, thereby necessitating a feud between the two that causes Achilles to temporarily withdraw from the war
[187] reference to Sarpedon, king of Lycia and Trojan ally

And our great ally and comrade King Sarpedon
Stout of heart and loyal to our imperiled cause
After bravely confronting the ferocious advance of Patroclus
Falls to him as he wields the weaponry of Achilles

So far away from his sumptuous realms
As wife and son are left behind to mourn his death
Our great friend sadly perishes for the sake of holy Ilium
As the son of Zeus is slain by the impersonator

And we commence the fight over the corpse of Sarpedon
For honor and duty overcome any apprehension
I, determined to rescue the fallen body of the Lycian king
Come face to face with the Myrmidon's cousin

Mistaking Patroclus for his much fearsome kin
As we battled near the Scaean Gates
And concerned Dardanians witness our struggle
And by Apollo's consent, I effortlessly conquer my foe

Stripping his body of the glorious armor of Phthia
Spoils befitting my tremendous feat at arms
Accordingly we again send the Achaeans fleeing
In sheer terror they stumble to their besieged ships

And the death of Patroclus swiftly reaches
The ears of the anguished Myrmidon monarch
And he is determined to revenge his kinsman
Undeterred by my dangerous reputation in battle

Fierce Achilles sets forth in all his ferocity, and
Never before had my armies witnessed such degree of fury!
The Myrmidon growls and grovels as if he is a hungry beast
Akin to a madman is he as he attacks our overwhelmed ranks

Without effort he routs the Trojans, Dardanians, and its allies

Slaying many of my dearest comrades, swelling Xanthus[188]
Streams with a multitude of Trojan corpses!
As his rage is assuaged only by irrevocable death

His gruesome handiwork displayed on the Idaean plains!
Aroused by the hatred of Olympians opposed to Pergamus
Fie the day of Paris' ill conceived judgment!
An inevitable slight of two powerful goddesses

And now revenge is embodied in the son of Peleus
As he lusts to meet me man to man
And I am forewarned by bright Apollo not to engage him
As he sends Anchises' son to meet the scourge

And Aeneas bravely stands against the Myrmidon
His valor apparent as he alone meets the furious advance
The Dardanian commander draws his sword and famed lance
To the dismay of Achilles, for the maneuver is unexpected

And the two champions engage in fatal battle
As Apollo lends courage to Cythera's[189] son
And the Myrmidon too has his divine benefactors
And thus fearlessly takes up Aeneas' challenge

To the disadvantage of Anchises' progeny!
For he is no match for the foremost of the Argives
As the Myrmidon's lance barely misses its mark
And nearly accomplishes a magnificent feat of arms

And the son of lovely Aphrodite is grateful
As he escapes only through divine intervention
For the Trident Bearer pitied his impending doom
And saves Aeneas from the cold and cruel steel

---

[188] another reference to Scamander
[189] another reference to Aphrodite

And so mighty Achilles continues his onslaught
In pursuit of my famous golden shield
And as I saw the scourge slaughter those I loved most
I could no longer hang back from the epic struggle

As my panicked armies rush inside the city
I alone wait for Achilles fearsome approach
Firmly gripping my lance and jeweled sword
Standing close by the entrance to the gates of the city

Ignoring the pleas of my own exalted parents
As they yell to me from the high walls of Ilium
And Queen Hecuba[190] tears her regal tunic
Beating her breasts in a frenzied sadness, and deaf am I

To the poignant entreaties of my beloved Andromache
As she begs her Hector to also swiftly enter
The safety of the strong walls assembled by Poseidon
And refrain from engaging the maniac Achilles

I even overheard the screams of my dear son
As young Astyanax cries for his mighty father
And the fervent prayers of my brothers and sisters
Chiefly Helenus,[191] Cassandra,[192] and Creusa[193]

And of Helen, her beauty the envy of the gods
For whose sake the Great War is unfortunately waged
The outcome predetermined the day she abandoned Sparta
For the sake of her love for Paris Priamides

---

[190] wife of Priam and queen of Troy; mother of Hector and Paris
[191] brother of Hector and famed seer
[192] sister of Hector and a famed prophetess; destined to utter truthful prophesies, but never to be believed
[193] wife of Aeneas and sister of Hector

Too I hear supplications of the Trojan elders
As Anchises and wise Antenor[194] state their appeals
These were the unison of voices in chorus
Imploring me to enter under the protection of the walls

But the hour of fate had at long last arrived
And the will of the great Olympian cannot be resisted
For merciless Pallas Athena plots my demise
And grants Thetis' son a tremendous victory

As Zeus' daughter takes the form of Deiphobus[195]
Hastening me to confront the fierce Myrmidon
And engage in the deadly game of war
And so our battle commenced, and the stratagem is complete

As Atropos takes her dreaded shears
Severing the thread of life once attached to this apparition
And before you now stands the once proud Hector
Father of Astyanax and tamer of horses[196]"

And so after a brief pause which seems like an eternity
After the sorrowful recounting of the final moments of his
Life, and of the travails of the revered son of Priam
Elysian Hector dutifully continues his narration

Pivoting from his own tragic ending
And eagerly addressing the inquiry the son of the goddess
Comforted in the knowledge that his beloved Ilium
Would soon welcome an incomparable hero to its holy gates

Respite for his besieged and troubled people

---

[194] Trojan elder and counselor to Priam; father of Agenor, a Trojan captain
[195] brother of Hector; Trojan captain
[196] reference to Hector, whose equestrian skills were unparalleled

And to the Troy's distressed allies alike
And a hopeful end to the Myrmidon's bloody exploits
In sight brought by the advance of the son of the goddess

Inevitable humbling of the haughty Achaean armies, and
Retreat contemplated by the once resolute sons of Atreus
As they abandon enterprise of retrieving Helen
And hastily return to the faraway lands of Argos

With these vivid ambitions in mind, Hector begins,
"My illustrious cousin, hounded by the Trident Bearer
Since your departure from the holy lands of Aethiopia
Much you have suffered for the sake of ancestral homage

As you bravely make your way across the torrent seas
Encountering fearsome monsters and delightful lovers
Your fame a testament to your esteemed lineage
Yet much more you shall endure for Priam's sake

Sufferings apportioned to you and your illustrious comrades
Once your glorious contingent makes arrival in Ilium
And engage the Achaean armies in fierce battle
As the enemies of Pergamus menace the Trojan phalanx

And with utmost certainty I can profess the knowledge
That if I be still alive wielding the cold steel
And allied with the invincible forces of Aethiopia
The walls of Ilium would remain steadfastly unblemished

For your prowess at arms are legendary!
Equaled only by your incomparable beauty
And impossible would be the task of the Argive armies
In opposition to our undeterred and united vanguard

But alas! The Fates thwart such an audacious plot
And the city of Priam is permitted a lone protector

And since I now am an inhabitant of Elysium
The defense of our homelands is within your purview

And so now I shall reveal what you honorably seek of me
A pathway to the holy lands of Dardanus
Unmolested by the passionately angered Trident Bearer
Unjustifiably infuriated by your perceived transgressions

First, dear cousin, make the preferred offerings
In deference to the indignant lord of the seas
To appease his provoked and raw emotions
And attempt restoration of Poseidon's good will towards you

Too offer fervent sacrifices to the remainder Olympians
Lamb, mutton, and other savory venison
The finest that you possess in your herd
All to be dispersed amongst a great conflagration

Afterwards, and without haste, navigate the Aegean due east
Then north, under the shadow of the invaders
Commencing from the holy city of Chalcis[197]
Mimic the vessels of the Achaeans

A massive undertaking after Atreus' scorned son
Implored his war lusting brother for assistance
To retrieve divine Helen from the saffron bed
Of handsome Paris after his forbidden seduction of her

For solely by this route shall you proceed without further
Incidence, imperiled are alternatives by Trident Bearer
And in due course your arrival to Ilium shall transpire
Along with imminent conflict with the Argive battalions"

---

[197] Greek city where the Argive armies assembled and departed to
Troy

And as mighty Hector concludes his wise counsel
And provides to the Aethiopian contingent the necessary
Directives, final pleasantries are exchanged by the cousins
As they sadly depart from one another after a brief reunion

The son of the goddess, along with his illustrious comrades
Determined to arrived to Troy without further incidence
Patiently await the ancient vessel of Hade's ferryman
With fare in hand in exchange for entry onto the transport

And the accommodating Charon again allows the living
To board his vessel usually reserved for the deceased
Ferrying the incomparable band across Hade's expansive
Realms, back to the forbidden entrance they dared to breach

And the son of the goddess along with his chosen men
Are again joined with the remainder of their comrades
Delighted by the return of their venerable king!
From his descent into the abyss of the underworld

And after each man cheerfully greets one another
As tales of the adventure are thoroughly recounted
All hastily make way to the lofty ships
And the offerings suggested by Hector are duly made

And once again the Aethiopian fleet set oars to the seas
In great anticipation of reaching its Dardanian destination
And at long last engage the feared armies of Atreus
For determined are they all for fame and glory everlasting

VIII. The Reunion of Memnon and Priam

And great Helios steers his glorious golden chariot
Bringing reprieve from the darkness of the night
As hopes is renewed within the bosom of mankind
Along with hardships as ordained by high Olympus

On this day great fortune smiles graciously upon
The sea harassed Aethiopian contingent
Led by the enduring son of the goddess
As he and his glorious comrades continue across the seas

With guidance obtained from the deceased Hector
The illustrious men set course for the Trojan shores
And sibling jealousies are momentarily abated, as
The turbulent sons of Eos relent against their famed brother

And acquiesce to peaceful navigation of Memnon's fleet
Too assuaged are the emotions of trident bearing Poseidon
For he supposed the son of the goddess to be preoccupied
And accordingly the ocean remains temperate

And the rich sacrifices by the Aethiopian contingent
Appeases the unpredictable Olympians, as great Zeus,
Apollo, and his huntress sister are duly honored
Also celebrated are the deities opposed to great Memnon

And immortal discord and strife are momentarily set aside
As the son of the goddess is permitted safe passage
No Echidna to subdue, nor fiendish giant to slay
Nor diversions of maternal meddling in Aethiopian affairs

Or seductions from lovely goddesses and Naiads
As only the calm blue green seas lay between
The son of the goddess and a triumphant arrival to Ilium
Unmolested as they cross the expanse of Poseidon's realms

And as the vessels effortlessly drift under these auspices

The Aethiopian contingent swiftly traverses the Aegean
Taking the same pathway as the Achaeans did before them[198]
When the armies of Agamemnon first set sail for Troy

After the blasphemous slaying of his own daughter[199]
As punishment for an offense to the huntress goddess
A horrid and steep price for a father to pay
For privilege to reach the far away Dardanian plains

Leto's infuriated daughter requiring atonement
For the careless slaying of her sacred antelope
And so Clytemnestra,[200] deceived by the stratagem
Is eternally deprived from embracing her beloved daughter

And thus the son of Atreus is permitted to proceed
In his ambitions to menace the Trojan citadel
Supported militarily by the Myrmidon scourge
To the dismay of Priam and Queen Hecuba

Such is the background of the select route at Aulis
Though Eos' radiant son is more fortunate in departure
As his men eagerly anticipate a wondrous homecoming
In the ancestral homelands of their mighty forefathers

To at long last hold privy council with the wise King Priam
And to hear the prophecies uttered by lovely Cassandra

---

[198] the Achaeans set sail for Troy from Aulis, a port near Boeotia;
Hector directed Memnon and his comrades to take this same route
to Troy in order to evade further incidence
[199] the Oracle at Delphi prophesied that Agamemnon could not
depart for Troy until he sacrificed his eldest daughter Iphigenia
[200] wife of Agamemnon; Agamemnon tricks Clytemnestra into
thinking that he is arranging marriage between Iphigenia and
Achilles, Accordingly, Clytemnestra allows Iphigenia to depart
Argos for Aulis

Though unheeded are her warnings in accordance to the will
Of Apollo, to the unfortunate doom of her many skeptics

The men are too intrigued to behold
The famed beauty of Paris' wife Helen
No less a daughter of Zeus the thunder lord
And for whose sake the mighty war is waged

And the comrades of the son of the goddess aspire
As they dined in the great halls of the palace
To engage her Trojan seducer, handsome Paris
Though he be the most hated man on earth

And eager are the men to demonstrate their skills
Wielding the lance and brandishing the sword
Conducting war maneuvers with pious Aeneas
The great commander of the Dardanian forces

Cyprian Aphrodite conceived this mighty man
On the Idaean plains to lord Anchises
The great goddess giving her love to a mortal
And bears an incomparable champion of Troy

The Aethiopian fleet is desirous too
Of audience with wise Antenor,[201] Helenus, and Deiphobus
Brave Agenor,[202]Glaucus, and mighty Polydamas[203]
As well as the other famed inhabitants of Ilium

These thoughts went through the minds of the men
For each held anticipation and yearning for glory everlasting
As the winds guide the vessels due eastbound

---

[201] a Trojan elder and counselor to Priam
[202] son of Antenor; captain in Trojan army
[203] son of Panthous; captain in Trojan army; companion of Hector,
as both were born on the same night

Then swiftly northwards at a brisk pace

And as these favorable events unfurl and transpire
And the son of Eos steadfastly makes approach to Troy
Whispers of the arrival of the mighty Aethiopian fleet
Swiftly are dispersed by rumor engendering Ossa

Reaching the ears of the concerned Argive captains
To the utter dismay of Diomedes Tydeus' son
And dually conveying shivers both to Telamonian Ajax
As cunning Odysseus too alarmed by the impending event

For the famed exploits of the son of the goddess
And his greatly acclaimed reputation and prowess at arms
Uniquely designates him as a formidable opponent in fierce
Combat, and accordingly deference is afforded to him

And so distressing is the impending approach of Memnon
That immediate council is held at the behest of Atreus' son
To formulate a coherent strategy in response to his arrival
And to stem the swelling panic growing amongst the ranks

For the presence of the vaunted son of the goddess
Incites great fear within the Argive armies
An emotion not experienced since the demise of Hector
As the son of Priam wielded his weaponry with deadly effect

And so Agamemnon candidly addresses his commanders
As well as the subject kings allied under his banner
All with purpose to capture the riches of Troy
And now an earnest exchange transpires amongst them

First to speak is the wily son of Oileus[204]

---

[204] king of Locris; father of Ajax the lesser, a captain in the Argive
army

Ajax the lesser, as compared to his namesake
"Achaean lords, why attempt to alleviate
What deprives us all of restful slumber?

The clarion calls from wondrous Aethiopia
Heard from the halls of Athens to the faraway Italian shores
Reaching Troy herself of the glorious arrival
Of the incomparable son of the goddess

Redoubtable Memnon, to even speak his hallowed name
Sends shudders throughout my very body!
For although he has endured the wrath of the Olympians
Matched against the monstrous Chrysaor

With Echidna lurking as a contingency
The son of the goddess has endured and triumphed
At this very hour great Memnon swiftly approaches Ilium
And will no doubt enter the Scaean Gates, embracing Priam

This mighty man determined to unleash destruction!
Upon our armies as he comes to the defense of his kinsmen
And all within such a short time after the fall of great Hector
Compelled are we to face yet another invincible champion!

As he leads the allied ranks we now devastate at will
And whom we have driven into the city in droves
As they cower behind Troy's lofty and stubborn walls
Built by no less than Trident Bearer and Leto's exalted son

During their famed servitude to King Laomedon
A fortunate mortal commanding two great deities
An impregnable invention and obstruction to our ambitions
And so for many years we toil far from our homelands

And yet now we are destined for more death and destruction!
For the ferocious prowess of Eos' son is widely known

And the famed lance of Memnon never misses its target!
And we shall surely suffer much more bloodshed!"

And all those assembled sadly nod in assent to these words
For none of the Argive captains dare to dispute their validity
As grumblings of concern spread through the audience
So revered was the strength of Memnon Tithonides

Next to speak is Tydeus' mighty son Diomedes
Though fearless during his exploits versus Aphrodite[205]
As she protected her beloved fallen son, for he was buoyed
By Athena as she sought her own vengeance

Now the tremendous man is suddenly humbled
At the mere thought of encountering Eos' feared son
Dreading close combat with him as he whirls his huge lance
And he slowly stands before his comrades and makes reply

"My fellow comrades whom labor beneath these walls!
It has been quite some time since we first embarked for Troy
And though we possess within our exalted ranks
The greatest warriors and commanders ever assembled!

The walls of Pergamus still remain stubbornly intact
For that magnificent city is loved by radiant Apollo
And that god would gladly see every Argive sadly perish
If this would save the famed citadel of King Priam

And at no such time before since our waging this awful war
Could I predict with undaunted certainty the breach of the
Lofty pillars of Troy, until the great victory of Achilles
As he slays mighty Hector near Scamander's banks

---

[205] after Diomedes wounds Aeneas during a confrontation,
Aphrodite intervenes to save the life of her son Aeneas; Diomedes
subsequently attacks the goddess Aphrodite

And though we be within proximity of our mission
Of conquering Ilium and recovering lovely Helen, with
Prospects of at last setting sail for our beloved homelands
Yet another plague is commissioned by Leto's son!

For we are all aware of the dangerous Aethiopian king!
And how mighty Memnon adroitly wields his lance
With deadly aim, such a fierce and difficult opponent is he!
As no man alive has yet to overcome him in battle

And if he is permitted to fight alongside mighty Aeneas
Panthous'[206] son Polydamas, and brave Glaucus
Or form a deadly alliance with courageous Agenor
The son of the wise councilor of King Priam

Such illicit plans pose significant concerns to our ranks
For the son of the goddess, his feats at arms notable, his
Skills in battle far more superior than even those of
The best man reared in all Troy, Hector himself!

Notwithstanding the son of Priam himself a terror for us as
He scattered our phalanx! And only one Argive could
Withstand his wrath, finally bringing down that mighty man
With the divine assistance of Olympus"

Then rose Menelaus, Atreus' aggrieved son
Longing for his divine wife, Zeus' own daughter
Nuptials carelessly abandoned by lovely Helen
As she eloped with Paris across the Aegean straits

An act engulfing two mighty nations in strife
For the sake of one luckless man
And so many brave men thus slated for Tartarus
Never again to see homeland and kin

---

[206] a Trojan elder and counselor to Priam

And so Atreus son sadly replies, "Achaean lords
I know all too well your sufferings!
For my sake as I seek to retrieve
My wife, the unfaithful queen of Sparta!

Leaving behind your realms and luxurious abodes
For my vengeance against the beguiling Trojan prince
And so the Argive armies endured that mighty man
Apollo loved Hector, as he raged in awful battle

Finally overcome by fierce Achilles and Zeus born Athena
To the relief of our embattled battalions, and yet more
Disheartening news suddenly arrives! Brought upon us by
The merciless Olympians as they announce to our armies

The arrival to Troy of that dreaded son of the Dawn!
Memnon Tithonides, a strong and dangerous foe!
As he dutifully supports his besieged Trojan kinsmen
More woe and folly for the Argive ranks!

He will undoubtedly slay many of our men
And bring havoc to our beloved comrades
Bloodthirsty, confident as he whirls his famed javelin
Fulfilling his aspirations to repel our determined assault

And though we are destined by fate to suffer these agonies
We too have formidable men in our ranks
And our travail must not be in vain
Nor unaccomplished our mission of laying waste to Troy

And with these words Menelaus beseeches his peers
Even though concern floods their minds
As the son of Atreus appeals to these concerned monarchs
And to the commanders and famed Achaean captains

To set aside thoughts of abandoning the campaign

And depart the Trojan beaches and wide ranging plains
Permitting the vaunted city walls to remain solidly intact
As a result of the intervention of Memnon into the conflict

And Menelaus' saddened pleas are persuasive
As the rank and file are sympathetic to his plight
Accordingly it is concluded to continue the siege of Ilium
Despite the enormous challenges ahead they faced

And king Agamemnon issues decree affirming this
Consensus, as he wields his indestructible golden scepter
A validation of his supreme reign of all assembled
As the various rulers of Achaea reaffirm their loyalty to him

And so the council of Argive lords solemnly adjourns
After deciding it best to withdraw from the city walls
And alternatively assume a defensive posture
Awaiting the ferocious advance of the Aethiopian king

And so the massive armies of the proud son of Atreus
Once thought themselves impregnable from anxiety in battle
Now voluntarily retreat to the familiarity of the ships
Despite the absence of fire hurling Hector

And the Trojan watch is flummoxed by the sight!
For all within the strong walls supposed entrenchment
Of the Argive armies around the perimeter of the city
Taunting the Trojan command to engage in fatal warfare

And the observers swiftly depart from their perch
Dispatching couriers to bring word to King Priam
Of the latest maneuver of their hated foe
As withdrawal from the periphery of the citadel is apparent

And once these developments are independently confirmed
Of the sudden vanishing of the Achaean encampment

The heartened peoples of the Ilium suddenly rejoice!
As hope springs anew in the face of certain annihilation

For all supposed the destruction of Troy is proximate
And that the women and children would surely be enslaved!
Since the sad and untimely death of great Hector, strong and
Courageous champion slaughtered for the sake of his people!

And none of Trojan stock could match the son of Peleus
For he is as swift as the northern winds
And strong as if he were made of bronze
As he deftly wields his fearsome sword and lance

And the deluge of relief within the city is pervasive
For the unexpected Argive retreat surely portend
The anticipated arrival of the famed son of the goddess
And his courageous armies to the defense of Ilium!

The elated Trojans fervently praise the Olympians
With abundant offerings of choice mutton and lamb
The best of the stocks within the royal stables
Honoring the immortals in anticipation of their salvation

And revelry is dispersed throughout the city of Laomedon
As pensive and dour moods hastily dissipate
And a war wearied nation suddenly rejoices
Sanguine expectations of succor from a powerful ally

And in the morn after the evening festivities
And subsequent to the earnest council hastily convened
By the best and foremost of the Achaeans captains
Followed by their evacuation across the shores of Scamander

The son of the goddess and his loyal comrades
Begin to make approach to the lands of Priam
And within a short time they make land fall

At long last docking their vessels at Trojan beaches!

And all of Memnon's battle famished comrades rejoice!
As their long and arduous journey mercifully reaches its
Terminus, consummating the Aethiopian triumph over the
Seas, respite from the harsh wrath of the Trident Bearer

And shortly thereafter the men disembark from the vessels
And due sacrifices are made to honor the Olympians
Even to those who oppose their arrival to Troy
As was the genial custom of the famed son of Eos

And the Aethiopian commanders are astonished!
That they are not met with Achaean resistance
For so effortlessly are they able to dock their exalted ships
And to raise the colorful and regal banner of Aethiopia

For great Memnon is unaware of Argive deference
Afforded him by unequivocal and unanimous consent
The Argive captains abstaining from initial confrontation
Revering the prowess of the son of the goddess

And so after the vessels are thoroughly garrisoned
As a precaution against an Argive ambush
The son of the goddess and his illustrious captains
At last proceed to the long sought after Trojan citadel

Bountiful gifts in hand from their wondrous homelands
Including gold, silver, bronze and rare spices
And exotic creatures native only to Zeus loved Aethiopia
To be presented to the principals of the Dardanian lands

And the Trojan sentries readily acknowledge the banner of
Aethiopia, without hesitation relax their stringent vigilance
As the famed entrance into holy Troy is flung open wide
For the son of the goddess and his glorious comrades

As the famed men regally approach the walls of the city
Marching resolutely through the Scaean Gates, and are
Immediately welcomed by King Priam and the Trojans
As their advent is met with wild and hopeful jubilation!

A joyous spectacle in the lands of Laomedon
Happiness not felt by the besieged Dardanians
Since incomparable Hector himself guarded holy Ilium
As Trojan vanguard, menacing the Argive ranks

And all are enamored by the masculinity of Eos' son
Well deserved is his reputation as the handsomest man alive
Unparalleled is his splendid and divine beauty
Comparable to that of his feminine counterpart from Sparta

For never before since genial Gaea first nurtured mortals
Had the world beheld such physical prowess
As that of venerable son of the goddess
Kin to the divine cupbearer Ganymedes himself

He too descended from the royal line of Tros
The Olympians enamored by his incomparable beauty
Hence this honor was bestowed upon a mortal
Even his physical attributes paled in comparison to Memnon

And so all of Troy is thoroughly entranced
As they watched the son of the goddess and his procession
Taking in his great length and sculpted torso
As he strides upright and majestically towards the great hall

Draped in his regal Aethiopian trappings
As they cover his famed golden bronze armor and tunic
And the crest of his helmet enriched in wrought palladium
As he humbly kneels before the wise King Priam

And that old monarch would have none of it

Hastily gesturing the son of the goddess to rise
And the revered king is followed by all the elders of Troy
As each bow respectively before the Aethiopian king

Affording him respect and honor as is his due
For no man alive more accomplished than mighty Memnon
Eos' mighty son endowed above all others in prowess
And his skills in battle paralleled only by his piety

And the just King Priam rises to address the gathering
Exuberantly, he begins, "Son of the goddess!
Your presence is most welcomed in these hallowed halls!
As a son of Troy returns to the lands of his descendants

Unfortunately our reunion is under the duress of conflict
And you return to defense the lands of your beloved father
As war is being waged against these sacred provinces
Such was the lot cast against our besieged peoples!

Your arrival could not have come a moment sooner!
In especial after the fall of our venerable Hector
More like the son of a divine Olympian
And not of one born from the loins of a mortal

For the extent of this accursed war our bulwark in battle
His life and limb taken by the Myrmidon scourge!
Supported by that aegis bearing daughter of great Zeus
Woeful to me and those of my royal household!

As an aging monarch outlives his mighty progeny
And my old eyes compelled to witness his untimely demise!
As he bravely fought against irresistible forces
Maintaining the honorable name of the house of Dardanus

And yet much worse suffering for Troy lay ahead
As the savage Achilles desecrates the prince's corpse

Piercing the limbs of his vanquished adversary
And in a fit of madness he drags the body around the walls

Satiating his insane appetite for vengeance, as we all
Look on and watch in sheer horror at the despoiled and ill
Treated body of fallen Hector, as the merciless Achilles is
Permitted to dishonor that mighty man

My joy forever lost in that moment of his demise!
And all anxiety and fears are suddenly vanished
And disregard I now have for my own existence
For Hector was the most beloved of all my progeny

And so with insistence from the lord of Olympus
I make advance upon the harsh Argive encampment
Alone I sought the barracks of the Myrmidon king
To request of him the recovery of my son's remains

And though my deep disdain for Peleus' son is apparent
I beseech the heartless Myrmidon for the swift return
Of his opponent's body for proper burial and honors
And for safe passage until I am within the walls of Ilium

The son of the Nereid is astonished by my presence
And by how effortlessly I enter his abode undetected
And by my overt and unexpected supplications to him
As I make my fervent request of conquering Achilles

A rare concession by the Myrmidon monarch
As he acquiesces to the pleas of a broken man
Returning to me the body of Apollo loved Hector
Thereby affording courtesy and kindness to his sworn enemy

In addition the Myrmidon genially offers a brief truce
For purpose of conducting the funeral games in Hector's
Honor, and to properly mourn the loss of our great champion

Conferring all due honors upon the mighty tamer of horses

Promises given in spite of the haughty son of Atreus
And I willingly accept the overtures of my foe
As I steer the cart bearing the corpse of my son
And the tears flow liberally as I depart the Myrmidon

And we Trojans duly honor our fallen protector
Commemorating the life of this godlike man
As the forlorn Dardanian women lament our great loss
Contemplating the course of this sad war in his absence

And after we bury with pride the bulwark of Ilium
And setting the fires to the grand funeral pyre
The Great War commences shortly thereafter
And the fierce son of Peleus slaughter runs amok

And though our bravest men present challenge to Achilles
Our armies are unable to withstand his furious advance
As his deadly lance fatally pierces all within proximity
For he fights more like an enraged god than a mere mortal

And succor unexpectedly arrives to the peoples of Dardanus
Shortly proceeding your own glorious homecoming, as the
Vessels of Amazonian Penthesileia[207] docks at the beaches
Her contingent determined to repel the invading Achaeans

And the warrior queen wreaks havoc amongst their ranks
As none are able to resist her dangerous javelin
All those who oppose Penthesileia are slaughtered
As the Argives again are driven to the safety of the ships

And once again our armies are heartened by these events

---

[207] daughter of Ares (god of war); queen of the Amazons and a
Trojan ally

As we give chase to the fleeing and panicked Achaeans
Led by the swift footed daughter of fierce Ares
Hopes anew of at long last defeating the Argive forces!

Until the scourge of the Dardanian peoples
Brandishing armor made by divine Hephaestus
Impenetrable to the weaponry of mortal men
Presents challenge to the Queen of the Amazons

And effortlessly ruthless Achilles pierces the breastplate
Effectuating the death of the beautiful Penthesileia
Renowned benefactor of the Trojan citadel
As another great warrior is slain by the house of Aeacus[208]!

And so we mourn the loss of Ares' brave daughter
For she afforded our besieged nation temporary respite
As she drove the Achaeans to their massive vessels
And now sadly she falls, far away from her beloved realms

And the Myrmidon continues raging across the Idaean plains
His lance and shield overmuch for any of us
As no man is able to withstand his fury
For he is protected by Olympus and divinely nourished

And thus permitted to senselessly ravage our city
To the dismay of all Trojans and Dardanians!
As hopeless fighting and death endures
Until your glorious arrival upon these shores

And our spirits are now uplifted!
For your godlike presence provides renewed hope
Your appearance striking to that of your famed progenitor
My beloved brother, the venerable Tithonus

---

[208] son of Zeus; grandfather of Achilles

Numerous years since my aging eyes have last seen you!
When you were a vibrant and handsome young boy
And full of vigor as you amused yourself near Scamander's
Banks, along with your cousins Deiphobus and Hector

The pride of your exalted Dardanian lineage!
And though destined by the Fates to be earthly heroes
Back then unaffected by the affairs of the world
And permitted to partake of the pleasures of adolescence

And now you return to us an accomplished champion!
The most famed and celebrated man in all the world
Your reputation validated by your glorious feats at arms
As even sad Troy receives word of your tremendous exploits

Entrenching your esteemed legacy during your journeys
Overcoming ancient Echidna and Chrysaor Medusa's son
And the continual obstructions of a concerned Thetis
Manifested in the sad Amphitrite and ravishing lake goddess

And your encounter with wily Triton
All these events known throughout these realms
For the entire world possesses knowledge of the enterprise
Undertaken by the Ilium bound son of the goddess

And so incomparable son of Troy, welcome home!
And freely partake of all that she has to freely offer
And if so desired, supreme command of our armies accorded
And you shall be regarded as equal to myself in rank"

Next rose to speak is the venerable Anchises
Chosen by divine Cyprian Aphrodite herself
For notable is the male beauty of the line of Dardanus
And so a goddess consorts with a mortal as her chosen lover

Their offspring the redoubtable Aeneas of Dardania

Second only in prowess to horse taming Hector
A conundrum for the Achaeans in awful battle
Such is the strength of the revered Trojan commander

And so revered Anchises speaks, "Great Memnon,
Son of my cousin, I see much of you in him!
The day as youths we battled the haughty Phrygians[209]
As we expanded the sovereignty of holy Ilium

Handsome Tithonus raged across the plains
Scattering our opponents as he brandished his lance
And his shield, dreaded by all with temerity to oppose him
A mighty man who I proudly fought with side by side

His accomplishments before exchange of vows with Eos
That bright goddess enamored by the mighty Trojan prince
Making him her consort, and their union brought forth
An incomparable hero whose great fame is unparalleled

We welcome your presence in this ancient city
The beloved son of mighty Tithonus at long last returns!
Howbeit a wretched homecoming, as beyond these walls
Lies a deadly foe that is divinely supported

And permitted to ravage our beautiful homelands
Freely roaming our plains, sacking our villages
Pillaging cities steadfastly loyal to King Priam
And plundering at will to appease Argive greed

And many brave warriors have stood against the Myrmidon
All either vanquished or barely escaping with their lives
Antenor's son Agenor, and my own beloved Aeneas
Both surviving through the grace of the Olympians, and thus

---

[209] inhabitants of Phrygia, lands near Troy

Continues the fiendish slaughter of Peleus' barbarous son
Choking the riverbed of wide ranging Scamander
For dire are the straits of the armies of Troy
As many sons of our lord Priam are mercilessly slain

Most notably the incomparable Hector himself has fallen!
And many other brave men fighting for homeland and family
Against the insurmountable force led by Atreus' son
For none are able to withstand fierce Achilles

And now your presence is enlightenment to all assembled!
For your virtue and prowess is wholly unmatched by any
As you dangerously wield your lance in battle
And the Trojan citadel may yet be saved!"

And the Trojan elders rejoice at the words of old Anchises!
Including the women, men, and children alike
As all are elated at the prospect of the defeat of Achilles
Accomplished at the hands of the son of the goddess

And all continue to behold the striking Memnon
For his regal appearance and demeanor elicits awe
And dire in need are the peoples of Ilium for such inspiration
After years of enduring the menaced of the Achaean assault

Attentively the people await the anticipated words of great
Memnon, as all eyes peer at his handsome and solemn
Countenance, veneration abounding for his famed deeds
And at last the son of the goddess addresses an exultant city

 "Holy Troy, famed Dardanian nation loved by Zeus!
Known for your abundant riches and hospitality
Excesses of gold, silver, and fertile estates
An incomparable metropolis menaced by the sons of Atreus

Long have you suffered under the aggressive Argive siege

And the sad loss of so many brave and loyal men!
Spillage of Dardanian blood over these ancient lands
An affliction suffered since Spartan Menelaus lost his wife

Your plight is well known throughout the world and beyond
As peace loving nations sympathize with your plight
Resulting in many faithful allies coming forth in support
Chiefly Zeus' own unfortunate son King Sarpedon

And his comrade Glaucus as they departed far away Lycia
Along with a vast and formidable fighting force
And many others too come to aid the Trojan nation
In deference, loyalty and due reverence to these great lands

And the Achaean advantage is slightly muted as a result
As the aforementioned allies of Ilium arrive
Without precondition to the shores of Pergamus
And no ancestral attachment directs them to Troy's defense

I would be remiss to abstain from this war!
For my blood is linked to your own blood
And your sufferings are therefore my sufferings
For are we not both descendants of famed Dardanus?

Accordingly I am bound by duty to intervene
For my own father drank from the very waters of Scamander
And reared near the Idaean foothills as a youth
And many times crossed these very gates I recently passed

As has mighty Hector and the pious Aeneas
And Cassandra, Paris, brave Agenor, and Deiphobus
Anchises, Antenor, and King Priam
Accordingly our fates are intertwined, as is our lineage

And if the Olympians ordain an encounter with Peleus' son
And even if the scales of the Fates are tilted against me

As the gods chose to favor Achilles swift foot
I will battle him to the utmost, man to man!

For there lies honor in undertaking this fatal match
And never shall I dishonor my famed lineage
Or eschew the chance for everlasting glory
That which is my due, as allotted by father Zeus"

After great Memnon delivered his rousing response
Not a dry eye could be found in sight amongst
The throngs of Trojans, Dardanians, and Lycians gathered
And the multitude of allies seated in the great hall

For many witnessed the works of the reckless son of Thetis
And from prior experiences they are knowledgeable
Of how fearsome swift Achilles is in the midst of battle
Often the end result being fatal to his unfortunate foes

And thereby the brave words of the revered Memnon
Elicits tears from all participants of the council
As they are in awe of the mighty man before them
And for his willingness to undertake their own sufferings

And thus the elders of Troy laud the well presented oratory
Matching his physical beauty and comeliness
And his regal appearance and exalted mannerism
More like a divine god descended from lofty Olympus

Than that of a mortal man foraging the earth
As renditions of his fame are exceedingly validated
And pride anew swells within the Trojan peoples
As they place high expectations upon the son of the goddess

And the battle wearied men are roused to meet the Argives
And fears of Achilles Peleids gradually recede
For such a formidable man presently leads the advance

And the Dardanian commanders brim with sheer confidence

And a rejoicing and hopeful Priam, bold in his supposition
That his famed kinsmen would undoubtedly rescue
The Trojan citadel, proclaims the venerable Aethiopian king
Supreme commander of his forces

And as the undisputed salvation of besieged Ilium
Predicting the son of the goddess and his comrades
To accomplish immense honor and glory
And effortlessly repel the haughty Achaean invaders

Thwarting the intent of the determined sons of Atreus
And their stated aims pronounced as they docked the ships
One seeking to expand his dominion across the Aegean
The other seeking swift return of his divine wife

And shortly after this proclamation, the joyous reunion
Adjourns, as spirited merrymaking commences in honor of
The arrival of the son of the goddess, Trojan revelry not
Witnessed since the commencement of the Great War

And the Trojan elite, those belonging to the house of Priam
Seek the company of the great Memnon and his comrades
Wondrously they behold his divine countenance
And admire his speech and regal demeanor

And as the potent wine flows liberally
A comparable companion to the sumptuous feast
Libations are poured in honor the Olympian deities
In hopes that divine support would be afforded holy Troy

And after the appeasement of hunger and thirst
The son of the goddess and his venerable armies
Hospitably received by the whole of Troy, slumber within
The city walls, anticipating the tremendous battle ahead

Bringing to an end the joyous and festive evening
As serenity at last reigns in the absence of apprehension
The gentle breeze of the winds wafts through the trees
As the warm night air comforts the inhabitants of Ilium

IX. Battle upon the Trojan Plains

And while the city of Priam tranquilly slumbers
Without harsh anxiety which plagues the minds of the
Unfortunate, a mighty man lies restless in his palatial
Chambers, for the heart of great Memnon is deeply troubled

Despite adulations from those allied with the Trojan nation
And though the praise is acknowledged by the son of Eos
Unfazed is the Aethiopian monarch to its powerful seduction
A much lesser man would have readily succumbed

For the unfortunate death of Hector is pervasive in his mind
As King Memnon desires to speak with his cousin's widow
And so he seeks out the grief stricken Andromache
Finding her within her sad and somber abode

As she is too unable to enjoy the sanctuary of sleep
Instead holding her young son Astyanax in her arms
And declining to participate in revelry of the prior eve
For the recent death of her Hector is painfully unbearable

And so while the rest of Ilium's inhabitants sleep
The son of the goddess seeks company with Hector's wife
As he gently solicits her audience
For purpose of delivering to her comforting words

And though his presence is entirely unexpected
The son of the goddess is acknowledged by Andromache
As she wholeheartedly welcomes him into her quarters
And Memnon takes her by her hand and solemnly begins,

"Sad Andromache, princess of sprawling Dardania
Your pain more prevalent that all of us in sum
From the loss of such a brave and incomparable husband!
Hector's greatness will be eternally remembered by us all

As my illustrious comrades and I endured our perilous

Journey to these ancient lands, we encountered the slain
Son of the good king Priam, and my own famed kinsmen
That mighty man, your very own beloved spouse

My heart is heavy even now from the experience!
As I sadly beheld his proud apparition
That whom I recognized as the great horse tamer, all this
Transpiring while I was deep within the realms of Hades

But fear not, my sweet and dear sister
For the Olympians bless Hector Priamides even in death
As he blissfully dwells in the field of heroes
Eternally honored and celebrated as is his due

And now I must make peace with Hector's soul
For my dalliance and needless dawdling
As I failed to assist in the defense of the citadel, and now
We have lost the mightiest of men to the shades of Tartarus"

And sad Andromache replies consolingly,
"Son of the goddess, the depth of my pain is immense
Attributed to the loss of my beloved and brave Hector!
For no wife shall ever have a better husband

This mighty man, honored in all earthly realms
As he bravely withstood the best of the Argives
Time and time again, he was Troy's stubborn resistance
Ensuring that these lofty walls never fell to Agamemnon

Much suffering and strife has been undertaken by all
At the hands of the Myrmidon, as our loved ones
Sons and husbands mercilessly slaughtered by the Achaeans
As they covet the ancient treasures of King Dardanus

This dreadful war waged for the sake of Zeus's daughter
For like you, her divine beauty entrancing to look upon

As the enraged King of Sparta seeks her return
With willingness to destroy Ilium to accomplish his ambition

And a descendant of the house of Tros is wholly culpable
As calamities are brought upon us all by an indulgent Paris
That woeful day that he gave judgment in favor
Of Cytherian born Aphrodite as the loveliest of goddesses

To the chagrin of envious Hera and Pallas Athena
For the two vengeful goddesses sought the prize themselves
And thus concoct a fatal scheme to exact their revenge
Intent upon the destruction of the famed city of Laomedon

And now we all have to endure immense sufferings!
With many more to come, much to our lament!
And yet you, handsome and brave Memnon
So far away from the lovely Aethiopian shores

From which you departed for the sake of your uncle Priam
Along with your courageous contingent of men
And your stout heart is greater than all combined, yet
You attempt to shoulder blame, after all you have endured?

No, you are the last in line for shame!
And your words have given me immense comfort
Knowledge that my earthly husband is forever honored
As he graces the fields of Elysium

And knowing that my son Astyanax
So much like his great father in appearance is he
Is now protected by the strong Aethiopian lance
Never compelled to acquiesce to the haughty Achaeans!"

And so Memnon and the resolute wife of Hector
Both consoled by eloquent speech of the other
As pain is assuaged over the loss of the Trojan prince

And both are afforded temporary respite and peace of mind

Meanwhile as bright Eos follows her familiar heavenly trail
Across the peacefully serene blue skies
Concern for her beloved son abounds within her
Compelling the goddess to abandon her celestial duties

And she swiftly goes to her magnificent son
In hopes of assisting him in awful battle, for deep
Within her troubled heart she possesses knowledge
That an encounter with the Myrmidon scourge looms near

And Memnon's unshakable conviction would not entertain
Abandoning besieged Troy in its darkest hour
And set sail for his homelands of lovely Aethiopia
Thereby averting the epic conflict over Priam's city

So an anxious mother instead shifts tactics
For Eos is determined to immortalize his glorious name
And dually set about the awful slaughter of the Argives
As they madly dash for their envied vessels

Fleeing in a sheer panic from the raging son of the goddess
As he wields his mighty Aethiopian sword and lance
With deadly aim against his opponents
Driving them away in droves from the Scaean Gates

Such were the thoughts of the anxious goddess
As she descends upon the lands of King Priam
Unbeknownst to the slumbering Olympians
She hastily seeks the whereabouts of mighty Memnon

And Eos finds her son standing near the walls
Gazing upon the massive ships of Atreus' son
His heart emboldened by the impending challenge
As odds are heavily stacked against the line of Dardanus

And his goddess mother suddenly appears before him
As her shimmering robes freely flow, and golden
Light illuminating the announcement of her presence
As Eos displays herself as the Olympians would behold her

Too much for the eyes of a mere mortal to absorb
But effortlessly is Memnon able to be
In the company of his divine mother
Just as the day she bore him in lovely Aethiopia

And so great Memnon embraces his maternal beginnings
"Mother, welcome you are to these lands, its golden
Grains that nurtured my father, your beloved husband
Tithonus, reared near the waters of the great Scamander

And treated by his people more like a god than a mortal
Much honor he has brought to all descendants of Troy
Both in his prowess of arms and keen wisdom
Accordingly such a man is chosen by you as consort

I, your son, having escaped the terrors of the sea
And Chrysaor no longer consumes mortal flesh
Nor does Echidna menace the Theban lands, for I
And my glorious comrades are now safely within Ilium

So why the distraught look on your face?
And where has your bright smile escaped to?
Your welcoming demeanor is no longer present
A comfort to men against the varied ills of the world"

And the goddess of the Dawn replies to her heroic son
"My darling favorite, much like your wondrous father
And despite all of your famous sufferings
You have truly acquitted yourself marvelously!

Matched against irresistible divine forces

Determined to prevent your sea faring vessels
From docking at the ports of holy Ilium
In an effort to avert your onslaught upon the Argives

And yet still more you shall encounter
As your imprint is made on this epic conflict
For much you shall accomplish and much you shall suffer
As your influence in this struggle is indelibly etched

My son, are you still firm and resolute?
Is your stout heart steadfastly unwavering?
To persevere in war upon the plains of Troy
For the sake of the unfortunate Dardanians?

And yet it is futile for me to indulge in making inquiry
As the outcome is already predetermined
For your virtue will not allow you to reconsider
Alternatives to partaking of this awful conflict!

And so I now humbly beseech you my son
To consider a distressed mother's appeal
Prior to entering these blood stained fields
Troy's fate since Paris' ill advised judgment

Let me fetch marvelous arms for you
Divinely forged by Hera's crafty son himself
Splendid armor for an incomparable bearer
So that the entire world shall speak of its magnificence"

And so the goddess of the Dawn entreats her son
For permission to seek from handy Hephaestus
Armor befitting such a man as himself
So that future generations would reminisce of them

And the son of the goddess readily acquiesces to her request
As Memnon bids his gracious mother farewell

Humbled is he to don the great handiwork of Hera's son
For such honor is reserved only for the most favored of men

And so lovely Eos takes her leave of Troy
And makes her advance to the palatial abode of Hephaestus
And the concerned mother humbly petitions the god
To forge armor of steel befitting her incomparable son

"Hephaestus, will you hear my distressed pleas?
For heavy with worry am I for my courageous son
As he imports Aethiopian valor and arms
Into the Great War waged over the lands of Priam

His mighty deeds at arms imbued by ancestral pride, in
The most unfortunate war the world has ever witnessed, nor
Shall the earth again experience such a conflict, and future
Heroes shall endeavor to the heroic feats accomplished in it

And so I stand before you, crafty son of Hera
On bended knee to make a heartfelt request of you
Will you have pity upon my troubled heart?
For your unmatched skills alone can accomplish my wishes

I simply request a set of battle attire for my magnificent son
Along with accompanying sword and hardy lance
To match an impenetrable shield and helmet
Tempered by the fires of your wondrous forge

Equitable to those donned by the dreaded Achilles
His sole advantage as he battled unfortunate Hector
And thereby the Myrmidon overcame the bulwark of Troy
Despoiling his body, an affront to the Olympians!

So now I appeal to you to allow my beloved Memnon
To be on equal footing versus Thetis' hardy son
Granting both a fair opportunity when they meet one another

In dreaded battle, which is not for the faint hearted"

And so Eos eloquently states her case to Hephaestus
Recounting both her past and future sorrows
And though the god of fire supports Argos
He agrees to make divine armor for the Aethiopian king

And Hephaestus swiftly sets about his task at hand
Nimbly that hobbled god[210] moves about his forge
Clutching his heavy tongs and anvil
As Hera's son commences the work as promised to Eos

He first creates the breastplate inlaid with bronze and gold
With a diamond crescent set in the middle
The object itself too heavy for tenfold men to bear
Such were the quality of the magnificently contrived work

Next great Hephaestus effortlessly fashions the helmet
Forged entirely of copper and hardened bronze
And upon it he places the insignia of Helios the sun god
Fastening it firmly in place as testament to the ancient deity

Next the lame god focuses his attention to creating the shield
Fortified with five thick layers of inlaid silver
And upon it the thrifty son of Hera craftily depicts
The divine lineage of great Memnon Tithonides

Beginning on the left side with his divine mother
Saffron robed Eos, along with her siblings
The sun god as he appears in his bright fiery chariot
Bringing respite from the uncertainties of evening

---

[210] while intervening in a dispute between his parents Zeus and
Hera, Hephaestus is hurled to the earth by an angry Zeus and
becomes disabled as a result

Next depicted is silver streaked and elegant Selene
A beautiful oasis in the darkest hours of the evening, and
Respite for mortals against the horrors of the night, as the
Moon goddess provides light while all peacefully slumber

Both of these great deities – the Sun and the Moon
Respectively uncle and aunt to the great Aethiopian king
Along with his radiant mother, goddess of the Dawn
For a triumvirate of light is the maternal lineage of Memnon

And on the right side of the great shield
Depicted is his famed paternal lineage
Outlining his great Dardanian ancestry
A nation descended from thunder lord Zeus himself

Mighty Dardanus, Ilus, and lusty Tros[211]
Too inscribed upon the shield is King Erichthonius
Richest monarch on earth during his reign
And overseer of wondrous mares grazing the Idaean plains

Next depicted are Tithonus, Ganymede, and wily Laomedon
Their regal images emblazoned with workmanlike perfection
And thus the great lineage of the son of the goddess is
Eternally honored by the divinely wrought arms

And after his arduous task is completed
Crafty Hephaestus delivers the handiwork to Eos
And the dawn goddess graciously thanks him
Swiftly taking her leave of the god's household

Eos then proceeds with utmost haste to the city of Dardanus
To present the divine armor to her beloved son
Thereby ensuring a tremendous victory for mighty Memnon
Rendering upon him invincibility as he ravages the Argives

---

[211] former kings of Troy and ancestors of Memnon

A tremendous force not yet encountered by the Achaeans
And though in the past the Argives rebuffed the dangerous
Onslaught of Hector and Anchises' son Aeneas, a much
Deadlier opponent awaits the armies of the son of Atreus!

Eos appears before her son as he makes war preparations
The radiant goddess delivers the divine armor to Memnon
Replete with lance, shield, and a glorious helmet, and
His heart rejoices at the sight of the marvelous battle attire!

For these arms were the best in the entire world
Never before donned by any until this moment
And a perfect fit for the son of the goddess
As they adorn his magnificently sculpted body

And heavy hearted Eos makes her solemn exit
Leaving her incomparable son to prepare for war
As great Memnon confidently strides into the city epicenter
And all before him behold his divine armor in sheer awe

For the Trojans revered him as though he were an Olympian
Similar in appearance to golden Apollo himself
Descending in defense of the famed Trojan citadel
Welcomed salvation to King Priam's besieged nation

And the wondrous sight emboldens the Dardanian resolve
As the armies are inspired to fight their fearsome adversary
Under the supreme command of great Memnon Tithonides
Resolute in expelling the haughty Argives from their lands

And so the Trojan elders Panthous and Ucalegon
Dutifully address the armies before departure
Exhorting the men to do battle to the uttermost!
For the sake of the Trojan women and children

Reminding them of the consequences of failure

If the breach of the walls is accomplished
For enslavement and death await the survivors
And long enduring shame for them all!

And next the son of the goddess prepares to deliver an
Incomparable speech and to utter stirring words
To inspire the very hearts of Aethiopians, Trojans
Dardanians, and Lycians, and the other allies of Pergamus

"Brave men, I implore you to summon all of your courage
For we are poised to accomplish a tremendous victory!
And the Olympians favor our cause this fortuitous day
To the utter dismay of the invading Achaeans

Atreus' son boasts of overcoming our walls
And subjecting our peoples to his cruel authority
A foolhardy and false proposition indeed!
For much blood shall be shed for this exalted capital!

As for the man some say possesses the strength of tenfold
And the quickness of the fastest steed on earth
I speak of Myrmidon Achilles; there will be no retreat
For I shall battle him man to man, come what may!

And whether he slays me, or I slay he
We shall encounter each other this faithful day!
And he will come to know that before our firm gates
Stands a resolute defender to protect these walls!

And so I entreat each of you to stand strong with me
As we steadfastly face our fierce opponents
And let almighty Zeus determine our fate
Whether it be prosperous or wholly doomed

For my objective is to send those haughty Argives
Fleeing in a hurried panic to their sea faring ships

And give respite to our peoples and allies
While the sons of Atreus reconsider their lofty goal"

And all of the men cheer these brave words
Roused are they by the call to arms by the son of Eos
As confidence emanates from godlike Memnon
And infectiously takes hold of the armies of Troy

And after the Aethiopian and Trojan commanders assemble
The allied battalions prepare for the fierce struggle
As each general is assigned a respective legion
With everyone under supreme command of fierce Memnon

And the armies of Priam are dutifully marshaled
Primed to encounter the superior Argive forces
And to reconvene the greatest of earthly conflicts
Commenced by Helen's precarious escape from Sparta

And the inspired armies buoyantly depart holy Ilium
Massive in size as they stream through the Scaean Gates
And next crossing the waters of flowing Scamander
To set about the destruction of the Achaean forces

And opposite them stands ready their determined foes
Equipped with the cold steel and chiseled bronze
With morbid intentions of sacking the famed city
And bringing about a great victory for the sons of Atreus

First strong Diomedes gathers his Calydonian[212] forces
As does Telamonian Ajax from far away Salamis[213]
And wily Odysseus marshals his Ithacan forces
As does Idomeneus[214] and Molus' son Meriones[215]

---

[212] inhabitants of Calydon; lands famed for being ravaged by a
mighty boar sent by Artemis to punish its people
[213] lands near Cyprus, birthplace of Aphrodite

And the Cretan archers stand poised to launch their deadly
Shafts, and lurking within proximity are the sons of Atreus
Menelaus, along with his haughty brother Agamemnon
And also present the most dreaded of all the Argives

Fierce Achilles, along with his strong Myrmidons
More like a god than a man is the son of Thetis
As his lance salivates for fresh Trojan blood, accordingly
The foremost Achaeans stand poised to resist great Memnon

Such are the sights witnessed by the son of the goddess
As he surveys the landscape of the impending battle
For he is eager to defend his ancestral homelands
And to attain more honor for his already heralded name

And after the two great armies come very near one another
Aligned diametrically in opposition as fatal adversaries
The son of the goddess suddenly roars audibly
Causing the Argives to tremble at the fearsome din

"Haughty Achaeans, why such close proximity to the walls?
Are you that eager to die, such folly indeed!
For much shall be suffered for Troy's sake
And many Argives will descend to dark Tartarus this day!

For my famed lance will strike down many in your company
As my glorious generals ravage your demoralized ranks
And the funeral pyres will burn incessantly
As your slain become overmuch for them to bear

So take heed of my forthright advice
As it is only to your vital advantage

---

[214] king of Crete

[215] captain in Achaean army; nephew of Idomeneus; prince in Crete

Cease from encircling these Dardanian walls
And return to your sea faring vessels

And at long last depart these ancient lands
Which you have plagued for many a woeful years
And embrace peaceful coexistence with Priam
Or massive sufferings shall be your alternative"

And the Argive commanders are silent in response, as they
Ponder the provocative words of the son of the goddess
A wise maneuver, for a dangerous warrior stood nearby
Teeth gnashing, his lance hungry for Achaean flesh

And great Memnon's reputation is well deserved
For he was by far the best to take up arms
In resistance to the Achaean aspirations
Of conquering the greatest kingdom of all earthly realms

And as the Argive leaders momentarily pause
To contemplate great Memnon's recommendations
And begrudgingly consider a negotiated truce
With the buoyed peoples of holy Ilium

A brash Trojan youth named Polymorenes[216]
Discerning hesitation by the Argive commanders to attack
As Achaean egos are somewhat abated
By the presence of the fierce son of the goddess

Rashly makes decision to seek attainable retribution
Avenging the death of his brother Eudoros
Slaughtered at the hands of Tydeus' brave son
During a particularly brutal and relentless battle

---

[216] a Phrygian captain allied with the Trojan army

The very same day that he furiously ravaged the Phrygian
Lands, as he overcame redoubtable Pandarus the archer
When that brave man attempted to prevent further slaughter
At the hands of heartless Athena and Diomedes

And so now Polymorenes sees his opportunity
Of exacting vengeance upon Diomedes
As he is exposed near the Argive vanguard, and
Without delay he cast his angry lance with all of his might

The dart strikes not its intended target
But a Calydonian captain named Cepheis
Piercing his liver and disgorging his bowels
For the weapon is hurled with such ferocity

And the unfortunate Cepheis succumbs to his wounds
As he falls to his knees, darkness covering his eyes
The Calydonian grips the arm of his lord Diomedes
As his soul hastily descends into dark Erebus

And in a panic the Argive armies grasp their weapons
As signs of the Great War's abatement swiftly vanish
And utter chaos prevails outside the walls
As anxious men resume the awful conflict

The son of Tydeus, distraught at the loss of his beloved
Comrade, and eager to avenge the death of his childhood
Friend, angrily hurls his lance at the Aethiopians and Trojans
A perfect strike, it pierces the breastplate of Laopios

A fearless Trojan captain and cousin to brave Agenor
Raised in the household of wise Antenor since his
Precocious boyhood shortly after the untimely death of his
Beloved mother her demise attributed to the bite of a serpent

And now his unfortunate life comes to an end

To the dismay of his forlorn comrades
A victim of the furious anger of the son of Tydeus
After witnessing the death of his own fallen captain

And Diomedes begins to rage across the battlefield
As his bloodthirsty aims become increasingly apparent to all
For he is determined to accomplish a great victory, and
Accordingly sets about the slaughter of the Dardanian armies

And the Argives take heart at his tremendous exploits
As initial fears of the son of the goddess gradually subsides
Foolish men indeed! For unbeknownst to the Argives
Massive suffering for their rank and file awaits!

And as Diomedes advances against the Trojan vanguard
Great Memnon, angered by the spillage of Trojan blood
Violently takes up his huge and heavy lance
And hurls it furiously at city conquering Diomedes

The divine javelin strikes its target! And the victim would
Have surely perished far away from his homelands, his life
Saved only by the protection of gray eyed Athena
Fortunate is strong Diomedes, a terror for many Dardanians

As Zeus' daughter turns aside the fatal missile
It pierces the bicep of the revered Achaean captain
As Diomedes falls stunned to the ground, immobilized, and
The hungry lance continues until it hits a Calydonian captain

The fatal weapon strikes Diomedes' charioteer Phylaos[217]
As he instantly falls from the famed chariot
His soul swiftly departing the corpse
And hastily flees to the realm of grim Hades

---

[217] cousin of Diomedes

And the fierce son of the goddess
With his revered Aethiopian commanders
Ergamenes, Agathon, and redoubtable Aithops
Along with their battle hardened divisions

Vigorously attack the awed Achaean armies
And cause ensuing havoc amongst their ranks
As dangerous Memnon slays many unfortunate Argives
Like a conflagration set upon a helpless forest

First Actaeon, namesake of his famous kin
Theban born and raised by the venerable Chiron[218]
The famed centaur, mentor to heroes, and
Unfortunately his pupil engenders the wrath of Artemis

As Actaeon exuberantly partakes of the hunt
She transforms him into a boisterous stag, subsequently
Destroyed by his own hounds, similarly his kinsman suffer
An unfortunate fate at the hands of great Memnon

Who next falls to the raging son of the goddess?
Next Euryalus, Maeon, and the herald Stentor
Whose shape Olympian Hera once assumed
During the Great War to encourage her beloved Argives

Next to fall before the son of the goddess
Zeuxippus,[219] a young and rash prince of Ithaca
As haughty boasts are made before the commencement of
War that he alone would slay mighty Hector Priamides

Hollow words made after consumption of wine
He now begs for his life as he flees in terror

---

[218] a wise and varied skilled centaur whom tutored many future
heroes in their adolescence
[219] cousin to Odysseus

Too late, he falls before the Aethiopian sword
And effortlessly succumbs to the might of the son of Eos

Too falls the fleeing Ornytus, Panopeus, and Iasus
And many more Argives are slaughtered by the fearsome
Lance of Memnon, as none is able to withstand his wrath
Thoroughly demoralized, they flee for the safety of the ships

Panic not witnessed since great Hector lived
And with regularity ravaged the armies of Agamemnon
Now torment anew at the hands of the son of the goddess
As his destruction of the Argives continues unchecked

And the devastation does not go unnoticed by the Achaean
Leaders, as Peleus' son Achilles and King Idomeneus
Along with Odysseus, Menelaus, and huge Ajax ponder
The appropriate response to the exploits of fierce Memnon

Agamemnon too joins the hastily arranged deliberations
With wise Nestor[220] and his son Antilochus, and they
Swiftly come to agreement that Memnon must be deterred
Though none desired to confront his massive onslaught

For a few days prior they stood before the walls of Ilium
Poised to finally subdue Priam's armies, and now
Trepidation swiftly spreads amongst the battalions, as the
Incomparable might of the son of the goddess is on display

Evidenced by the mad rush to the vessels
As any trace of courage departs from the Achaeans
And father Zeus obviously now favoring their opponents
As the son of the goddess triumphs over the battlefield

And so wise Nestor begins, "leaders of blessed Argos

---

[220] king of Pylos and Achaean elder

We are surely doomed by the Olympians!
To perish so far away from our lands, as great Memnon
Permitted to exert his will upon our demoralized armies

He relentlessly slaughters our besieged men
Look at how his famed steeds move like a whirlwind!
As Tithonus' son is indiscriminant as to whom he ordains
To live or die during his brutal rampage!

And now he threatens to destroy our very ships
For it is clear his deadly intentions are to slay all of us!
And undeterred is he by the fame of our captains
Look how effortlessly the son of the goddess overcame

Our own Diomedes, a terror for the Trojans!
And unfortunately he encountered Eos' mighty son
No match is he for the Aethiopian king!
Tydeus' son saved only by the grace of the Olympians

Else the son of the goddess would attain
A tremendous triumph indeed!
A crushing blow to our beleaguered forces
Would be the loss of Calydonian Diomedes to our forces

So now I beseech all of you men assembled before me
For one of you must take your stand!
No matter how fearsome Memnon Tithonides may be
Whether you vanquish or be overwhelmed

For though he were made of hardened bronze
And moves as swift as his windy brethren
We must summon our courage and pray to the Olympians
And do our best to repel this plague upon us!"

And an eerie pause follows Nestor's heartfelt pleas
As the best of the Argive commanders ponder his words

Each fearing to directly oppose the son of the goddess
But equally ashamed to refuse the deadly task

And finally Peleus' son courageously steps forth
As he pledges to challenge Eos' redoubtable son
His confidence validated by his many exploits
Most recently by his slaying of the feared Amazonian queen

Lovely Penthesileia, as she ravaged the Argives
Along with her formidable Amazons in alliance with Priam
And none could resist her as she attacked the Achaean ranks
Until at last she fell to the savagery of Thetis' son

As did many warriors caught in Achilles' murderous path
Evidenced by his slaughter of throngs of Trojans and allies
Including many of Priam's own exalted sons
All perishing at the hands of the feared Myrmidon

And so two men, best among all upon the Trojan plains
Memnon Tithonides versus Achilles swift foot
Furiously drive their chariots towards one another
Determined to test the mettle of the other in the awful war

And in an effort to dissuade the son of the goddess from
Engaging him in single deadly combat, haughty Achilles
Speaks stern words to great Memnon, "Son of the goddess,
Do you think you alone shall drive our armies from Ilium?

Long we have toiled under Priam's high walls
And we shall continue to persevere until the citadel is
Destroyed! As punishment for Paris' ill advised indiscretions
That woeful day Helen left the Spartan kingdom

And now I am here as a scourge to all Dardanians
And a curse upon the famed peoples of Priam
For many have bitten the dust from my sword

And many others more shall lose their lives

Do you fancy that you will save them from my dreaded
Lance? For I have accomplished overmuch already
For not even strong Hector could defeat me in battle
Nor Ares' daughter, and many other brave heroes

As all are laid to the ground by the cold Myrmidon steel
Divinely fashioned by great Hephaestus himself
For the Olympians love me above all other mortals
Even above you Memnon, great though you may be

For your own exploits are too known throughout the world
As you freed holy Thebes from its monstrous bondage
By subduing the feared and gruesome Echidna
Mother of all horrid beings ever birthed

And the slaying of Medusa born Chrysaor
His cannibalistic appetite no longer plagues mankind
As your mighty sword and irresistible lance
Abruptly ends his nightmarish practice

In spite of these lofty accomplishments
And your physical beauty and prowess at arms
These will not avail you against me
So I advise you cease your ambitions"

And Memnon responds to the audacious taunt of Achilles,
"Son of Peleus, your words mean but little to me
Nor shall they deter our swords from clashing
Your reputation and my own are both well deserved

And both our lineage is famed throughout the world
Mortal are you on your paternal side
As the goddess Thetis was given to your father as his bride
And their marriage is celebrated by the immortals

And though you are honored by the Olympians
And your senseless slaughter of Trojans tolerated
For all of your boastful speech and prattle
You too shall die beneath these revered walls!

As immortal blood does not flow through your veins
And my lance may very well end your life
For I too am loved by Zeus thunder lord
As he granted me victories over mightier foes than you

For in your callousness you desecrate the body
Of mighty Hector, a man by far your superior
In piety and in admiration of the world
For he fought for his revered homelands

Equally brutal the slaying of Penthesileia
As the Amazonian queen defended the walls
For no man could withstand the daughter of Ares
And she finally falls to your Olympus supported lance

For your bloodthirsty aim is suffering
And vainglory, both deplorable attributes
Killing for the sake of sport and torment
And so unabated you slay the piteous Dardanians

Less savage was the monster Chrysaor, for he is
Unable to contain his cannibalistic urges, and his
Nature dictated his inhumane behavior, an affliction
Suffered as a result of his horrid maternal beginnings

So I forewarn you to prepare for a struggle to the death!
And I remain resolute in my solemn pledge
To meet you man to man in deadly war
And allow the Olympians to select their champion

And this faithful day either Thetis swift foot

Or my own mother radiant Eos
Shall mourn the loss of a beloved son
For your pretentious words fall on deaf ears"

And following this retort, the son of the goddess
Hurls his mighty lance with all his strength
At the body of Peleus' son Achilles
Determined to end his murderous ways

The dangerous weapon penetrates both shield and armor
Piercing through three thick layers of gold
Fashioned by Hephaestus at Thetis' insistence
And the fire god's gift barely saves Achilles' life

As the best of the Argives is driven to the ground
Stunned by the sheer power of the strike
Never before experiencing such dangerous conflict
With an opponent more daunting than himself

Sensing hesitation from the son of Peleus, mighty Memnon
Swiftly advances, drawing his shimmering sword from his
Waist, with purpose to slay the Myrmidon outright
And avenge the death of countless of his victims

Achilles recovers, aware of his impending doom
And swiftly the son of Peleus takes up his own sword
And prepares to meet the Aethiopian king
Though now a little less audacious is the Myrmidon king

And both men lash furiously at one other
As each hero wields the divine weaponry
Requested by two concerned goddesses
Commencing a clash unlike any ever before witnessed

As mighty Memnon strenuously attacks his foe, keeping
A bewildered Achilles on the defensive, as the magnificent

Tug of war ensues, and both Trojans and Achaeans stop
To witness the otherworldly encounter

And finally fierce Memnon deals a stroke
Leveling Achilles Peleids to the earth
And he is dazed from such a devastating strike
His first ever encounter with mortal vulnerability

And a bewildered Achilles strength begins to wan
Yielding to the might of the son of the goddess
Akin to his struggle with divine Scamander[221]
That day the river intervened to save Priam's armies

And only through the intercession of Olympus
Hera, Athena, and crafty Hephaestus
Concerned that his destruction was imminent
The Myrmidon was able to survive this encounter

And now Poseidon, determined to set in motion
The demise of Eos' incomparable son Memnon
Intervenes on behalf of Thetis' son
Cloaking him in the disguise of a cloud

As Achilles is swept from the battlefield
And whisked away to the safety of the Achaean vessels
Far away from the dangerous sword of Memnon
His life saved by the lord of the Sea

And a confused Memnon looks about
Amazed that his quarry has suddenly vanished
As cessation of affliction suffered by the Trojan nation is
Near, and a mighty triumph taken from within his grasp

---

[221] in the *Iliad*, Scamander intervenes on behalf of the Trojans as
they fled from Achilles

The son of the goddess says to himself
"My boastful opponent has suddenly disappeared!
Certainly the work of some Olympian whom loves him
Just before my glorious lance is set to take his life

For it appear as though his prior triumphs
Attributed to assistance from the gods
Not possible but for Olympus' intervention
And now his great fame is somewhat tarnished!

So now to assess the mettle of his comrades
To ascertain if they shall stand before my dangerous advance
For surely all are disheartened subsequent to my wounding
Their best warriors, Tydeus' son Diomedes and Achilles"

And so Memnon marshals the Trojan forces
Exhorting them to fight to their uttermost
And to drive the Argive forces to the seas
Far away from the Scaean Gates

And the son of the goddess leads the furious charge
Overmuch for any of the Achaeans to resist
Casts his dangerous lance at the unfortunate Agrius
A cousin of Idomeneus on his paternal side

And the shaft pierces the sinews
It plunges into his body through the shoulders
As the soul escapes the conquered body
And is hastily claimed by the lord of Erebus

Next to fall is Lycurgus, then Butes
The latter named for his great uncle
Who once stood stubbornly against Thebes
As one of the seven men besieging her gates

And the son of the goddess furiously rages on

Slaying Canthus, Euryalus, and unlucky Eumedes
Himself a son of lion hearted Heracles
The great sacker of Troy during King Laomedon's rule[222]

And now his progeny is slaughtered by the son of the
Goddess, under the very walls once subdued by his father
And like a whirlwind commenced by swift Boreas
Memnon continues his furious attacks on the Argives

And all flee in terror after witnessing his awful work in war
And the demise of their revered commanders
As King Memnon lords over the blood stained battlefields
Leading the Trojans to a mighty victory over their bitter foes

And as the son of the goddess exacts his will
An indignant Antilochus, Nestor's stubborn son
Resists flight as he foolishly ponders encountering
Eos' son, though none other would dare to do so

For he is afforded courage by gray eyed Athena
As the goddess is determined to save the Achaeans
From great Memnon's dreaded prowess at arms, for he
Threatens to destroy them all far away from their homelands

Zeus' daughter convinces naïve Antilochus he is a match
Against the might of the son of the goddess
And that he shall repel the triumphant Aethiopians from the
Ships, causing them to madly retreat back to Ilium's walls

And Telamonian Ajax sees Antilochus as he idly stands by

---

[222] in exchange for killing a sea monster ravaging Troy, Laomedon
promised to give to Heracles horses given to him by Zeus
(compensation for the abduction of Ganymedes); when Laomedon
reneges on his promise after the sea monster is killed, Heracles
sacks Troy as vengeance

And in a panic calls out to the fleet foot Pylian commander
"Antilochus Nestorides, why do you engage in dawdling?
Did you know that sad Diomedes lies stunned by the ships?

And ferocious Achilles no longer rages in the plains?
As both these brave men have succumbed to Memnon's
Dreaded lance, for no Argive alive can withstand his
Rampage as he is permitted a great triumph this day

My advice to you is very plain and simple
Abandon the battlefield along with the rest of the captains!
And cede this day to the triumphant armies of Aethiopia
For our very survival takes precedence in this hour of doom"

But the intransigent son of old Nestor
Ignores the wise counsel of gigantic Ajax
For he is buoyed by the gray eyed daughter of Zeus
And thereby decides against retreat to the ships

Foolhardy and ill advised judgment indeed!
For the son of the goddess was much stronger than he
And shortly thereafter Antilochus spots Aegialus, son of
Caunus, as he advances against the fleeing Achaeans

His father Caunus[223] fled to the Lycian lands
Escaping the incestuous advances of Byblis
His twin sister as she was passionately overcome
By maddening and forbidden lust for her own brother

And his son Aegialus accompanied King Sarpedon
That faithful day he set sail for Priam's city
Shortly after pledging his wholehearted support to Troy
In its epic struggle against the Argive forces

---

[223] grandson of Apollo, son of Cleochus, a Cretan princess

And as the Lycian captain gives chase
To the panic stricken armies of Agamemnon
Antilochus steadfastly launches his lance
And strikes Aegialus through the neck

As the shaft enters a vulnerable opening in the breastplate
And the son of Caunus falls from his chariot
Perishing far away from lovely Lycia
Slain by the hands of Nestor's indignant son

And as Memnon continues his ravage of the Achaean flank
Unbeknownst to Eos' raging son, emboldened Antilochus
Wrecks unexpected havoc upon the Lycian contingent
Providing much needed respite to the distressed Achaeans

Nestor's confident son next overcomes Polycaon
His mother Aethilla a sister to King Priam
She bore him on the shores of the Scamander
The very same day as Hecuba begat peerless Hector

The unfortunate Trojan falls to Antilochus and Athena
Overmuch for a mere mortal to endure, accordingly
The Trojans and allied forces are briefly thwarted
From annihilating the defeated Argive armies

According to the designs of the vengeful gray eyed goddess
And thus saving countless of Achaean lives
For the son of the goddess would have undoubtedly
Slaughtered many more of the fleeing Argives

The Aethiopian king takes notice of the gruesome handiwork
At the hands of Nestor's swift footed son
As he is supported by the gray eyed goddess, and without
Delay, great Memnon drives his chariot towards Antilochus

The son of the goddess is determined to encounter him at the
Height of his fury, heartening the dazed armies of Priam
Accordingly he guides his magnificent steeds forward
In the direction of Nestor's son and Athena

And the son of the goddess shouts to his imminent foe
"Which great Olympian descended from the heavens are
You? For no mere mortal has courage to defy my dangerous
Lance, can you not see the Argives as they flee me in terror?

No man is fated to withstand me this day
For I am overmuch for the best of the Achaean captains
As Diomedes now lies wounded by the invading fleet
And the son of Peleus himself barely escaped with his life

Both Achaean commanders had the temerity to oppose my
Will as I rampaged across these plains which nurtured my
Beloved father, in support of my ancestral brethren
For I am now the undisputed champion of their cause

And I will destroy yet many more hopeless Argives
For I am divinely favored beyond all men alive
And my famed lance shall provide reprieve
To the besieged and overwhelmed peoples of holy Ilium

So take heed, brave Argive captain
I advise you depart for the safety of your vessels
For my lethal reputation is well deserved
And you shall surely lose your own dear life"

And a defiant Antilochus stands his ground
His impressionable mind directed by Athena
Though the goddess knew his doom was near
The son of the goddess was by far much stronger than he

And Nestor's son replies, "Lord Memnon, son of the radiant

Goddess of the Dawn, you have accomplished much during
Your reign over the Trojan plains, more by far than the sum
Of all of the good King Priam's famed allies

For the Trojan king is kinsmen to your incomparable father
Himself the chosen mate of the iridescent goddess
The day she saw him near the shores of Scamander
Great Tithonus, pride of the venerable line of Dardanus

And so lovely Eos begat a peerless son
Handsomest of men with none your peer
Equaled only by your piety and prowess at arms
A calamitous combination to the armies of Agamemnon!

Your lance dreaded throughout all realms
And your fame known throughout the world, and due
Reverence is freely afforded for your tremendous exploits
As only a dishonorable man would offer dispute

The men of Argos call me Antilochus, son of Nestor
My fate determined after amorous pursuit of Helen
And thus compelled to swear allegiance to her eventual
Spouse, or forego any matrimonial claims to Zeus' daughter

Dutifully I kept this oath before the Olympians
When Helen fled east with Priam's son
Across the Aegean, violating her vows
Enamored by Paris' handsome features

And a distraught Menelaus seeks her swift return
So I accompanied Atreus' sons to Ilium
Along with my venerable and respected father
Wise Nestor, the king of lofty Pylos

Misfortune encountered by us since departing our homelands
And docking upon the Zeus loved beaches of Troy

Many brave men slain, and yet many more shall perish!
In this long conflict, commenced for Menelaus' sake

And though your beauty is beyond comparison
And your strength unmatched by any man alive
I will endure you for as long as the Olympians permit
Though you may well slay me this fateful day!"

And with the conclusion of these words
Nestor's son foolishly launches his javelin
And it harmlessly strikes Memnon's divine armor
As it falls lamentably to the cold hard ground

And redoubtable Memnon takes pause
Dismayed by the predetermined notion of slaying
Nestor's son as he is urged on by gray eyed Athena
To foolishly present challenge the son of the goddess

And while the Aethiopian king hesitates
Rash Antilochus takes up another lance
Intent upon slaying the famed Aethiopian king
As he hurls it with full force at Eos's son

It passes by its intended victim, and
Unfortunately strikes brave Aithops!
Memnon's beloved cousin and dear comrade
As he stood near his revered godlike commander

And stunned silence spreads through the Aethiopian armies!
As great Aithops falls lifeless to the ground
And his soul departs for dark Tartarus
Validating a tremendous victory for Nestor's son

And the son of the goddess falls to his knees
Agonized by the death of his dear cousin
So far away from their exalted homelands

As Aithops perishes on the plains of besieged Ilium!

And fury builds up within Memnon's stout heart, as he is
Engulfed with thoughts of avenging his comrade's death
For the son of Eos, intent to slay Nestor's son
Orders his charioteer Oeipios[224] to drive his chariot at him

And Antilochus, under the false protection of Athena
Audaciously meets his godlike opponent, confidence
Emanating in him resulting from earlier triumphs, though
Unaware is he that the daughter of Zeus abandons him

And so great Memnon angrily takes up his lance
Heavy for tenfold men alone to handle, but the
Weapon is light in his magnificent hands, as the
Son of the goddess flings it with all his awesome might

And its incomparable power inflicts horrible death, with
Ease the dangerous weapon cuts through the Pylian armor
As it plunges deep into the body of unfortunate Antilochus
And Nestor's son is violently flung from his chariot

And a stunned silence sweeps through the ranks of the
Saddened Argives, as they are anguished by the fall of swift
Antilochus after he foolishly challenged the fierce
Aethiopian king at the behest of Zeus' daughter Athena

And no Argive dared to defend the vanquished Antilochus
As he lay on the ground, bleeding and gasping for air
For they all were terrified to encounter the son of Eos
And meet the same fate as Nestor's deceased son

For so effortlessly the son of the goddess overcame him

---

[224] nephew of Memnon, son of Emathion

Accomplishing a great triumph for the Aethiopian and
Trojan armies, and the Dardanian retreat is temporarily
Halted, as the Achaean flight to the docked vessels resumes

And the son of the goddess approaches his victim
His heart still heavy at his own tragic loss
Brought about at the hands of Nestor's dying son, whom
Feebly begins to utters final words to his executioner

"Glorious and triumphant son of the goddess
No better man would I hope to fall to! For my long,
Dark journey to deep Erebus is near, as I was foolishly
Encouraged to try and match my strength with your own

Buoyed by my taking the life of great Aithops
That revered Meroitian prince of vast eastern Aethiopia
And your own beloved cousin and faithful comrade
As he bravely stood by in your vanguard

A fatal act indeed! I too should have retreated,
As you ravished our armies, like the rest who wisely fled
And now here I lay pierced by your fatal hurl
Will you graciously grant the request of a dying man?

For I remember well the dreadful and sad day
When Achilles insanely attached the cold hitch
To the feet of great Hector as he lay dead
Dragging the corpse around the high walls of Pergamus

An awful sight for both Argives and Dardanians!
And a most profane and sacrilegious act!
For though us men of Argos dreaded Priam's great son
We afforded deference to his tremendous war prowess

Shameful indeed is the despoilment of incomparable Hector!
At the hands of the aggrieved and maddened son of Peleus

And so now I humbly beseech your mercy in requesting
That I not suffer a similar fate at your own hands

And Memnon makes his sad reply, "Antilochus,
I have most reason to hate you of all earthly men! For the
Slaying of my dear cousin and comrade! Undertaken even
With the knowledge that a more powerful avenger awaited

Though I could cut your corpse to pieces
And devour your flesh to appease my fury!
Still troubled is my heart for your death
For your demise was not my foremost intention

And though your foolish deeds cause me immeasurable pain
And your brash acts necessitate the conclusion of two lives
I respect the irrefutable will of the Fates
And reverence is due to the honorable house of Neleus

And so as long as the Olympians allow this mighty heart
To freely beat within my chest
Despoilment of your body I shall not condone
By any Aethiopian, Trojan, Lycian, or Dardanian"

And a relieved Antilochus attempts to offer gratitude to his
Benefactor, as murky blood spews from the orifices
And his shattered body begins to violently convulse
As the soul hastily departs for Hades' sanctuary

And a saddened Memnon orders his battalions to gather
And preserve the lifeless bodies of two fallen men, that of
Nestor's son, and of his beloved cousin Aithops, this
Commandment accomplished in the mist of Argive flight

But one aggrieved Argive orders his charioteer to remain
Aged Nestor, trusted councilor to the son of Atreus
As word of the demise of his beloved son reaches him

His desires become fixated on avenging the slain Antilochus

And so the son of Neleus advances his horses towards great
Memnon, daring the son of the goddess to do battle with him
As he feebly brandishes his ancient sword, and
With trembling arms he casts his lance at the divine armor

And Nestor's weapon falls harmlessly to the earth
As it barely grazes the divinely constructed shield
A testament of the wondrous handiwork of the fire god
Himself, Hera's son Hephaestus, at the behest of Eos

And great Memnon, ashamed to encounter Nestor
And empathetic towards the aged Argive councilor
For the old man reminded him very much
Of his own beloved father King Tithonus

Refrains from retaliating and instead shouts to him,
"Aged Nestor, terrible is our losses this faithful day!
As the rash Antilochus was laid low by my very own hands
Accomplished even after I petitioned him to cease battle

He refused my advice, as he and Athena takes Aithops' life!
By that ill fated lance intended to strike me instead!
Such folly that Antilochus' aims were not consummated
For great Aithops would still be alive at this moment!

And bound by duty, my famed lance ends the life
Of this brazen Argive, your own beloved son
And if young Antilochus heeded my wise counsel
Great Aithops and your beloved son would both now live"

And a dejected Nestor makes his ominous reply,
"Son of the goddess, you speak the truth
For I know the brazen heart of my son
And his sometimes stubborn intransigence

Culminating in his demise by your famed lance
You acted as any true commander would
But now my life is hopeless and meaningless!
For my joy has at long last come to an end!

Antilochus, my favorite amongst mortal men
Lies dead, far from our accursed vessels
And lofty Pylos is deprived of its fated monarch
And shortly thereafter I too shall suffer a similar fate

For I refuse to depart until you slay me, son of the goddess!
Which I have no doubt you shall surely accomplish
For your strength is by far greater than any Argive alive
So take heed and prepare for a taste of my sword!"

And Memnon, admiring old Nestor's immense bravery
And willingness to avenge his son's violent death
Against immeasurable and overwhelming odds
Again implores him to reconsider his foolhardy decision

"Nestor, your heart is as great as tenfold men!
And surely in your famed wisdom
You are aware that your own imminent demise
Will not bring about the return of your beloved son

Nor the return of magnificent Meroitian Aithops
My own beloved and revered kinsmen
Never again to see our lovely homelands again, for his burial
Shall take place beneath the high walls of Pergamus

And in my respect for your heralded lineage
I have ensured the preservation of the body
Forbidding the despoilment of Antilochus
So that it may be returned to you for proper rites

And further, I hereby grant a truce to you and your peoples

Thoroughly ravaged this day by my superior forces
To commence funeral games honoring both our fallen
And for ten days hence we refrain from awful war"

And Nestor the old councilor responds,
"Such a magnanimous offer, son of the goddess!
The rumors of your piety are well deserved, for no greater
Sympathies have ever been proffered to an enemy

And I do not doubt that it is within your power
To completely destroy our allied forces
As our armies perish so far from our beloved Argos
While magnificent Troy still endures as long as you deem so

And though you too are stricken with overwhelming grief
At the loss of your own comrade Aithops
You offer reprieve to another grief stricken man
To properly bid farewell to his beloved son

And so I shall graciously accept your benevolent offer
For it would be discourteous to refuse your act of kindness
And we shall refrain from this awful conflict
To properly honor our fallen with funeral rites"

And so the Aethiopian king convinces aged Nestor
To depart from the dreaded battlefield
Littered by the bodies of the many unfortunate Argives
As the handiwork of the son of the goddess is apparent

And the grateful Achaeans complete their mass retreat
As due sacrifices are made to the merciful Olympians
In appreciation of escaping the awful fury of great Memnon
As the vessels once again spared from being set afire

Contemporaneously the Dardanians buoyantly cross the
Flowing Scamander, flushed with victory over a mighty foe

And King Priam himself goes to meet Eos' son
As he enters the famed Dardanian capitol

The aged monarch grateful for his kin's presence
As confidence floods the heart of the famed king, an emotion
Not felt since the day the Achaeans first arrived, for at last
Thetis' son suffers defeat at the hands of a mightier foe

And all manner of preparations are made
To honor the tremendous military feat accomplished
As sacrifices are duly made in honor of the Olympians
In hopes of soliciting a replication of the successful day

And all of Ilium revels at the prospect of swift departure
By the defeated Argives from their ancient lands
As they head homeward bound across the Aegean waters
Demoralized, for much blood is spilled in a futile effort

And after all are gathered within the Great Hall, King Priam
Exclaims, "The great Olympians have at long last restored
Divine favor upon our beloved city! And has benevolently
Sent to us one of our own as its stalwart defender!

For the son of the goddess alone withstands
The awful might of Peleus' hated son
And as difficult as he is to overcome in this despised war
The dreaded Myrmidon now retreats before fiery Memnon!

And the scales of Zeus are now tilted in favor of the line of
Dardanus, as our scourge has been mercifully humbled
And though he is supported by powerful Olympians
The day of his fate is now close at hand

For the Argives are reduced to trembling before the
Aethiopian lance, forged by the divine fires of Zeus's son
Hephaestus, wielded by a man more like a god than a mortal

And his weapon does not stop until it fatally pierces flesh!

As the rout of the Achaeans is set in full motion, and
They seek refuge from war in the sanctuary of their vessels
As the sons of Atreus fear the destruction of their forces
For their strongest captains are rendered powerless in battle

And the great champion Memnon shall surely succeed
In driving away our powerful enemies
And liberating our hallowed ancient lands, for the
Famed walls of Ilium shall continue to remain unbreached!

As riches and prosperity return to the countryside, and our
Women and children again gleefully play outside the walls
As in the days when our beloved great bulwark in battle
Horse taming Hector still walked these lands

Those foregone days when lovely Helen
Was still the stately Queen of the Sparta, and the
Faithful and loyal spouse of sad Menelaus
And lusty Paris is yet to be her lover and betrothed

And Pandarus, playmate of great Aeneas
Both in the flush of joyful youth
Yet to encounter the ferocious son of Tydeus, and
The mares[225] of Assaracus are still in Trojan possession

And trusty Sarpedon yet to reach our besieged shores
Or to face the Myrmidon's brazen cousin
Nor before the breach of Scamander's lovely brooks
By Trojan corpses, utter sadness transpiring in these lands!

---

[225] in the *Iliad*, during a battle between Aeneas and Diomedes,
Diomedes kills Pandarus, then wounds Aeneas and takes his horses
(descended from Boreas)

But now we return to our glorious heyday!
For the moment of our salvation is near
And the son of Tithonus shall lead our crushing assault!
Against the Argive contingent as they retreat in humiliation"

And King Priam happily welcomes home his armies
Prideful in their tremendous defeat of the Achaeans
And in the retreat of Thetis' feared son
After facing such a dangerous and fierce opponent

And the entire city loudly cheers the words of King Priam
As they confidently accede to his bold edict
And the Trojan commanders readily assent as well
As the Trojan elders dutifully follows suit

And praise is continually heaped upon the son of the goddess
From the rank and file of the Trojan elite
As they promise the destruction of the armies of Atreus' son
Brazen they are in their short sighted proclamations!

But wise Memnon refrains from offering concurrence
Remaining cautious in his assessments of the conflict
Constantly wary of the plans of the mighty Olympians
Namely those who professed hatred against holy Ilium

Zeus' wife Hera and aegis bearing Athena
Both scorned in favor of Cytherian Aphrodite
Paris' judgment precipitating strife for the Trojan kingdom
As vengeful goddesses remain determined to sack the citadel

Also on the aggrieved mind of the son of the goddess
The woeful death of his cousin at the hands of Antilochus
For deep sadness envelopes the heart of great Memnon
As he hastily orders the Aethiopian contingent

To make preparations for the upcoming funeral games

In honor of the illustrious Meroitian prince Aithops
As the body is cleansed and bathe in incense
And subsequently attired as befitting an Aethiopian monarch

And after the careful preparation of Aithops' corpse, due
Sacrifices are made honoring Olympus, as all are grateful for
A tremendous yet bittersweet victory, for the defeat of Argos
Is tempered by the loss of their beloved comrade

And the Aethiopians subsequently prepare for the events in
The morn, while their Trojan counterparts happily return to
Their wives, parents, and rejoicing children, as once again
All are hopeful the siege of Ilium may soon be lifted

X. The Funeral Games

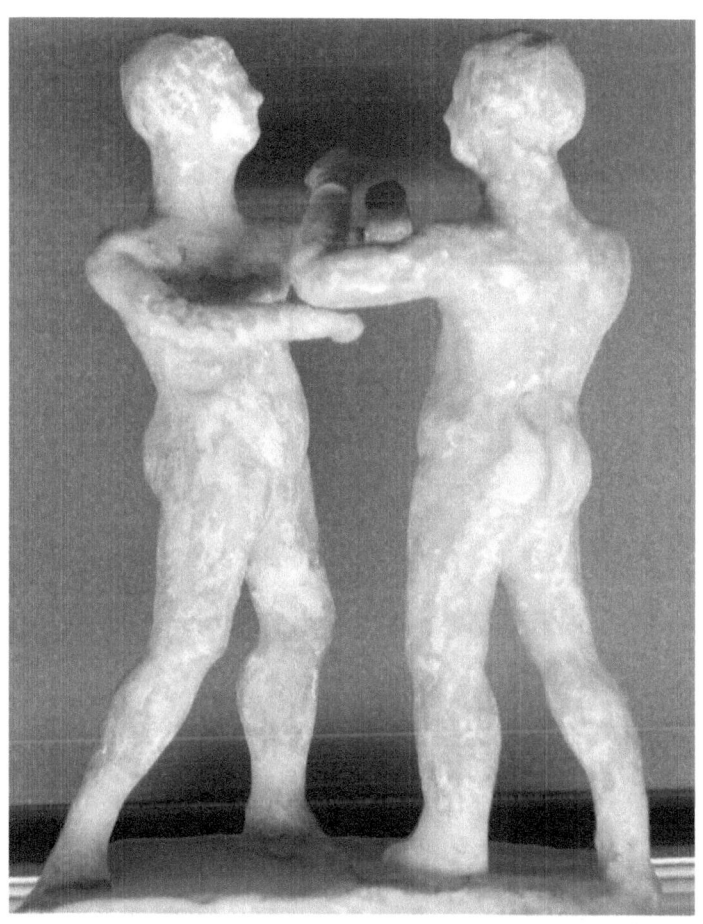

After the long evening of celebration by all within Ilium
Duly honoring the tremendous exploits of the son of the
Goddess, palpable confidence reverberating throughout the
City derived from the recent triumph against the Argives

One man, best by far, resisted the premature celebration
As great Memnon is unable to revel in the spoils of war
Or partake of the luscious and abundant venison and wine
As his heart is heavy at the painstaking loss of Aithops

And so while all of Troy engages in such merriment
And offers rich sacrifices to the divine Olympians
The sad son of Eos mourns the loss of his brave companion
Blaming himself for the fall of his beloved cousin

As he approaches the lifeless body of his comrade, and
Gently strokes his dark hair, matted with dried blood, taking
Into his own hands those of great Aithops, for the pain is as
Intense as the moment of the Meroitian prince's demise

And great Memnon agonizingly shouts out,
"Dear cousin, please forgive my shortcomings!
And wretched failures in regards to your defense
So far away from our beautiful Aethiopian lands!

For you have stood with me through all tribulations
Those both mortal and divine in nature
And even when the tides were woefully turned against us
We could always rely on the courage of the other

And now I am sorrowfully deprived of your desired
Company! Alone in this world to face the perils of life
Without you by my side, lacking your wise council
Tremendous is your loss to all inhabitants of Aethiopia!"

And the tears flow freely down the handsome face

Of Iridescent Eos' heartbroken son
As no person within the walls of Troy or beyond, is
Able to console the mourning Aethiopian king

For great Memnon's mind is duly preoccupied
With the death of his fallen cousin
And the impending preparations for his funeral games
And the final honors for the redoubtable Aithops

Accordingly the son of the goddess is unable to rest
As the Trojans and their allies slumber in jubilation
For all are again joyous, as prior to the commencement of
The Great War, and hopeful at last of salvation

Meanwhile the daughter of Hyperion[226] keeps watch
As her beloved son agonizes over the death of his comrade
For the sights witnessed by lovely Eos are too much to bear!
Accordingly she makes approach to the city of Dardanus

For maternal concerns abounds as to the well being of
Memnon, for she knows the day of reckoning draws eerily
Near, as ordained by the Fates, and accordingly desires to be
In the company of her magnificent progeny

And as Eos descends to grieve along with her troubled son
Heavy is the heart of the forlorn goddess of the dawn, for
She too is saddened by the death of great Aithops, and
Without delay Memnon is tenderly embraced by his mother

And in that instance, the goddess says to her beloved son,
"My darling favorite, your pain is wholly justified!
Brought forth by the unfortunate loss of our Aithops
So far away from the shores of lovely Aethiopia!

---

[226] another reference to Eos

His demise saddens even the Olympians
As he was loved for his dedication and piety
And he was a true friend and loyal comrade
And a constant companion to you throughout your life

And while the entire world mourns for our Aithops
Know that he is honored even in his untimely death
For he takes his rightful place amongst the chosen few
In the Elysian Fields with all other earthly heroes

Enjoying eternal prosperity as is his due, cavorting with
The fellowship of the exalted, a tremendous honor!
For his lofty and abundant accomplishments
And for his bountiful sacrifices to the Olympians

So rejoice in the knowledge of the current state of affairs
And pay tribute to his esteemed legacy
By collecting the wood necessary for his glorious pyre
And properly initiate the final burial rites

And by serving as steward of the games held in his honor[227]
As you distribute the accompanying prizes to the victors
In recognition of exceptional endurance, strength and skill
And valor amongst the best in the lands of Priam"

And so radiant Eos speaks uplifting words of encouragement
In hopes of raising the lowly spirits of Memnon
And to assuage the anxiety of her grief stricken son, for
He is enormously tormented by the loss of his fallen cousin

And as suddenly as she appears before him, lovely Eos
Swiftly departs for holy Olympus, making her return to

---

[227] the funeral games were held in honor of the recently deceased
and traditionally included athletic competitions such as wrestling,
archery, boxing, and chariot races

The realm of the immortal gods and goddesses, and into the
Divine chambers she shares with her beloved companion

And without haste the son of the goddess commands his men
To gather the necessary firewood and timber
From the wondrous forests surrounding Ilium
For construction of an expansive pyre for great Aithops

And the Aethiopian contingent set to work immediately
Erecting its final monument to the great Meroitian prince
Working feverishly to complete the massive project
And thereby commence the final funeral procession

And the comrades of famed Aithops toil with heavy hearts
Remembering the exploits of their illustrious commander
As each man reminisces about experiences long since past
Until their awesome task is accomplished at last

And all allies of the honorable Trojan king Priam
Including Aethiopians, Trojans, Lycians, and Dardanians
And many other great nations allied against the Argives
Gather solemnly near the epicenter of the city

And everyone present is adorned in full military garb
Brandishing shield, sword, bow, and lance
And each battalion stands with precision and in alignment
As due reverence is afforded to Memnon's fallen comrade

And from his magnificently fashioned golden throne
The venerable Priam stands adjacent to his queen
Along with the sadly widowed Andromache
As she tenderly embraces her young son Astyanax

And adjacent to her stands Helen of Troy
Her grief readily apparent at yet another death
Resulting from her ill fated abandonment

Of Atreus' son as she followed Paris to his homelands

And standing nearest to her is the saddened Cassandra
Along with various elders of the Trojan nation
As all in Ilium stand in unison as a final grateful gesture
To the beloved cousin of the son of the goddess

And great Aithops' corpse is duly accompanied
As it makes its final journey to the hallowed pyre
And select Aethiopian nobility are chosen to be his escort
Each bedecked in armor of gold and sparkling silver

And the procession begins as the Scaean Gates are flung
Open and the women of Troy beat their breasts in anguish
And not a face in the massive gathering remains tearless
As all mourn the loss of the good and brave Aithops

And the epic Aethiopian commanders
Along with the entire contingent of their loyal men
Dutifully shear a lock of beautiful dark hair
As a final offering to their beloved comrade

And through his flowing tears, great Memnon passionately
Speaks, "Redoubtable Aithops, my dear and beloved cousin!
And constant companion in all undertakings, including
Those both great and in those that were more humble

It was you that always stood by my side through all
Conflicts, as we conquered our foes across vast Aethiopia
Establishing our dominion over those wondrous lands, and
Effortlessly overcoming those that dared to challenge us

And equally you stood with me against fiendish opponents
As we subdued the venomous and hideous Echidna
And overcame horrid Chrysaor as he emerged from his lair
And now both are obstructed from their evil intentions

It was your brave optimism during these dark hours
Imminent throughout our varied fatal ordeals
That encouraged our men to strenuously persevere
When all felt overwhelmed by our immense challenges

And now you rightfully take your hallowed place with the
Exalted, as you dwell amongst the heroes of the Elysian
Fields! Assembled with the elite in the realm of Hades, and
Forever shall you be in the memories of your comrades"

And so great Memnon speaks these stirring words
Emanating from the depths of his pained heart
In remembrance of his great companion and friend
For his tremendous life is lost so far away from Aethiopia

Next the body of Aithops is carried to the wooden structure
And shortly thereafter the son of the goddess takes up the
Fire, and with a burdened heart he steadies the great torch
As the magnificent pyre is ignited by incomparable Memnon

And so the final farewell to great Aithops concludes
Accomplished magnificently by his beloved comrades
As the whole of Troy honors his legacy, with further
Remembrances of the Meroitian prince on the horizon

And at the request of the son of the goddess
King Priam orders the commencement of the funeral games
To further honor the cousin of the Aethiopian monarch
Overcome as he vigorously defended Troy

And the best of the Aethiopians and Trojans assemble
Along with Lycians, Phrygians, and Dardanians
As they all eagerly vie for the elaborate prizes
And the accompanying honors bestowed upon the victors

And so the games begin with competition in archery

With the finest archers lined up ready to take aim
For determined are they to display their prowess
And artistry in wielding the bow and arrow

The participants gather near the eastern wall of the city, and
Each of the man assembled is of distinguished birth and
Pedigree, amongst those gathering are peerless Astylus,[228]
Lichas, [229]and Eupolemus, the latter a cousin of Agenor

Also engaging in the revered competition
Is an incomparable Aethiopian commander
Agathon Aknatides, the famed Nubian prince
And trusted counselor to the son of the goddess

His peoples famed for impeccable archery skills,
Evidenced by the son of Aknatus' exploits, as he
Ravaged the Achaean rank and file with his arrows
Compelling those whom he encounters to flee him or die

And the last to step forth as a competitor in the glorious
Affair is Paris, the husband of lovely Helen
And though he is scorned above all men present in the games
His prowess at the bow is undisputed by any man alive

And great Memnon steps forth to reveal the coveted prize
A gold and silver encrusted chalice
Depicting Leto's glorious son Apollo as he battled
The fiendish and fire breathing Python[230]

That monster set upon the torment of Leto, at Hera's behest
In envy of her dalliance with Zeus cloud gatherer

---

[228] a Phrygian prince
[229] a Dardanian captain and nephew-in-law of Anchises
[230] a great serpent sent by Hera to harass Leto and prevent her from
giving birth to Apollo and Artemis

Resulting in the beginnings of two great deities
The huntress goddess and her famed golden brother

Such a magnificent award allotted to the best of the archers
Along with the honors of being proclaimed the victor
As each participant is determined to contend to his
Uttermost, and lay his claim to the divinely wrought chalice

The task at hand arduous for even those assembled
For the one whom triumphed could only claim this wondrous
Prize by striking a target one eight a kilometer away
An impossible distance for an ordinary man

But not a daunting task for the contestants
For each are masterful in wielding the bow and arrow
To the utter dismay of their opponents in battle, such is
The reputation of the participants in the archery events

Confidently they stand behind the apportioned marker
And each man steps forth to take their respective shot
Undaunted by the distance of the far away target
As a deafening silence takes hold of the captivated audience

And commencing the heralded event is lusty Astylus, shortly
After he strings the bow inherited from his grandfather, and
Though he unleashes his arrow with tremendous power, the
Shaft falls short of the target as it harmlessly grazes the earth

Next to attempt the feat is the incomparable Lichas
A fearsome foe to the armies of the son of Atreus
For his famed arrows battered the Achaean forces
As they fled in terror across eddying Scamander

That faithful day that great Hector laid low Patroclus

As the panicked Argive horses trample over each other
During flight, and the dust whipped up is blinding to all, as
Those commanding the reigns are pierced by Lichas' arrows

Such was the pedigree of the next contestant
And though his fame is well deserved for his feat at arms
His prowess in battle is of no assistance to him, as he
Barely misses the target after launching the bitter arrow

Similarly too does strong Eupolemus' misfires his shot
For though the accuracy of his aim is undisputed
The launch of his arrow lacks both force and distance to
Strike, and accordingly the target remains unmolested

And next to step forth and make attempt is Paris
Gingerly Helen's lover makes his approach to the marker
And the Trojan prince is aware of the resentful glares, for
Embitterment abounds in his imperiling Troy for a dalliance

And without delay handsome Paris strings his bow
Next notching his self crafted arrow to it
And with a prayer to the lord of all archers[231]
The son of Priam let flies his well launched shaft

And great Apollo consents to Paris' invocations
As Helen's husband is granted a tremendous
Accomplishment, for his shaft effortlessly strikes the target
To the subdued admiration of the astonished audience

For none forethought the Trojan prince to succeed
And those that did bore ill will towards Paris
And accordingly prayed against his success
And now all eyes turn to Agathon Aknatides

---

[231] reference to Apollo

And that incomparable Aethiopian captain takes up his bow
Now widely recognizable by the Argive forces, for that
Mighty man overcame many in their ranks in recent days
Thereby necessitating their panicked flight to the ships

And so Agathon takes careful aim at the target
As he assuredly unleashes his shaft with all its force
And with relative ease the famed archer strikes the mark
Though it was positioned at a near impossible distance

And of all the men to take part in the challenge
Only two were able to strike the far away target
The first being the Nubian prince Agathon
And the second being Priam's son Paris

And since there is only one prize to be awarded
It is decided that the two men would again compete
And this time a pomegranate is strategically placed
On top of the high branch of an aged oak tree

With the victor expected to strike from a considerable
Distance, and Paris is first to position himself at the marker
As he steadies his bow and takes careful aim at the apple
And the Trojan prince deftly hits his intended target

And the men loudly applaud this magnificent feat!
As Priam's son is poised to claim the chalice, not so fast!
Agathon struts forward confidently, as another pomegranate
Is placed on the high branches of the ancient tree

And the Nubian prince lightly strings his bow
And takes another trusted arrow from his quiver full
Then Agathon aims for the beleaguered apple
As mighty Apollo easily guides the precise shaft

Striking the unfortunate fruit through its center

And the core is pierced and shatters instantly
As the assembled men all look on in awe and reverence
Lauding the splendid performance of the Nubian prince

The son of the goddess steps in as final arbiter
Declaring both Agathon and Paris Priamides
As co-equal and rightful claimants
To possess the divinely crafted chalice

And Agathon in his infinite gentleness
Unselfishly renounces his rightful claim
Instead deferring to a grateful Paris
As mitigation against the incessant scorn of his countrymen

Endured by the Trojan prince since the arrival of lovely
Helen, for they blamed him for their sufferings, as the
Great War is brought about by her departure from Sparta
And so Paris bore the blunt of condemnation of these actions

And the son of Priam thanks the venerable Aethiopian
Commander for his magnanimous gesture towards him
And the other contestants look on in sheer admiration
As the already outsized prestige of Agathon is multiplied

And next the boxers take their respective places, men
Renowned in all earthly realms for their skill and strength,
Including Epheseus,[232] strong Callippus,[233] Philostratus[234]
Also Laodocus, a son of Priam, and peerless Ergamenes

---

[232] nephew of Priam and son of Hesione; the Trojan princess was
rescued by Heracles from a sea monster after he was promised a
reward by Laomedon (Hesione's father); when Laomedon reneged,
Heracles sacked Troy
[233] a Phrygian prince; brother of Astylus
[234] nephew of Aeneas and son of his sister Hippodamia

The latter accompanying the son of the goddess
On the long and arduous voyage to holy Ilium
And now called upon to display his awesome strength
As he did the day he overcame the great lion in childhood

Thus rescuing his beloved younger brother, his physical
Prowess an attribute to his exalted lineage, and evidence
Of divine favor bestowed upon him by Olympus
All of these factors a testament to his fortunate fate

And again the son of the goddess presents to the contestants
A greatly sought after award allotted for the victor
A magnificent pair of steeds from his palatial stock
Sleek, beautiful, and reared in the lush Aethiopian grasslands

For these magnificent steeds at one time or another were
Harnessed to the glorious chariot of divine Memnon himself
As the son of the goddess lorded over the battlefields
And now would be possessed by the champion of the event

Without delay the competition begins, and within
A short time the contest is narrowed to two contenders
The best by far of all participants being strong Ergamenes
And prince Laodocus, the venerable son of King Priam

And so the two men begin their anticipated duel
Both aware of what was at the stake if they triumphed
And hopeful that the Olympians would bring victory
For each desire the honors of triumphing in the elite event

From the outset the favorite of the combatants is discerned
As mighty Ergamenes aggressively pursues Priam's son
Strenuously attacking his beleaguered and embattled foe, as
An overwhelmed Laodocus meagerly defends himself

And denied the opportunity to go on the offensive

As relentless Ergamenes effortlessly holds his advantage
And finally great Memnon mercifully intercedes
Proclaiming his beloved comrade the victor of the event

And all those who beheld the match are awestruck
By the display of tremendous strength of the Kushian
General, as Ergamenes effortlessly batters poor Laodocus
Bringing immense honor to his already famed name

And following this glorious victory by mighty Ergamenes
The son of the goddess announces the commencement of
The time honored and renowned wrestling competition
Along with his intent of bestowing choice oxen to the winner

A tremendous prize afforded the victor of the vaunted event
Requiring a degree of skill that few earthly men possessed
And accordingly such a magnificent prize is apportioned, as
The participants courageously step forth to participate

First Eupolus,[235]Sotades,[236]and wily Polycto,[237]
And Polydamas, courageous son of Panthous
And trusted confidante to great Hector
Though his measured advice unheeded after the demise

Of haughty Patroclus at the hands of Priam's son
Also to enter the wrestling competition
Helicaon,[238] son of highly regarded Antenor
And so the field is set to begin the match

With Polydamas and Helicaon emerging as the best
Amongst all of the contenders for the prize

---

[235] charioteer of Aeneas
[236] cousin of Pandarus
[237] a Lycian captain and counselor to Glaucus
[238] a Trojan captain

As they effortlessly dispatch their rivals in the event
And at last engage one another in hopes of claiming the oxen

And so Polydamas shouts brazenly to his opponent
"Son of Antenor, why even attempt a futile task? And
Dually the loss of your honor before all of these great men
Assembled? For I shall surely triumph in this contest

As I am by far the best amongst the Trojans, and I shall
Win the oxen awarded by the famed son of the goddess
So take heed and withdraw your claim to the coveted prize
Or suffer a humiliating defeat at my hands"

And brave Helicaon answers this audacious boast,
"Son of Panthous, your words shall not deter me!
Nor will your bold speech intimidate me from my intentions
Of engaging you for possession of the coveted oxen

So I implore you to summon all your skill and might!
For I shall not hold back in my relentless assault
As the Olympians above decide who shall be victorious
And to which of us will be apportioned dishonor

And with these words the two captains of Ilium engage
With the advantage being exchanged on several occasions
As the two Trojans continue the uttermost struggle
Each strenuously pushing the limits of their strength

And suddenly Panthous' son gains the advantage
As he deftly pins the limbs of a surprised Helicaon
And presses his upper body into his opponent's spine
In a concerted effort to force him to capitulate

And the bewildered son of Antenor looks to swiftly recover
As he upends Polydamas with a mighty thrust
And Panthous' son suddenly crashes to the ground

Instantly ceding his hard fought edge to Helicaon

And Antenor's son in an instance becomes the aggressor
As he begins a full on assault of his opponent
The lord of the Olympians grants him endurance
And Polydamas' strength slowly declines

Next Helicaon grasps the stunned son of Panthous
And furiously hurls his foe to the ground
With awesome force as Polydamas concedes the match
After enduring such a violent conclusion to the competition

And all of the men thunderously cheer
For the son of Antenor after his great victory
In the closely contested duel of champions
As lord Memnon dutifully awards him his prize, and

Immediately preceding is the commencement of chariot
Races, as the final component of the funeral games begins
And there is no shortage of contestants for the competition,
For many coveted the grand prize awarded to the victor

Rare gold and precious silvers from far away Aethiopia
Accompanying the son of the goddess and his comrades
In their magnificent vessels to the shores of Ilium
And now allocated to the winner of the famed chariot games

The competitors amongst the best at Troy!
Including redoubtable Glaucus, the Lycian monarch
And great ally to Priam's besieged city
Also participating is Priam's son horse taming Deiphobus

And the son of the Aphrodite too lays claim to the prizes
Great Aeneas, his famed exploits well known by
As he approaches with his chariot and steeds
With nary a doubt considered the favorite to win the event

- 256 -

And finally the last entrant confidently steps into the fray
Venerable Tanutamen, the great Aethiopian commander, and
Loyal subject of mighty Memnon, the stout-hearted
Axumian king is the best horsemen in all of lovely Aethiopia

And the markers are set to a predetermined distance
In the expanse of approximately twelve kilometers
Nearly a quarter the length of the high walls of Ilium
With the victor being the first to reach the opposite end

And so these godlike men approach the starting point
Exhorting their mares to perform to their absolute uttermost
And each is determined and poised to claim the rich prizes
Generously awarded by the son of the goddess

And great Memnon gives the starting signal
Each champion whips the reins to rouse their horses
And Aeneas Anchisides takes the early advantage
Only a few paces ahead of the Axumian king Tanutamen

While the others continue distant pursuit of them both
And the Cytherean born Aphrodite, along with Artemis
Observe the race from high atop the walls, each
Supporting one over the other of the two competing heroes

For Tanutamen is the champion of the huntress goddess
While Aphrodite assuredly supports her own beloved son
And as the goddesses are determined to intervene
On behalf of her respective favorite contestant

Both thought it best to allow the Fates to decide
For a conflict over sport was unbecoming, and each assume
The role of neutral observers, while the Axumian king and
Aeneas make final approach to the marker

And swift Tanutamen utilizes his gifted skills by

Maneuvering his chariot and disciplined steeds, narrowing
The gap between he and the son of Aphrodite, and by the
Final kilometer both men possess equal chance to prevail

And unease slowly infiltrates the confident Aeneas
As Tanutamen begins to open a slight lead
His determination for victory obviously apparent
For the Axumian king had never before lost a chariot race

And Aphrodite's son summons all of his remaining strength
And prepares for one final effort
To conclude the highly contested competition
And upend the hopes of great Memnon's trusted comrade

And as Aeneas exhorts his mares to ride even faster
An axle buckles under the intense pressure
As the famed chariot immediately takes a fall
And the steeds of Tros are liberated from their bridle

And so by default Tanutamen is declared victor
But in his pride and sense of honor the great Aethiopian
Commander refuses to accept the splendid award
And renounces his rightful claim to the treasures

And famed Aeneas, also a man great in piety
Urges the Axumian king to accept his prize
And praises him above all other earthly men
As the greatest to steer and maneuver the chariot

And the chorus grows for Tanutamen to acquiesce
As the rightful claimant of the gold and silver
Even the son of the goddess gives his explicit assent
Inducing the Axumian king to relent in his unwillingness

And so the participants of the festivities all gather beneath
The lofty walls of holy Pergamus, and the victors of the

Funeral games are duly honored before all, and revered by
The assembled Aethiopian, Lycian, Trojan, and Dardanians

While consolation prizes are unexpectedly awarded to all
Contestants by the benevolent son of the goddess
As the battered egos of the defeated are assuaged
Restoring unity once again amongst the varied battalions

And so all return to Priam's glorious citadel
To partake of meat, fruits, bread, and wine
Celebrating the famed life of Memnon's beloved comrade
As he sacrificed his life for the sake of Troy

And the son of the goddess rises before all of Ilium
Expressing his gratitude for the deference shown
To himself and his Aethiopian comrades
For they are honored more like the Olympians than men

And the spring lambs and oxen are slaughtered
As due sacrifices are made to the Olympians
Acknowledging the success of the funeral games
Held in honor of great Aithops, famed seeker of adventure

And after the glorious conclusion of the funeral games
And the revelry following the solemn event
The emboldened armies of King Priam
Are eager to engage their hated foes near the vessels

Confident with Memnon Tithonides at the helm of at last
Repelling the haughty and unmerciful Achaeans! And
Avenging the deaths of beloved comrades long since slain
While wrecking havoc upon the enemy Argive ranks

And so the Aethiopian, Trojan, Dardanian, and Lycian
Generals begin preparations to aggressively engage their

Demoralized enemies, Anchises' redoubtable son Aeneas
Commences the discussion, "Son of the goddess

A mighty accomplishment indeed! Attributed to your
Spectacular feat at arms! Vanquishing many of our
Fearsome opponents, concluding with the defeat of old
Nestor's boastful son Antilochus, he no longer flings taunts

As he is pierced by the Aethiopian lance
Along with many other Argives champions
Corpses that have bitten the Trojan dust
As they hysterically flee your indomitable advance

A complete victory as we ravaged their battalions
And the Argives are compelled to flee to their ships
A triumph not witnessed since Peleus' son
Angrily left the battlefield in protest against Agamemnon

And horse taming Hector wielded his mighty lance
For no Achaean was able to withstand his fury
In his pursuit they too fled to the vessels
As we set fires to the very ash wood ships from Ithaca!

The Achaeans in a panic solicit the return of Achilles
And the stubborn son of Peleus instead sends his beloved
Cousin, bearing the breastplate and armor well known to all
As the Trojans and Lycians are initially tricked by the ruse

Only through this stratagem are we turned away
From destroying the Argive fleet set afire
And now we are thankfully presented yet again
With opportunity to destroy them once and for all!"

And all of the men loudly cheer Aeneas' exhortation
As all within the ranks are inebriated with overconfidence
Due to witnessing Myrmidon Achilles, for the first time ever

Departing the battlefield due to great Memnon's prowess

And Deiphobus Priam's son adds his own encouraging
Speech, "Incomparable Aethiopian king, commander of our
Triumphant forces! Aphrodite's son speaks the Truth! For
We may at last accomplish the terminus of this war

Complete annihilation of the Argive armies!
If we advance upon them in all our fury as they are
Disjointed and in sheer trepidation! For Atreus' son steadily
Loses grip on his once firm control of his panicked armies

And never before has the morale of Achaeans been lower
Nor the Argive leader's appetite for our riches diminished
As Menelaus' resolve is drastically lessened
At the retrieval of his divine wife"

And Deiphobus words furthers the call to arms, as the
Chatter amongst the growing chorus desires immediate
Attack of the Argives as they cowered near their vessels
Contemplating return to their lands across the Aegean

But Priam's son wise Helenus the great seer of Ilium
For the will of Apollo he effortlessly interprets
Though his advice is equally embraced and rejected
Intercedes with counsel as he addresses mighty Memnon

"Son of the goddess, I beg you to heed the Olympians!
For even as great and heroic as you are
You too must yield to their divine will
For no great triumph shall occur this day

Can you not see Queen Hera as she succors the Argives?
Or Cronus' son Poseidon wielding his feared trident?
For the Achaeans are fortified under their vanguard
As aegis bearing Athena stringently protects their ships

The divine enemies of Troy are thoroughly allied, as fear
And adrenaline runs through the Achaean commanders
Much like a cornered boar surrounded by a self assured
Village, the Argives are now at their most dangerous!

And we should not take this opportunity
To hasten an assault on our dejected enemies, for it was
Recently that we made such a proposed advance, only to
Later flee to the sanctuary of our strong walls

As the son of Peleus was angered at the untimely demise
Of his beloved cousin, and his fury was unmatched, and
Though we have a champion amongst our armies that
Possesses might greater than the Myrmidon

We must remember that the great Olympians themselves
Descend from the heavens to participate in this epic struggle
And many are assuredly aligned against our aims, for no
Man can prevail against the will of the divine immortals

And so great Apollo advises against immediate attack
And instead await signs from the high heavens
For we shall not be successful in our lofty endeavor this day
Of driving away the mighty armies of Agamemnon"

And the warnings of prophetic Helenus give pause to the
Men as they begin to ponder the words of the respected seer
As many concurring with his wise counsel
But yet many more foolishly and blindly opposed it

Such misgivings expressed by the son of Priam
Dictated to him by the divine will of father Zeus
And his concerns too shared by the son of the goddess, for
Always mindful of the will of Olympus is wise Memnon

Accordingly the son of Eos acquiesces to Helenus' counsel

His decision having the dual purposes of
Not alienating the powerful deities above, nor to
Foolishly overplay the victorious achievements of his armies

And so the son of the goddess commands the Aethiopian
Ranks, along with their Trojan, Lycian, and Dardanian allies
To remain within the walls of the holy city
And respite from horrible war, though desired by Ares

Dually honoring his promise to the venerable Nestor
Allowing the proper burial of his son Antilochus, when
The son of the goddess forbade despoilment of the corpse
And permitted safe passage for return to the Argives ships

And subsequent to the decision of great Memnon Tithonides
All of joyous Troy continues its revelry and merrymaking
As libations are poured on behalf of the Olympians, with
Peaceful slumber bestowed to all within the city afterwards

But two within the high walls were unable to partake of rest
First was the great Aethiopian king himself
The most celebrated man in the entire world
And the second is his cousin, lovely Cassandra

The former, particularly troubled and cognizant
Of the fickle tendencies of the Olympians
For in the morning they favor one party of the conflict
Only to swiftly change alliances by the evening

Similar to the glorious rays of the Sun in its splendor
And in the next instance Helios' chariot cedes to darkness
And just as the triumphant Aethiopians and Trojans prevail
One day, without a moment's notice become the vanquished

For now Zeus takes sides with Aphrodite and Apollo
And concedes victory to the Aethiopian battalions

- 263 -

But then at his discretion acquiesce to Hera's vengeance
And permit Pallas Athena to ravage Priam's lands

Such were the thoughts of incomparable Memnon
As he lay in his sumptuous palatial chambers
Guarded is he against excessive optimism, as the son
Of the goddess contemplates the next military maneuver

His thoughts beset by the fierce conflict ahead
Assessing what went well in battle and what did not
Astute are his observations of Argive techniques, as he lay
The groundwork for the next chapter to the Great War

And Cassandra, her mind and thoughts always restless
For she is gifted with divinely granted prophetic abilities
And able to discern the will of the Olympians, and this eve
The daughter of Priam is deeply troubled by her visions

For the plans of mighty Zeus are made clear to her, and the
Decisions that lay ahead are not favorable to Troy, for a sad
Outcome awaits no matter the determination, such are the
Thoughts of Priam's lovely daughter as she seeks Memnon

Her concern borne out of love for her epic cousin
And though her warnings are often unheeded, a curse from
Leto's son, she is not dissuaded from approaching the son of
The goddess, and so Cassandra enters his royal chambers

And immediately she kneels before the Aethiopian king
For her actions are undertaken in hopes of discouraging him
And sadly Cassandra begins to describe to Memnon her
Visions, "Oh cousin, will you listen and heed my counsel?

For the words I bring forth are not encouraging, and are

Selfishly uttered for the sake of your well being, for you
Have been forewarned by your concerned mother, and your
Decision was rendered prior to the arduous journey to Troy

And yet the Olympians love you dearly, son of the goddess!
For your tremendous piety and purity of heart, I, employed
As a vessel to reiterate your destiny, bring forth a stark
Choice that the immortals willingly present to you

For only one man alive can withstand the Myrmidon scourge
As the son of Peleus cannot overcome you in awful battle
And the Olympians shall not permit him to be slain by your
Glorious hand, commencing an eternal struggle

And the Argives shall remain encamped at our lovely shores
While many more men die on both ends of this conflict, as
The feared Argive captains succumb to your awesome might
And one by one your beloved comrades are slain

And the awful sack of Troy shall inevitably be accomplished
Swiftly set about by the hands of the fierce Myrmidon king
Amidst the fires, holy Ilium razed to the ground in utter ruins
As the sacred pillars of our ancient city fall one by one!

And the very body of Priam himself desecrated!
As the hopeless women of Troy, including myself
Forcibly taken and compelled to Achaean servitude
Achilles' victorious rampage wholeheartedly completed!

As our sons are tossed from the high precipice!
And mercilessly slaughtered by the Achaean sword
Bloodthirsty Argives exacting cruel revenge upon innocent
Children! Too dreadful a sight for any of us to endure!

And you too shall sadly witness these distressing events
For even as irresistible as you are in dangerous war, unable

You shall be to obstruct the Argive conquest of the city, for
Your lance is powerless to prevent the walls from falling

As haughty Achilles triumphantly returns to his faraway
Lands, welcomed as the undisputed conqueror of Ilium
Bearing children that will reign over Phthia, as swift footed
Thetis witnesses the aging of her beloved son

Son of the goddess, your armies shall be destroyed, and
Only you alone survive, setting oars to the wild seas
Departing these accursed plains, never to return
Your mission unaccomplished, as doomed Troy is sacked!

And yet even though these sequence of events are intolerable
The alternative causes yet even more grief to my heart! For
The demise of the Myrmidon coincides with your own fate
And he shall survive only for as long as you continue to live

And though none shall ever match your dexterity with the
Sword, nor overcome you in the midst of ferocious battle
Except only by your own unequivocal consent, this lofty
Decision is apportioned to you alone to make by Olympus

And so I implore you to painstakingly consider all options
For though you have journeyed a far and perilous distance
Tormented and plagued by the jealous Poseidon
And seduced by the lusty goddesses you have chanced upon

And famed throughout the world as conqueror of Chrysaor
Your great exploits well known in the halls of Olympus, and
Your renowned achievements are justly earned, the
Alternative does not permit endeavors beyond these lands

And people of all realms shall be deprived of your beauty
And virtue, and your indomitable spirit! For undoubtedly

You are the most handsome man in all the world, and
Equally blessed with prowess in wielding the lance

So my dear cousin, please heed these measured words
For I know deep down in your brave and stout heart
Which of the two options you shall avail yourself of, but just
This once, be selfish and depart for lovely Aethiopia!"

And tears flow freely from the face of the Trojan princess
For she knew that her words fell on deaf ears, and the
Character of Memnon would not permit him to contemplate
Abandoning the birthplace of his father in its darkest hours

And fully aware of the consequences of his impending
Actions, and without nary a thought to reconsidering his
Determination, the son of the goddess lifts his lovely cousin
From her knees, as he attempts to comfort and console her

And so an empathetic Memnon gently speaks to Cassandra,
"Fair cousin, our lot in life is predetermined
Though it be cloaked in the guise of choice
All is known to the great Olympians prior to our decisions

For the risk I undertook preceding my journey to Troy
Outlined in great detail by my beloved mother
She whom bore me and my unfortunate brother
On the Aethiopian shores to my incomparable father

A mortal chosen as the consort of a goddess
And now my own fate lies within proximity, for bravely
I shall confront my destiny, as I am compelled to do!
And adhere to the will of the divine Olympians

And though I may be the handsomest man alive
And the son of a radiant and the most revered of goddesses
And my prowess at arms unmatched by any

Even I am powerless before the irresistible Fates

For I too must cede to the awesome will of Zeus
Nor shall I ever be accused of cowardice
Or refraining from my allotment in this life
Though your caring words are acknowledged"

And a forlorn Cassandra begins to weep uncontrollably
Beating her breasts, the outcome now painfully conclusive
As her anguish emanates throughout her entire body
That such a sacrifice is selflessly made for all of Troy

And the son of the goddess embraces the Trojan prophetess
Taking Priam's daughter into his strong arms
As he attempts to comfort her uncontrollable grief
And provide assurance that all would be well

And subsequently great Memnon and Cassandra depart from
One another, as she returns to her quarters in very low spirits
While the great son of iridescent Eos, resigned to his fate
Enters his chambers to prepare for the upcoming day

And that mighty man did not once consider retreat, nor
Entertains acceptance of a less ominous path, but instead
Great Memnon ponders how best to inflict utmost damage
Before the frigid Atropos wields her dreaded shears

XII. The Ascension

And as Helios despondently steers his flashing chariot
Bringing forth daylight to grateful men and women alike
Though within the heart of the deity lies deep sadness
For the forthcoming day promised to be the most wretched!

Replete with utter sadness and despair! Manifest by the
Dimming lights of the Sun god's transport, for even eddying
Scamander's immense sorrow is apparent, and
Disconsolation is not relegated to these two gods alone

For anguish too consumes the halls of high Olympus
And the impending events of the day are very much on the
Mind of Zeus, as he swiftly summons before him all
Immortals in privy council to reveal his divine edict

And most intense of anxieties are endured by lovely Eos
And by swift footed Thetis, Nereus' daughter
As both are concerned over the fate of a son
And so with heavy hearts both goddesses are restive

As too are the other immortals in a state of unease
Each knowing the gravity of the impending events
On one side sits Hera, Athena, and gray bearded Poseidon
Along with crafty Hephaestus and Hermes

And opposite sits glorious Apollo and the huntress Artemis
Along with lovely Aphrodite and war mongering Ares, and
Countless lesser deities accordingly divided amongst the
Factions favoring opposite sides of a dispute amongst men

And great Zeus begins to speak to the gathering,
"Hear my words, inhabitants of the celestial heavens!
As I am by far more stronger than you all in sum
And therefore I compel you to obey my commandments

For this day I desire you all to abandon

The blood stained plains of divine Troy
And to cease your intrusion into this epic military struggle
Though many of your progeny are participants

I deem that you transform yourselves into active spectators
And witness the conflict from your lofty and palatial
Accommodations, atop the heights of our wondrous abode
And refrain from intervening in the Great War this day

For shortly the greatest battle ever to take place
Shall occur between two men – best by far! Between
Redoubtable Memnon, the exalted son of the goddess
And Peleus' son Achilles the swift footed king of Phthia

And it has been determined by the Fates
That this struggle shall occur uninfluenced
By any concerned Olympian god or goddess
Despite your otherwise inclination to the contrary

As both of these venerable men are truly beloved by us all!
In especial Tithonus and Eos' divine son
For he is the handsomest man alive!
And his physical beauty is the equivalent of his courage

And it shall be his judgment alone as to his destiny
As recently foretold by his cousin the Trojan prophetess[239]
Whether to sacrifice his unparalleled mortal life
Or return to those delightful lands in wondrous Aethiopia

And though he is godlike amongst earthly men, and
Has prerogative to espouse a vainglory direction, his stout
Heart only allows him to choose unrepentant confrontation
With the consequences of his brave endeavor"

---

[239] reference to Cassandra

And with these words lord Zeus forewarns the Olympians
As each deity acquiesces to his edict to avoid fearsome
Wrath, and Cronus' son leaves the comforts of his celestial
Estate, swiftly arriving to the fortified walls of holy Troy

And the greatest of all Olympians makes his will known to
Memnon, and Eos' son swiftly obeys the king of the
Immortals, for Zeus desires him to commence awful war
And accordingly redoubtable Memnon makes preparations

Next, disguising himself as a great golden eagle, thunderlord
Zeus perches himself high above the famed Scaean Gates
As he watches the great Aethiopian king appear before his
Armies, and give the order for the gates to be drawn open

As the son of the goddess marshals his forces
Exhorting Aethiopians, Trojans, brave Lycians
And Dardanians, as well as the other assembled allies
To fight to the uttermost, even if it meant dreaded death

Memnon shouts out, "Brave men, today we shall make our
Stand! In defense of the women and children of this famed
City! Even if the Olympians should be decidedly against us
We shall distinguish ourselves by fighting to our uttermost!

For it is incumbent upon us to wholeheartedly assure
That lofty Ilium is not ceased by Atreus' son this day, and to
Thwart the subjugation of its people to his rule, woe is the
Ill fated and sorrowful day if this should come to fruition!

And let there be little doubt that I shall very soon
Again encounter the Myrmidon leader and his battalions
As we are destined to battle man to man with the cold steel
For the day of reckoning has at long last arrived!

And though we have each tested the other's mettle

And by the grace of father Zeus I remain standing
While Peleus' son is rescued from my strong lance
The Fates may render alternative results this time around

But I fully promise you, my illustrious comrades, that I shall
Stand beside you in the heat of battle for as long as I may
And accept whatever destiny the Olympians bestow upon me
For no mere mortal can go against their divine will

And so I entreat each of you to stand strong with me! Even
In the face of the awesome challenges that we may face this
Day, I implore you to stand firm against any divine
Headwinds, thoroughly acquit yourselves in the battlefield"

And great Memnon concludes his words of encouragement
To his men, so rousing is the speech from the son of goddess
That all whom heard is undoubtedly moved by its content
For the resolute call to action by great Memnon is inspiring

And accordingly the men are buoyed by the exhortation
Delivered by the redoubtable son of Eos and Tithonus
As the sun splendidly illuminates his armor and shield
His regal appearance resembling that of an Olympian god

And with this image the armies again stream through the
Gates, led by brave commanders ready for the struggle ahead
And each captain marshals his contingent of men
As they all await the command to engage the Argives

The son of the goddess moves ahead confidently
Primed to yet again encounter the armies of Agamemnon
In the latest battle of the seemingly everlasting Great War
Precipitated by the union of Zeus' daughter and Paris

And the Aethiopian and Trojan contingent continue its
Advance, marching in unison as they cross the war wearied

Plains, courageously march across the flowing shores of
Scamander, resigned to the outcome of the day's events

And heightened are the anxieties amongst the enemies of
Troy, as the sunken morale of the Achaeans is apparent
Its resolve for sacking holy Troy wholly deflated
And thoughts of departing Priam's lands are prevalent

As the Argive commanders begin the task of marshalling
Their forces, first Sthenelus,[240] trusty comrade of Tydeus' son
Along with the aggrieved lord of far away Sparta,[241] entreat
Their battalions to resist the coming Aethiopian onslaught

So too does Acamas, the son of great Theseus
His mother Phaedra[242] bore him in lovely Crete
After her rescue at the hands of his father
From her half brother the horrid Minotaur

And Agamemnon, accompanied by his trusty herald
Talthybius, attempts to rouse his men with encouraging
Words, this action echoed by Oileus' son Ajax the lesser, as
He exhorts his Locrians to endure fierce Memnon

And Achilles too joins the Achaean rally and advance
His formidable Myrmidons following closely behind
Armed and thoroughly prepared for awful war, and
Determined to accept the judgment of Olympus for that day

And the two armies stand on opposite ends of Scamander
Each side anticipating yet another epic clash
For godlike men stood on both ends of the battlefield
Employed as pawns in a conflict amongst the immortals

---

[240] a Calydonian captain and comrade of Diomedes
[241] reference to Menelaus
[242] a princess of Crete

And commanders on both sides are poised to engage one
Another, as the emboldened armies of Troy and its allies
Buoyed by recent successes against their foes, stand ready to
Assail the apprehensive Argives as they defend their vessels

With more ambitious designs of repelling the enemy forces
From Troy, for their enemies sorely dreaded the ferocity of
The son of the goddess and his magnificent commanders
from Aethiopia, along with their battle hardened battalions

And despite the fact that amongst the Argives
Stood a dangerous and fearsome warrior
The haughty confidence of the son of Thetis is shaken
After barely escaping the might of great Memnon

And so the conflict begins with the son of the goddess
Intent upon ravaging their armies and spreading panic
Amongst the ranks, takes up his heavy lance into his mighty
Hands, and launches it at the Argives with deadly aim

No miss! It pierces the fine Eleian made armor
Of Onesimachus' honorable son Amarynceus[243]
He came to Priam's citadel with nineteen vessels
Along with his son the youthful Diores

Now he perishes far from his homelands
For he is unfortunately matched against a far mightier foe
As the fury of the son of the goddess is fully displayed
And he effortlessly slays the king of the Eleians

And his son is taken by utter trepidation
As he witnesses murky blood flow from the deadly wound
Of his beloved father at the hands of great Memnon
In sheer terror Diores and his men turn in full retreat

---

[243] king of the Eleia, lands near Achaea

Fleeing the advance of son of the goddess
Shamefully he abandons the lifeless body of his father
To the awe of all those in the vicinity
As Diores' fear caused this reprehensible act

And great Memnon retrieves his famed lance
And swiftly draws his deadly sword from sheath
Giving chase to Amarynceus' dishonored son
Intent on taking his life as recompense for his cowardice

And without difficulty the swift son of the goddess catches
Him, as Diores drops to his knees in supplication
Beseeching the son of the goddess to spare his life
And to excuse his actions in abandoning his father's corpse

And merciful are the Olympians to Amarynceus' son
For a lesser man would surely have ended his life
But the pious Memnon, more godlike than mortal
Bestows clemency upon the dishonored Diores

Commanding him to fetch the body of his father
For return to sea faring ships from Eleia, as the son of the
Goddess promptly lectures the youth on honor, admonishing
The son of Amarynceus for his immoral actions

The grateful Diores fulfills the commandment of great
Memnon, as he and his men collect the corpse of his fallen
Progenitor, and dutifully take it to the ships
Preparing the body for its final interment

And the son of the goddess continues his vigorous attacks
As the Achaeans begin a panicked retreat, and who was to
Fall to the lance of great Memnon in his furious assault?
First Abas,[244]Dolius,[245]Melas[246]and Toxeus

---

[244] cousin of Sthenelus

The latter named for his notorious uncle
Slain by his famous cousin Meleager[247] of Calydonian boar
Hunt[248] fame, during a heated dispute between the two men
Over the presentation of the prize to a female victor[249]

Next to be slain by the raging son of the goddess
Munichus,[250] courageous champion of the Molossians[251]
His father Dryas a famous Argive seer
As was his grandsire, both beloved by the gods

Such that after a surprise assault by thieves
Upon his family on its hallowed fields
The Olympians intervened on its behalf
Transforming them all into various birds and fowls

Such was the lineage of brave Munichus
As he departed for holy Ilium with six vessels
For the sake of grief stricken Menelaus
Now laid low at the hands of glorious Memnon

Next to fall to the fierce Aethiopian king is Thrasymedes[252]
Foolishly he boasts over wine to battle Memnon man to man
And now he turns in flight upon the sight of his famed armor
As the son of Eos promptly dispatches of the braggart

Also slain by fierce Memnon at the height of his fury, and

---

[245] an Ithacan captain and comrade of Odysseus
[246] Cretan captain and cousin of Idomeneus
[247] king of Calydon
[248] a hunt organized by Meleager to capture and slay a gigantic boar sent to ravage Calydon by Artemis
[249] a reference to Atalanta, heroine of the Calydonian boar hunt whom was the first to wound the boar
[250] king of the Molossians
[251] lands near Thessaly
[252] a Locrian captain and kinsmen of Ajax the lesser

Continuing his slaughter is Demophon,[253]lusty Rhexenor,[254]
And Leonteus, the latter a commander of the Lapiths
He came to Troy along with his comrade Polypoetes[255]

His father Coronus[256] accompanied peerless Jason[257]
And his band of Argonauts[258] on the sacred quest
As they encountered tremendous adventures
To recover the infamous Golden Fleece[259]

And many more Achaeans are slaughtered by the hands of
Memnon, as they flee in droves across the waters of
Scamander, in sheer fear of the awful might of the son of the
Goddess, and his unmitigated slaying of the Argives

And once again the Achaean commanders assemble, first
Diomedes, still recovering from injuries inflicted by Eos'
Son, and Odysseus, along with Ajax the greater, too joining
The assembly are Idomeneus and his comrade Meriones

Athenian Menestheus[260]also takes part in the deliberations
As does fierce Achilles, surrounded by his loyal men, and
Lesser commanders are also in audience, as the council
Is convened by Atreus' sons and sad Gerenian Nestor

---

[253] Athenian commander and son of Theseus; brother to Acamas
[254] Calydonian captain
[255] son of Pirithous
[256] a king of the Lapiths
[257] prince of Iolcos; led an expedition of the greatest heroes of his generation on a quest to find the Golden Fleece for the purpose of claiming the throne of Iolcos
[258] heroes assembled by Jason for the quest of the Golden Fleece; named after the vessel they sailed called the *Argo*
[259] fleece belonging to a golden haired ram in Colchis
[260] king of Athens; granted rule of the city by Castor and Pollux (brothers of Helen) after they rescued Helen (abducted by Theseus and taken to Athens)

As all unanimously agree that Memnon's slaughter must
Cease, for they feared that he would finally destroy the
Vessels along with all those who dared to assault holy Ilium
Though none of those assembled desired to confront him

For no man alive is able to overcome the famed Aethiopian
King, as he is permitted to slaughter their men at will
And the son of Eos is beloved by the great Olympians, as
Evidenced by the chaos he inflicts with his lance and sword

And by the fleeting courage of the devastated rank and file
As father Zeus himself rouses the son of the goddess, along
With his fierce Aethiopian contingent, accordingly Memnon
Lords over the battlefield as the undisputed champion

And Tydeus' mighty son Diomedes begins first,
"My beloved comrades, we are surely doomed by the
Olympians to be destroyed so far away from our homelands
For none of us can match the powerful son of the goddess

For whenever he takes up his divinely fashioned arms, and
Mounts his famed steeds from his blessed homelands, he
Descends upon us like an uncontrollable conflagration! And
The will of our battalions are swiftly overwhelmed!

And again he threatens to destroy our besieged fleet, along
With every Achaean that dared to set sail for Ilium, for
Memnon intends to bring a swift end to this sorrowful war
And triumphantly return to his vast kingdom as victor

I myself had an encounter with the son of the goddess,
Witnessing how huge he stands as he whirls his famed lance
Growling ferociously as he unsheathes his sword! And I
Surely would have been slain but for divine intervention

Great Memnon able to overcome our bulwark in battle, as
Achilles offers challenge to him as he raged near the
Corinthians,[261] and yet he too had to be saved by a great
Olympian, swept off the battlefield by Trident bearer

Such an adversary we are unfortunately matched against
And so now I offer this straightforward advice to you all
We must retreat to our seafaring vessels
And offer respite to our demoralized armies

For the son of the goddess again shall rule this day
And if he decides to launch further assault upon us
As he confidently aspires to destroy our besieged ships, and
Make desolate these very beaches we have called our home

Then shall we be compelled to confront our aggressor
Even if he be made of indestructible bronze
And his body forged in the fires of the waters of the Styx
For a retreat into the seas is an implausible proposition

And we must not despair if such is our fate!
For we too have benefactors amongst the Olympians
Gray eyed Athena, Queen Hera, and great Poseidon
Will surely save us from the fury of the Aethiopian king"

The Argive captains are in agreement with great Diomedes
Words, nodding in assent to the wise advice of Tydeus' son
And each offers fervent prayers to the immortal deities
Of merciful rescue from the rage of the son of the goddess

As they rally their men to make a final stand
Exhorting the armies to fight to its uttermost
As further retreat was simply not an option, for their very
Flank was positioned along the edge of the ocean

---

[261] inhabitants of Corinth

And the formidable Aethiopian king rages on, as the Trojan
Armies and its allies follow his lead in the ferocious assault
And presses its advantage against a hated foe
As the panicked Argives are pinned against the ships

And the son of the goddess continues his gruesome work
Sensing the demoralization of his beleaguered opponent
He next casts his lance at brave Olenus[262]
And the dangerous weapon strikes its target

As the unfortunate man spews murky blood
Disemboweled by the fatally hurled weapon
His guts spill onto the dusty plains
And his soul swiftly flees for dark Tartarus

Next to fall is Theiodamas,[263] then Polycaon[264]
The latter a cousin of brave Protesilaus[265]
Slain at the hands of mighty Hector Priamides
For he was the first Achaean to set foot ashore[266]

Holy Ilium after voyage across the tumultuous seas
And no other Argive dared to sacrifice life
And to die so that war upon Troy could commence
As prophesied by the Oracle at Delphi

And the comrade of such a man is slain by great Memnon as
He shifts his assault, unleashing his fury upon the battalions
Of Salamis, led by Telamon's son huge Ajax the Greater

---

[262] a Lelegian captain

[263] a Spartan captain

[264] a Phylacean captain

[265] king of the Phylaceans

[266] it was prophesied by the Oracle at Delphi that the first Argive to
step upon the beaches of Troy would be slain; this was a deterrence
for the Argives until Protesilaus essentially sacrificed himself

And his beloved half brother Teucer[267] the famed archer

As the son of the goddess approaches them in his rampage
The two brothers try in vain to defend the vessels
And Eos' redoubtable son draws his sword
And vigorously attacks the retreating brothers

And unconquerable Memnon deals a fierce blow to Teucer
As that Achaean commander attempts to his use his bow, for
His arrows are of no protection against the mighty son of the
Goddess, as he falls to the ground, darkness engulfing him

And powerful Ajax intervenes to save Teucer's life
Concerned that mighty Memnon is poised to slay him
He takes up his shield and draws his own lance
And deftly he casts his weapon at the son of the goddess

It strikes the divine shield of the Aethiopian king
As the magnificent armor absorbs the tremendous force
And to no avail is the weapon of the son of Telamon
As it harmlessly hits the ground at the feet of great Memnon

And the son of the goddess takes up his own lance
And launches the powerful missile at Ajax, and the weapon
Strikes the Argive commander just above his thigh, and huge
Ajax crash thunderously to the ground next to his brother

And the men of Salamis flee in sheer terror
After watching the fall of their venerable commanders
Teucer the famed archer and mighty Ajax
Both sons of Telamon by different mothers

---

[267] son of Telamon and Hesione; Hesione is a daughter of
Laomedon rescued by Heracles and given to Telamon as his wife,
thereby ancestrally linking Teucer to both Salamis and Troy

And now the besieged armies of Agamemnon, compelled
Into a precarious dilemma at the hands of raging Memnon
Either absolute destruction by the son of the goddess so far
Away from Argos, or continued flight into the very sea itself

And as the son of the goddess is on the verge of epic triumph
The Fates deem fit a different course of action
And father Zeus, though very reluctant to do so
Summons trident bearing Poseidon to holy Troy

And the lord of the Sea obeys his brother's commandment
Swiftly arriving to the high walls of Priam's city
Sturdy walls he himself built with his bare hands
During his and lord Apollo's servitude to King Laomedon

The two sons of Cronus assemble near the Scaean Gates
Zeus begins first, "Earthshaker, though it pains me greatly
For this man, more like a god, has always duly honored us
All, with abundant offerings and splendid sacrifices

For there is none his peer amongst the ranks of men
And none more handsome or regal in stature and appearance
These attributes equaled only by his piety and prowess at
Arms, for no Achaean can withstand him against his will

And his iridescent mother has my eternal love
For she has always been loyal to my divine reign
And a joyous delight to us all on Mount Olympus
And now she suffers in anguish as to what is to transpire

And with these saddened words I now command you
To rouse great Achilles and fill him with courage
To offer stern challenge to the redoubtable Memnon
Intervening in the struggle between him and Telamon's sons

For the moment of destiny draws near for both, two of the

Greatest heroes ever to walk upon the vast earth! And a
Dolorous decision remains to be made by the son of Eos
As Atropos takes up her inflexible shears as we speak"

And so without delay Poseidon appears before Achilles
Taking the mortal form of Gerenian Nestor
He begins to speak powerful words to Thetis' mighty son
Imploring him to confront the raging son of the goddess

"Achilles, why dawdle as if in a daze? As mighty Memnon
Lords over the plains, he goes from strength to strength
Slaughtering many Argives, while you flee before him like a
Frightened and meek lamb!

And they once called you the best in the entire world
As it pertains to the deadly art of war and strife, you
Effortlessly pinned the frightened Trojans inside their city
And now they threaten to set fire to our very ships!

What a spectacle for these aged eyes to witness!
For never did I venture to conceptualize such a sight!
That Achaeans would flee before any foe
So long as you were present on the battlefield!

And what would my old dear comrade Peleus think now?
To know that we have not one who dares to stand firm
And withstand the awesome might of the son of the goddess
For he is now the undisputed champion of this conflict"

And Achilles makes his reply, "Aged Nestor
Your intense words are but folly to my ears!
For the Olympians highly favor the Aethiopian lord
As he continues his ravaging of our battalions

And none can withstand his awful fury!
For he fights more like a god than a mere mortal

As evidenced by his mastery at wielding the lance
And swinging the sword with fatal accuracy!

He has already overcome the best of the Argives
Mighty Diomedes himself took an ignominious fall
As has Telamonian Ajax and his brother the famed archer
And I too barely escaped his ruinous might at arms

And sadly your own son is unable to survive, as Memnon
Took his life not far from where we stand, woeful be that
Awful day that many Argives were lost! As the son of the
Goddess drove our forces back to the Hellespont[268]"

And lord Poseidon responded, "Be of good cheer!
For you also have allies amongst the Olympians, and we
Now must make our stand against the son of the goddess
Even though he is strong and marvelous to behold in war!

And let the Fates decide whom shall live or die
For glory only comes to those who relentlessly seek it
And it is never simply given to any mere mortal
But seized by those confronted against immeasurable odds!"

And with these words Poseidon fills Achilles
With courage and renews his demoralized spirits, as the
Sea lord persuades Thetis' son to offer opposition to
Mighty Memnon as he rages in battle with divine-like fury

And the son of Peleus boldly drives his chariot forth
While the rest of the frightened Argives continue chaotic
Retreat, presents challenge to the son of the goddess, at the
Very moment Memnon is set to slay both sons of Telamon

---

[268] a narrow straight connecting Troy to the Aegean Sea

And his presence is acknowledged by great Memnon
Tithonides, as Eos' son swiftly moves away from where
Ajax lay, and makes his way towards the direction of Peleus'
Son, as two greatest of champions are set to duel yet again

And the son of the goddess begins, "Myrmidon Achilles
Again we are matched against one another
To test the mettle of the other in the dance of war
As pawns of the Olympians in this great conflict

And surely this shall be the greatest encounter ever fought
By men, for we are both loved by the divine immortals
And this shall be the day of our reckoning!
As both you and I are at last confronted by the Fates

So, son of Thetis, I implore you to battle to your uttermost!
And do not hold back with the lance and sword
Let us feel the full extent of the other's prowess, so that men
Of future generations shall not forget this great battle!"

And Achilles makes reply to great Memnon,
"Son of the goddess, great is your stout heart!
For I know that the words you speak are assuredly authentic
In that we both now at last face our destinies

And whether it is you or I that is to perish first, at no
Other man's hand would I choose to die, for your honor and
Fame are known to both mortals and deities, and your
Exploits are unparalleled by any man to ever walk the earth!

At one time prior to your arrival to besieged Troy
I effortlessly lorded over the lands of famed Dardanus
For no man born or allied with Troy at the time could
Withstand me or my dangerous sword, overmuch for all

And only one came as close as any to matching my skill

For Hector Priamides was indeed a dangerous and worthy
Foe, yet even his might pales in comparison to your own, for
Your prowess at wielding the dangerous lance is unmatched

Trepidation amongst our armies as your contingent alight
From the vessels, intent to defend Priam's renowned citadel
For his peoples are of your divine bloodline, accordingly
Your awful might descends upon us like a plague!

And you have overcome our feared commanders one by one
Including myself, saved from you only by lord Poseidon
As he mercifully sweeps me off the battlefield, and now
We are called upon yet again to test the other's endurance

Though you may slay me in these blood stained plains
As you have to so many other brave Argive men
I shall endure your strength for as long as I may
For no man alive has yet to conquer you against your will"

And with these words Achilles hurls his deadly lance, and
The weapon glides powerfully towards the son of the
Goddess, and were its intended target a much lesser man, the
Son of Peleus would have swiftly overcome his dreaded foe

But the lance and all its fury strikes Memnon's golden shield
Penetrating the uppermost layer of the divinely fashioned
Aegis, and the son of Eos is made safe from the dangerous
Weapon, as swift footed Achilles is denied a glorious victory

And now great Memnon aims his own mighty lance with all
His might, at the armor of his famed Argive opponent
Redoubtable Achilles, a terror for many Trojans, and yet the
Son of the goddess confidently engages him in fierce battle

As his brutal lance hits the right arm of Peleus' son
Piercing the area of the divine armor near the bicep

And dark, murky blood flows from the grievous wound
For so violently is the weapon cast by great Memnon

Achilles swiftly gathers himself and rebounds
And prepares to meet the raging son of the goddess
As both men draw swords and advance upon the other
Aspiring to battle one another to the uttermost

As they begin to furiously lash at the other, strong Memnon
Pursues his attack as the aggressor, while Myrmidon
Achilles shifts to a defensive posture, for deep in his heart he
Acknowledges Eos magnificent son as the stronger of them

And yet again Achilles' strength begins to fail him
As he slowly yields to the might of the Aethiopian king
For great Memnon's sword inflicts awful punishment
Upon the divine armor bedecking the body of Thetis' son

And then to the bewilderment of the beleaguered Achilles
And to the Aethiopians, Trojans, Lycians, and Achaeans
Eos' redoubtable son tosses aside his sword and shield
And his wondrous armor, exposing his beautiful body

And without hesitation the Myrmidon king swiftly takes his
Blade, and plunges it deep into the body of mighty Memnon!
To the disconsolation of his Aethiopian comrades!
As utter despair envelopes the Trojans and its allied forces!

And the son of the goddess falls to the ground, as the
Blood pours freely from his fatal wound, and a relieved
Achilles cautiously approaches his dying foe, curiosity
Engulfing his mind as to his sudden and unexpected fortunes

And Achilles begins, "Son of the goddess
Why are you suddenly now dying? When you
Undoubtedly held the military advantage just recently?

And you would have surely defeated me?

Thereby achieving a magnificent triumph to the dismay of
The Achaeans and my own beloved mother the Nereid
And you would surely have driven the Argives from holy
Troy, for no man alive can withstand your furious assault!

Instead you now lie perishing on the Trojan plains
Fallen as a result of my fortuitous sword
And your Trojan protectorate now flee in utter terror
After you benevolently sacrifice your life"

And the heroic Memnon replies with shortened breath,
"Peleus' son, though you are by far a capable adversary
Amongst the varied men, immortals, and monsters I have
Endured, I perish at your hands not because of your might

For the Fates offered an alternative to this outcome, and
I could effortlessly overcome you in battle again, as some
Olympian favoring you comes to your rescue, saving your
Life, while I continue my rampage against your comrades

But such actions shall not alleviate Trojan suffering
Nor can my feared lance repel the Argive invaders
And send them scurrying across the wide Aegean
Returning to Argos, defeated and dishonored

For only my demise offers a glimpse of hope for Ilium
And too draws near your own unfortunate end
As my death is directly linked to your own
As foretold by lovely Cassandra, the Trojan prophetess

And so I have chosen to forfeit my life, to the utter dismay
Of my loyal comrades, as iridescent Eos loses her beloved
Son this hour, so that Priam's long suffering citadel may
Shortly witness your own demise, long overdue"

And with these final words ends the mortal life of the son of
The goddess, and as water extinguishes the conflagration
The son of the goddess sanctions the lineage of Oceanus[269]
To triumph over the lines of Helios and Dardanus[270]

And Achilles shouts in agony through his flowing tears,
"Mighty son of the goddess, great is your spirit!
And your piety, virtue, and selfless manner!
Justly deserved is your worldly fame and honor!

For did you not refuse the desecration of Antilochus?
Even after he slaughtered your beloved comrade, great
Aithops, and you refused to encounter his grieving father
Though his death would have come swiftly at your hands

And even in the very midst of your own grief
At the loss of your cousin the splendid Meroitian prince
You granted a reprieve to our demoralized ranks
Allowing for the time honored funeral games to proceed

For your righteous nature would not do otherwise
Than what is moral and becoming before the Olympians
For you are the shining example of the greatness of
Humanity, and a much better and nobler man than I"

And so the saddened son of Thetis the Nereid
Shouts to the Achaeans to refrain from despoiling
And from stripping the divine armor and shield
From the body of the famed son of the goddess

---

[269] reference to the lineage of Achilles; Achilles' mother Thetis is
the daughter of Oceanus
[270] reference to the lineage of Memnon; Memnon's mother Eos is
sister to Helios, and his father Tithonus is descended from
Dardanus (founder of Troy)

He threatens instant death to any Argive that dares
To defy his determined commandments, thus duly
Showing his reverence for the godlike Memnon, for the
Son of Peleus held the Aethiopian king in such high regard

Yet even if the son of Peleus did not utter his dire warnings
So feared was the son of the goddess, even in his death
That none would dare to approach his corpse, and after his
Decree, Achilles advances against the fleeing Trojans

And all this is espied by Helen's Trojan husband
As Achilles moves from where great Memnon lay
Tremendous sadness mounts within his heart, along with
Fury at the death of the son of the goddess

For though Priam's son was hated by all in Ilium
And reviled by his Trojan and Dardanian countrymen
The only exception is that of great Memnon
As he supported his besieged kinsman and embraced Helen

Such were the thoughts of Paris as he took up his bow and
Arrows, for his skill at archery is famed throughout the
World, and Priam's son takes aim at the Myrmidon
As Achilles gives chase to the discouraged armies of Priam

And Paris lets fly his arrow toward Peleus' rampaging son
As great Apollo deftly guides the fatal missile
And the fateful shaft strikes the exposed heel of Achilles
For the fierce Myrmidon is otherwise invulnerable[271]

The Myrmidon king falls to the ground in agony

---

[271] Achilles' mother Thetis attempted to bestow immortality upon
Achilles by submerging him into the Styx River in the underworld;
she held him by his heel when doing so, and therefore he was
vulnerable only in this area

Within proximity of the body of great Memnon Tithonides
For the moment of his own death had arrived as well
As foretold a short while ago by the son of the goddess

And as the corpse of swift footed Achilles
And the son of the goddess lay next to one another
The soul of Thetis' son swiftly departs for Tartarus
To take his rightful amongst the heroes in the Elysian Fields

While godlike Memnon is borne to glorious Olympus
High honors bestowed upon him by the divine immortals
As the son of the goddess is duly granted immortality
For his incomparable exploits and lofty deeds

And for his physical beauty and prowess at arms, and
His comeliness and congenial demeanor, and for his
Humanity and kindly acts towards the inferior, and thus lord
Memnon eternally congregates with the great Olympians[272]

And the mourning comrades of the son of Eos, fiercely
Loyal to him as the day they departed lovely Aethiopia, are
Too honored for their bravery and service to great Memnon
As each is transformed into varied perennial birds

Beautiful falcons, eagles, sparrows, and ravens
To continue attendance and pay homage to their earthly
Monarch, duly implementing his divine commandments
And eternally faithful to the edicts of the great god Memnon

---

[272] for his selfless act of allowing Achilles to kill him, Memnon is
granted immortality by Zeus and becomes an Olympian god

www.ingramcontent.com/pod-product-compliance
Lightning Source LLC
Chambersburg PA
CBHW020345180626
46812CB00001B/342